VALOR

❖ S. M. SAVOY ❖

بساله

Published by
Ace Lyon Books
June
2017

Published by
Ace Lyon Books LLC
Acelyonbooks.com
Second Edition
Cover Design by S. M. Savoy
VALOR /S. M. Savoy
Library of Congress Control Number: 2017906516
ISBN 978-1-947122-11-6

Dedication

Thanks to Rapture and all my good friends on Mannoroth who inspired this book, and my husband who didn't mind waiting for dinner while I finished a game. Play On!

Zare

TABLE OF CONTENTS

VALOR

THE TEAM

The captain of Charlie's football team drew his sword and leapt. Charlie smiled. This would be an easy kill. His captain wore only old ragged jeans, like Charlie's, and held a two-handed broadsword. The choice of weapon was a mistake.

Charlie pulled his own sword, a one-handed gladius, and rose his shield. The surrounding crowd laughed and yelled insults. Directly overhead, the mid-day sun hung perfect for dueling. After the last football game they'd agreed to meet here on this grassy meadow to fight to the death.

Charlie had lost count of the duels he'd won today. The death of a challenger exhilarated him the same way a great play on the football field did. His teammates cheered him on unconcerned by the imminent death of their captain. Charlie had taken on all comers, and so far, remained undefeated.

They loved him.

He braced himself, letting his opponent waste his rage. The first few wild swings hit his shield unopposed.

When Charlie did nothing except block the attacks, the captain cast Berserk and screamed his war-cry, swinging wildly. Once the blows slowed, Charlie released his shield and pulled his other gladius from the sheath on his back, yelled his battle-cry, and attacked.

In moments, his opponent lay dead at his feet. Without a shield of his own, the captain couldn't defend from attacks against another warrior; a fatal mistake. A warrior's strength was in defense, taking hard hits on his shield and wearing his adversary down. A two-handed sword shouldn't be used with no healer in the group.

Not wanting to anger the people watching, Charlie resisted the urge to prod the body with his toe.

The crowd of spectators grew. By some

internet miracle known only to the gods of UBM, the entire server seemed to know about the duels. Half of his football team stood in the shade of giant, purplish-green trees with a cluster of girls gathered beside them, most wearing bikinis and dancing.

He thought they were the team's cheerleaders but it was hard to tell without the short skirts, and for all he knew, half his team might've chosen female characters.

"Who's next?" Blood dripped from his sword as he waved it at the crowd and one of the bikini-clad girls approached.

"Me, I guess." She laughed and disappeared.

Great, a rogue, Charlie thought and issued the duel.

He immediately cast Immune, knowing her first assault would be a knife in the back and an all-out frenzy. While he waited for her to attack, another bikini-clad girl strolled to the captain's corpse and prayed over it. A yellow light surrounded them and the captain stirred, stood and swung his sword.

The rogue attacked, using her most powerful spells, and Charlie turned his attention to his fight. With thirty seconds left on immune, he stood still and let her cast until she'd expended her strongest attacks before running from her.

As expected, she casted Waylay, appearing instantly behind him again. He leapt forward, landing twenty feet away in a single bound, and she intercepted again, showing up behind him right as he casted his drop weapon area-of-effect. *All new rogues were utterly predictable.*

The daggers in her hand clattered to the ground, and he laughed when she swore. Pivoting to face her, he slammed her with his shield, stunning her. Unable to evade his attacks while stunned, four sword swings later, she fell to the ground, dead. A rogue with more experienced would've been able to break the stun.

The priest in the bikini sauntered over and laughed at the corpse. "Good job, Hailey. You lasted two entire minutes!"

Yellow light surrounded the dead body, and Hailey stood.

"I bet *you* don't even last two." The rogue disappeared.

The priest snickered again.

Charlie narrowed his brown eyes. None of them had a prayer of beating his team. This noob-fest was a complete waste of time. Before calling for his next opponent he took a moment to view Team Valor fight.

Oz, Team Valor's mage, fought Mark, a fullback on the football team and a wizard. Mark's minion was dead already; a smoldering cat corpse still giving off sparks. Currently a sheep, Mark wandered aimlessly while Oz created a fireball.

Charlie winced. Unless Mark broke the sheep spell right now, he was toast....

The ball of fire between Oz's hands grew until it floated in front of him, a bright-orange ball four-feet in diameter. The center glowed dark orange, shading to radiant white on the edges, which shimmered with heat. Oz drew his arm back and threw.

Yep, Mark was toast.

Charlie turned his attention to Stasia who fought the captain of the football team. Not wanting to insult the people listening, he bit back a laugh as Stasia sapped the captain with a weighted blackjack, leaving him swaying in place unable to move. Then, she casted Pickpocket before attacking, not bothering to become invisible.

Stasia played a rogue. Usually, she attacked from behind while invisible, but a protection warrior with a broadsword wouldn't be much of a fight for her. She dodged his attacks, utilizing the same tactic Charlie had, letting her opponent cast his strongest spells and avoiding them before using any of her own.

Charlie delivered his next challenge, knowing how Stasia's match would end.

Another cheerleader approached. He ran his hand through his short brown hair when he noticed her nametag read MrsChief, and sighed hard, being careful to keep it off-mic. He supposed he should be flattered but he thought her a skank.

"Hannah, accept when ready," he said.

He issued his duel. His cheeks heated when she hugged and kissed him before accepting the duel, and he hoped Sara hadn't seen. A quick glance showed Sara busy fighting a paladin.

"Chief, we'll make a great team," Hannah

said in a flirty tone. "After school, you can come over and practice at my house."

Charlie sighed again, this time not bothering to hide it. "I have a great team. Valor isn't looking for any new members. The most you could hope for is a spot in the guild."

"I'm a better sun-priest than Seraphim." Hannah sounded smug now. "You'll see. I always top the healing meters in my raids."

"Let's just duel. I don't have much time tonight. Our flight leaves in a few hours." Charlie wanted this finished. He swung his sword in a skilled arc and issued his next duel while the body fell.

The next time he glanced around, Oz stood in the middle of the bikini-clad girls. Charlie rolled his eyes. *Trust Oz to be chatting them up instead of playing.* As Charlie watched, Oz singled one out and brought her over to Stasia. Sara dueled Mark now, and Hawk fought another ranger. Well, fought was an exaggeration. Hawk had trapped the other ranger and now sat with his back against a tree, petting a squirrel.

Charlie returned his attention to Sara—

Hawk's traps lasted five minutes. If he planned to sit there the entire time without attacking his opponent, it would be as exciting as staring at a loading screen.

Sara killed Mark but didn't touch his minion, which disappeared in a puff of smoke. Charlie smiled, the smile widening when Sara saluted him. Mark wasn't aware of it, but Sara loved cats. Using one against her was a smart move. Not that it had helped Mark; he still lay dead at her feet.

Stasia and Oz stood in a corner, talking with the bikini-clad girl. The queue was empty, so he joined them and logged into their chat channel. Gamers filled the main channel complaining about Hawk holding the other ranger in place.

Oz greeted him and introduced the girl, "Ah, Chief, this is Marcy. She's new in town. I'm teaching her the game, and she's going to the dance with me Friday."

From this close, Charlie saw she was an elf. Bright red hair covered her pointed ears and slightly slanted eyes.

"This is the first time I've played Ultimate Battle Magic. It's fun. It's kind of weird though how similar your game characters are to you. My character looks nothing like me," Marcy said.

Charlie glanced at Stasia and laughed. Marcy wasn't wrong. Sara was the only one who didn't resemble herself. She played an elf too. Seraphim had white hair, cut short, unlike Sara's golden-blond hair that almost reached her waist. The only similar trait was the slightly slanted eyes and thin body type all elves possessed. Seraphim was tiny and delicate while Sara was tall with well-defined muscles from dance and track. Sara had the 'Barlow' blue eyes her mother had made famous. Thick, black lashes framed her lilac-blue eyes. Charlie had never seen eyes as beautiful as Sara's.

Stasia's character, Stasis, was short and curvy, like she was, with long brown hair pulled back in a simple ponytail, the same color and style as her hair. Oz's character was tall and blond with a slim build, nothing like Charlie's own muscular character. Charlie's character was the tallest one offered, which fit his six-foot-two height. Already taller than his classmates, he was often mistaken for a senior.

In real life, Oz wore his blond hair in a much shorter ponytail than Stasia and had recently stopped shaving, trying to grow a Vandyke beard, but it never got past the thick stubble stage.

Hawk's character wore his brown hair in loose waves to his shoulders in the same style he wore in real life, but in real life Hawk limped. Two knee surgeries later, and the knee was worse.

Charlie sighed, *poor Hawk*. It would kill him to give up football and be a spectator as Hawk had to. Not that he wanted to be a professional ball player, he intended to join the Marines like his brother, but he planned to use football to get through college first.

Marcy spoke to him again, and he turned away from Hawk to answer.

"Oz says you'll return from Japan on Monday; I hope you win. I'll be watching." Marcy cleared her throat and then asked hesitantly, "Will you guys be at the dance next Friday?"

"I will be," Stasia said as Charlie said, "Yes."

"Who are you going with?" Marcy asked.

Stasia stared at her brother fight, answering absently, "No one. I prefer to go alone. None of those boys interest me— I like them older."

Charlie bit back a laugh, and Oz coughed to cover one. They both knew that for two years now Stasia had a crush on Charlie's brother Rick. He thought she would've been over it by this time, seeing as how Rick was stationed in Iraq and they never spoke, but apparently, her infatuation was still going strong. Stasia was pretty enough to get any guy at school she wanted, but she didn't have a chance with his brother. Rick would never date someone so much younger than him.

Marcy asking a question brought him back from thoughts of his brother.

What about you, Chief? Who are you taking?"

"I'm going to ask Sara."

"Seriously?" Stasia's voice rose, and Charlie heard the shock in it.

"Like on a real date ask her?" Oz sounded shocked too and shouldn't have. He knew how Charlie felt about Sara.

Charlie's ears burned with embarrassment, and he was glad they couldn't see him. "You think I shouldn't?"

"No, no. I didn't mean that. You surprised me," Stasia assured him, the grin clear in her voice. "By all means, ask her."

Marcy cleared her throat again. "I hope she says yes."

"Me too," Charlie mumbled under his breath, and hurriedly changed the subject. "Nice to meet you. Maybe we can meet for pizza or something before the dance." Without waiting for an answer, Charlie turned to see if Hawk had finished messing around with that ranger.

More small animals now circled the tree Hawk leaned against.

"What's with that?" he asked, frowning at Hawk.

Stasia giggled. "He pissed Hawk off the other day, and this is payback."

The crowd cheered as Charlie strode over and kicked Hawk in the leg. "Hurry the hell up, Hawk. We have a plane to catch. Let's go!"

Hawk gave a dramatic yawn, then rose

and shot his opponent with his bow, breaking the trap holding him, and ran behind the tree.

Charlie moved out of the way.

Hawk leaned out from concealment, cast Stun-Shot, and stopped to pet the squirrel again. When the stun was about to wear off, he cast Rapid-Shot. Ten arrows thudded into the other ranger in seconds, followed by a Knock-Back shot that threw the other ranger backward ten feet. Hawk kept the other ranger from the green leafy trees where his healing aura would work better and shelter him from attacks.

The other ranger tried to trap Hawk and caught the squirrel instead.

Hawk laughed as the squirrels and birds attacked his opponent while Hawk hid behind the tree. While his opponent was busy killing the wildlife attacking him, Hawk peppered him with arrows, stunning him between knock-backs while attacking from the cover of the tree. He was using low-level shots, toying with the other ranger.

This guy must have really pissed him off. It wasn't like Hawk to humiliate someone. Usually, he won and moved on, Charlie thought worriedly as he eyed the muttering crowd.

Hawk finally killed his opponent and kicked the corpse as a last insult.

Charlie rubbed his eyes and glanced at his watch. Holding tryouts for the guild before a tournament had been a bad idea. His annoyed grimace lightened. In three hours they'd be on a plane headed to Japan. Sara's driver would pick them up, and he couldn't wait to see her. A few more fights and he could log off.

- 2 -

HANNAH THE HARPY

Half of the crowd booed, and half cheered; Charlie winced. He'd be so glad to be done with this, and it was his own damned fault. When his fellow football players had asked to try out for his guild, he'd felt obligated to let them, and before he knew it, the cheerleaders were trying too. Stasia hated them and with cause. They were backstabbing, boy-crazy shrews— she wasn't wrong.

Stasia called them Harpies, mostly because the leaders of that pack of she-wolves had the same initials, H P, and it suited them, they were harpies. They couldn't even get along with each other.

Heather Perry was screaming at Hailey Perez right now about cheating, which wasn't possible in a duel. Charlie kicked them from his voice chat. *Let them call each other on the phone and scream.*

Oz's sudden laughter made Charlie glance back to the dueling area.

"Nice name, Hannah, but a bit premature," Oz said.

A groan escaped Charlie. Hannah still had to fight the rest of them, and they'd noticed her nametag. The ease with which Team Valor was defeating their foes should've discouraged her, but she wasn't giving up. Another blush heated his cheeks when Hawk snickered over her name.

"It's on bitch," Hannah sneered in the main chat room.

Charlie whispered to her privately, "Swear words aren't allowed. No name calling or derogatory comments. We play by tourney rules."

"Fine, whatever, Sara isn't the only good sun priest out there. I could easily heal your group. Being partners will be fun, Chief. We can see each other all the time then," she replied in the main chat channel.

"Your first duel is with Stasia." Charlie sighed and rubbed his forehead where a headache was developing.

Stasia giggled. "Her name is immature, not premature. She doesn't have a prayer with Chief, but let's go. You fight me next."

Showing no mercy, Stasia stealthed, blew her cooldowns, and killed Hannah in six seconds.

Hannah shrugged it off. "Everyone knows rogues own priests. Bring on the next one."

Her next duel was with Hawk. The foliage on the tree hid him between shots. Not one of her casts hit him. The crowd quieted as Hannah stepped up to fight Sara. Sara killed her in thirty-eight seconds, and the crowd roared its approval.

"Wait! That's not fair! She's wearing clothes," Hannah complained.

Instead of wearing the bikini the character started with, Sara wore a simple white dress. The dress had no stats, and no one else had complained.

"Those clothes have no stats, it's

allowed." Stasia's voice was sugary sweet, and Hannah growled.

Charlie saw this going downhill fast. Stasia wasn't above physical retaliation later if Hannah hurt Sara's feelings.

"It's fine."

Charlie jerked in surprised when Sara spoke. He hadn't realized she'd entered the channel. All her chats were usually off except officer's chat.

"If she wasn't expecting me to be dressed, and it threw her off, let her try again," Sara said as she moved her character, Seraphim, into the center of the grassy field and sat with her back to Hannah's character.

A large, dark-yellow ball tinged with orange formed between Hannah's hands and she flung it at Sara.

Sara rose and planted her staff but didn't cast.

The yellow balls became smaller.

When Sara had a hundred hit points remaining, a wave of golden yellow light rolled out from her staff and formed a ball of light above it that healed her completely. Then Sara used her staff to beat Hannah to death.

"Wait— that's not fair!" Hannah's voice was strident. "The spells she's using are upgraded."

"I used one spell, and you have it too." Sara sounded exasperated. "Magic didn't kill you. I beat you to death with staff expertise."

"Chief, give me one more shot and I'll prove I'm a better priest!" Hannah wheedled in a soft voice, "then we can be together all the time."

"Fine, accept when ready!" Sara snapped.

"No, that gives you the advantage, you accept," Hannah said.

"Actually, the advantage is to the person who accepts, not offers, but whatever you say. Any other requirements?" Sara asked, her tone cold.

"No, and don't get so hoity-toity. You got lucky. I'm as good as you are. I always top the healing charts in my raids."

"Ready when you are."

Charlie was worried. Sara sounded really angry now.

The tree was once more put to use as Sara hide from Hannah's casts in the gnarly branches. The watching crowd cheered and yelled insults at Hannah when Sara won again. The general chat channel became a confusing mix of voices yelling advice and criticism.

"I didn't know we could do that," Hannah whined. "One more chance, Chief. I'll show you."

"Fine," Sara agreed before Charlie could say anything.

The spectators quieted. Charlie could practically feel them willing Sara to win.

Hannah ran MrsChief to the tree and issued the challenge. Sara accepted and made no move to hide or run. Balls of yellow light flew from her hands and hit Hannah while Hannah tried to use the tree to hide. Hannah walked into almost every one of Sara's casts. The insults were getting so rough Charlie had to mute almost everyone in the general channel.

"Come on, Chief—" Hannah said.

Oz cut in, "Enough already. You aren't good enough! You're so far from good enough I need binoculars to see you. If you have any interest in getting better, talk to

Piper. He's an amazing priest in our guild. I'm sure he'd be happy to help you."

"I knew you only brought Sara along because—"

"Oh, for crying out loud," Oz interrupted her again. "I didn't recommend Sara as your teacher because she doesn't like *you,* not because she isn't as good!"

"That's not what I hear. I hear she's never first on the meters."

"Thanks for coming out, everyone, and have a great Thanksgiving," Sara said and signed off.

"We don't use meters, we use teamwork. None of us are ever first on meters; what does that prove?" Charlie snapped, angry now too. Sara still sounded upset to him, and he was kicking himself for letting the Harpies tryout. "The goal is to win, not show off our epeen. Sara is a team player who understands the mechanics of the game and plays accordingly. She doesn't mash one heal button and crow over large healing numbers.

"Ask any member of this guild, it's all about the timing, and she can do that. How do you think she won with one spell? It was timing, not luck. Once you'd casted your major damage attacks, she casted her biggest heal and had time to beat you to death with a stick before your cooldowns reset. You were so focused on killing her you didn't even try to heal yourself."

"With only one hundred hit points remaining, I thought I could push her over into death."

"Yeah, and she counted on it; it's a classic noob mistake. You see your target almost dead and you push the damage and forget the game mechanics. The spell she used applied a HOT to her. You should've backed down and let the heal-over-time tick off or dispelled it before you attacked. Instead you went all out while she killed you with her staff."

"No one is that good; it was just luck."

Charlie was rapidly losing patience with this conversation.

"She *is* that good. The spells a priest use are the same, and she knows them all. Every player in this guild knows every single spell each character has. Believe me when I tell you, if you'd stopped fighting and let the

HOT tick off, she had a plan in place for that. She wouldn't have cast wildly."

"That's so much to remember, no one could remember all that."

"We *all* remember all that, and the boss's abilities, and the room layouts, and how certain buffs work better than others in different situations. This guild is dedicated. We aren't the number one guild on this server by luck."

"Holy crap, you must be to memorize all that. I mean, I see you on every day, but I had no idea. I have better things to do than learn all that. Guess I'll stay and raid with the regular kids, not the super geeks." Hannah left the channel.

The remaining players broke out in a babble of voices asking questions and getting advice. All the officers bailed on Charlie, leaving him to deal with it.

"Well, that was a big, heaping pile of steaming poo." Hawk turned off his game, leaving officer chat on.

"The warrior has potential if someone can talk him into using his defensive spells. The need to top meters is holding him back.

His timing is good," Oz said.

Hawk made a sound of agreement. "Why the heck did you give her so many chances, Sara? It was obvious she was horrid after her first try."

"If Chief wants his girlfriend in here, that's fine with me, but if he wants her to replace me, she better prove she can. I earned my spot."

"Jesus, Sara, we weren't trying to replace you. Hell, I don't even like her." Oz sounded appalled at the idea.

"No, we'd never do that," Hawk agreed. "This is Team Valor. If one of us goes, the team falls apart."

"I need a break. I'll see you on the plane." Sara logged off and ran to the bathroom.

"Holy crap," Stasia said. "She thinks he wants to replace her with his girlfriend. He made her cry."

"Who's getting replaced?" Charlie asked as he entered the officer's chat room.

"Sara, you re-re! She left here crying. Good job, Romeo! She thinks you want your girlfriend to be the new sun priest." Stasia's voice vibrated with anger. "I told you those

Harpies were bad news."

"Wait… what— why would she think that? What did you say!" Charlie yelled back.

"Me? Did you fall and hit your head? MrsChief comes into a surprise tryout and you let her try four times, and then explain to her how she could become as good and I'm the one who said something? You're lucky you aren't here; I'd slap you myself."

Stasia yanked the headset from the computer and shut it off. After packing up her headphones and laptop, she brought them to the living room where the rest of the luggage was stacked, waiting for Sara's driver to pick them up.

Sara remained in the bathroom.

Stasia waited on her front steps enjoying the cool night breezes and the insect chorus. Cicada's drowned out the low hum from the television. Light from the windows cast shadows that hid Sara's expression when she sat beside Stasia on the stoop.

When Stasia spoke, the insects quieted momentarily before redoubling their efforts.

"None of us want to replace you. There'll never be a replacement— by a boyfriend, or girlfriend, or anyone at all. Your spot is secure for all time based on skill, not pity or friendship. I know for a fact she wasn't his girlfriend. She wants to be, there's no denying that, but she never was and never will be. But, it wouldn't matter even if she was. I swear to you, we'll always be Team Valor, us five— no others. Someday, one of us might quit, but that'll be the end of Team Valor."

Sara nodded but didn't answer or meet her eyes. The cicada chorus continued unabated.

Hawk approached the door and gave his sister a questioning glance.

The light from the opening door silenced the insects as Stasia went inside, leaving Sara sitting on the front stairs in silence.

"Let's move our luggage outside," Stasia whispered. "Give her a few minutes. Abandonment pushes all her buttons. Let it sink in we wouldn't do that even if MrsChief had been the best player on Earth."

Stasia grabbed her bags. Hawk took his and one of Sara's. Sara entered, took her bag from Hawk, and thanked Mrs. Morales for dinner. The folder Camila gave her for Mrs.

Hayes went into her laptop bag, and she returned to the front steps to await her driver.

"Is something wrong with Sara? Did you guys have a fight?" Camila peered out the open door after Sara.

"No, we're just eager to go." Stasia hugged her mother.

"Well, good luck, guys. I hope you win it. God knows you could use the college money." She gave her son a hug and drew him down to kiss the hair on the top of his head.

The limo pulled up to the curb where Hawk and the driver loaded their bags. Camila waved goodbye as the limousine drove away.

MISUNDERSTANDINGS

Charlie entered the public channel, thanked everyone, and wished them a happy Thanksgiving before rejoining Oz in the officer's channel. The rest of Team Valor had already logged off.

Uncharacteristically silent, Oz sounded stunned when he spoke. "Holy crap, I never saw Stasia that mad at you, and you made Sara cry."

The desk chair squeaked as Charlie squirmed uncomfortably. "Hawk said he didn't see her cry— she just left the room."

"We both know that's why she left the room. A backhoe couldn't reach her feelings they're buried so deep."

"God, and just when we were doing so well." Charlie ran a hand through his hair in agitation. "She's really opened up this last year."

"Yeah, Stasia says she believes we really are her friends. So many posers want to be her friend because of who her parents are it's hard to trust us. Even in the game, weird losers hound her like she's the last girl on Earth, but none want Sara, only Meredith Barlow's daughter. We're her only real friends. And, I don't want to twist the knife, but that had to really hurt if she thought we didn't want her."

"That's not how it was!" Charlie felt his face heating again, this time in anger.

"I'm not saying you intended it but look at this from her point of view. If she called a tryout out of the blue for MrSeraphim, and the exact same scenario played out with him being a warrior, how would you feel?"

Charlie groaned and dropped his head to his hands. "Those damn Harpies! I didn't even know Hannah's character's name. You know I don't want to replace her! What do I do, Oz?"

"Nothing. Stasia and I will handle this. Treat her like usual and let this blow over."

"If I've ruined this...."

"It isn't ruined. You hurt her feelings, but she'll recover. The fact this upset her is a good sign for you; it means she cares for you. Let her think about it without everyone making it a big deal. She'll realize you didn't intend to replace her, and we'll be fine."

"God, I hope you're right. I'll never forgive myself if I ruined our team. Come over. The limo should be here to pick us up soon.... Charlie trailed off as his father called him. "Gotta go. Rick is on the other line.

Stationed in Iraq, his brother Rick usually couldn't call home during the day. Both girls had told him to give him their love the next time he phoned.

"Tell him I say hey," Oz said and went offline.

Charlie ran downstairs and grabbed the phone from his father. "Hey, bro, how's it going there? Valor says hello and sends their best wishes." *No way was any of Sara's love going to anyone else.*

"Still playing games, huh?" Rick's deep laugh made Charlie smile. "When are you giving up the kid stuff to go play with the big boys? The government recruits the good gamers to run their drones. That sounds like the perfect job for you."

"Oh, har, har; don't be jealous I make more than you do a year from the comfort of my bedroom."

"Ha, that hurt. That was below the belt. I'm working hard for my dough while you get to stay home and eat Mom's cooking. Life isn't fair."

"Speaking of Mom's cooking, you should see the Thanksgiving spread she made." Charlie described his meal in loving detail to his envious brother. "The tourney will be streamed live on the web. Can you watch?"

"Don't know. We go on patrol tomorrow. If the squad is on base, we'll definitely watch. There's a pool going, and we can cash in if Valor wins. Tell Stasia and Sara thanks for the videos of your football games. When I get a chance, I'll watch them. And thank them for the snacks. My squad loves them. The snacks, not the girls, although they'd love them too if they saw my pictures. The entire squad wants to play UBM with Team Valor. When we return from this patrol, I'll set up a time."

"Tell them we look forward to that. I'll make them all guild members so they can use the guild bank to buy starting gear, and I'll try not to let you down in the tournament."

Charlie knew both girls kept in touch with Rick, but not that they sent him things. The momentary squirt of jealousy he felt made him smack himself silently in the head. Stasia and Sara had known Rick for years and cared about him. Charlie was glad his brother liked his friends and they liked him.

"Tell Team Valor I wish them luck. And, Charlie, keep an eye on the girls; Japan isn't America. I'd hate to have to come rescue you."

"I will, bro. Watch your back." Charlie handed the phone to his father and raced upstairs to his room to grab his suitcase. The sound of his father's laughter followed him up the stairs. He was telling Rick about a client who wanted hamster furniture, and Charlie laughed too. The manufacturing plant his dad managed produced specialty items in any amount needed and made some very weird stuff.

Charlie was pacing in the living room beside his packed bags when Oz arrived a few minutes later. He lived with his father in an apartment two blocks away and spent more of his time at Charlie's house than his own. Oz let himself in and rolled his eyes at Charlie. Charlie rubbed his forehead and flopped into an armchair.

Oz couldn't relate to his worry over losing Sara. Oz had a new girlfriend every week. He was happy playing the field, and the girls were happy letting him.

Charlie only wanted Sara. She wasn't replaceable. The time they spent together was the best part of his day. The last thing on Earth he wanted was to make her cry.

Oz patted his shoulder. "Stasia and I will handle this."

A rueful smile crossed Charlie's face. Oz had way more experience with girls, and he could trust him to patch things up.

The limo arrived to take them to the airport.

"Grab your bags, boys," Charlie's mother called.

Charlie's mother, Mary, had volunteered to escort them to the tournament in Japan. The accounting firm she worked for always laid her off from September until January. Right now, she had plenty of free time.

Sara handed the folder with the tickets and passports to Mary. Charlie's heart sank when she avoided eye contact, pretending to be busy reading her notes, ignoring everybody.

Check-in at the airport was quick, and they breezed through security, arriving in the waiting room with an hour and a half to spare. Charlie nudged Stasia when his mother headed to Sara who sat with her back to everyone else still pretending to study.

Stasia grabbed Mary's arm and tugged her away, saying, "Sara, can you guard the bags? We're getting food. Want anything?"

"No thanks, and sure I'll watch them." Sara didn't glance up from her notebook.

A confused expression on her face, Mary tried to pull from Stasia's grasp.

Stasia clung to her arm and pulled back.

With a last troubled glance at Sara, Mary followed Stasia.

Hawk and Charlie trailed them while Stasia explained the misunderstanding. "Oz will straighten this out. Once she realizes we didn't want to replace her, she'll be fine."

Mary patted Stasia's hand and then hugged her, saying, "Oh, honey, no she won't. I mean, yes, she won't be mad at you, but don't you see you made her realize how much she has to lose? Sara loves you, really loves you, and she just realized that it could all go away. That isn't a lesson you get over or forget. You take unconditional love for granted. Your mother will love you forever, you understand it, and accept love when you receive it. Sara never had that, not ever. Her father's never home, and her stepmother ignores her. The people she knows should love her, don't."

Tears sprang to Stasia's eyes. "What do we do?"

"Nothing, sweetheart, except be there unconditionally. The decision to risk heartache on love is one everyone makes. Risk is inherent in love, and her life experience makes it a bigger leap of faith. Give her time to think things through."

Stasia stopped walking. "But we *do* love her."

"It isn't about that. It's about being willing to trust that love. Try to imagine no adult on Earth loved you. Would you trust in love or would you isolate yourself from those feelings?"

Stasia looked thoughtful. "I can't imagine it. Even if my mother died, her love is part of me."

The group was quiet as they continued to the snack bar and ordered drinks.

Charlie felt sick. "Stasia, I never meant…"

The hug she gave him didn't comfort him.

"I'm sorry I yelled at you," Stasia said. "This would've happened eventually. I wish it happened later when she had more time to trust us, but she's brave, she'll love us back, I'm sure of that."

To give Oz time with her, they lingered over their drinks while Charlie paced.

Oz sat beside Sara and tweaked her ponytail. "What's up, buttercup?"

He frowned when she sobbed and clung to his shirt, smiling in embarrassment at the people who turned to stare.

"Whoa now! What's all this?"

More people stared as her crying escalated, and he awkwardly patted her back, trying to calm her. "You can't be this upset over that scrub. Seriously, Sara, get a grip."

"No, it's not her. I don't care about her. I just realized you could all leave me, and I'd be alone— so alone. I'm sorry." Her sobs lessened as she covered her face with her hands and tried to pull away.

Oz hugged her tighter. "It's okay. I'm here for you, but what's wrong? You aren't alone. We're here the same as always."

Sara pulled away and wiped her eyes. "I'm being stupid, crying over something that hasn't happened, but it hurt so bad, Oz." The shaking of her shoulders showed her distress as she leaned over, covering her face with her hands, crying silently now.

An older woman approached and handed Oz a stack of napkins. "Are you okay, sweetie?"

Sara nodded but didn't answer.

The woman glanced at Oz and frowned slightly. "Boyfriend troubles? Don't worry, there's always more fish in the sea, and good memories are better than no memories. *Carpe diem*, I always say. Can I get you anything? Do you need help?" She gave Oz another, longer glance.

"No, I'm okay. I'm sorry for causing a scene, it's just, he's leaving me, and I never thought he would, and it shocked me."

"There, there, honey. We've all been there." The woman patted Sara's arm.

Oz handed the napkins to Sara who wiped her eyes and tried to stop crying. "Sara, I'm not leaving. We'll be friends forever. Cross my heart and hope to die." Oz crossed his heart and hugged her again.

"Oh, the friend speech— that's a kicker." The woman gave Oz a sour glance.

Sara giggled at Oz's expression and held him tighter before pushing away and wiping her face with the napkins. "I'm okay. Thank you, ma'am. Sorry I disturbed you."

"Quite alright, young lady. True friends are the rarest thing on Earth. Don't toss one aside because of a wandering eye. Maybe he's not boyfriend material but give the friendship a chance. When you get to be my age, you'll regret not taking those chances."

"Thank you, ma'am, I will." Sara smiled and wiped her eyes.

The woman nodded and with a final harrumph at Oz and a muttered, "It's not you, it's me," she walked off.

Sara laughed again and turned back to Oz with red and puffy, but still beautiful eyes. "Sorry, Oz, I shouldn't have—"

Most of the staring people had turned away. He stopped her with another embrace and kissed her hair. "No, Sara, we're friends. Don't apologize. When you need a hug from a friend that's what we do. I do love you; you'll always be my friend—"

"No, not the dreaded friend's speech" – Sara leaned away from him and waved her hands in the air, an expression of mock horror on her face— "it's not you, it's me," she continued in a dramatic tone. He frowned, and she laughed. "There's other fish in the sea. Sorry, I'm throwing you back."

Oz and Sara were both laughing when the others returned.

Charlie ruthlessly stamped on his jealousy when he saw them together, blond heads touching, laughing. He was glad Sara was smiling, but he wanted to be the one with an arm around her.

Sara gave Mary a hug and apologized for being difficult.

Mary smiled and smoothed her hair. "There's nothing to be sorry for. Growing up is hard, and we can't pick when it happens."

Once more seated together, they talked normally about the trip, the tension gone. Mary smiled and opened a book to read on the way.

- 4 -

THE PLANE RIDE

Their plane was scheduled to arrive in Japan a little after three on Thursday morning.

Tired and stressed-out from the earlier misunderstanding, everyone was yawning except for his mother who was already reading a book. *This flight would take fourteen hours. They could practice when they woke up,* Charlie thought gratefully as he gave Sara his window seat, more to have her to himself than for the view; there wouldn't be much of one. He accepted two blankets from the flight attendant, using one and covering Sara with another.

Sara took her pillow and leaned against

41

the side of the plane.

Maybe I should've kept that seat and she would've leaned on me, he thought, then gave himself a mental shake. The faint strains of a Pat Benatar song emanated from Stasia's headset. Eighties girl bands were her favorite music. Stasia usually listened to old rock-n-roll during casual dungeon runs.

The cord from Oz's headset dangled into the aisle. He was already sleeping, using his headphones as earmuffs. The back of Stasia's seat blocked his view of Hawk. He'd need to lean over her to see him and he didn't care enough to bother. Golden strands of blond hair fell across Sara's face, and he couldn't tell if she was awake.

"Are you asleep?" he asked.

"No, not yet." Brushing her hair back, she turned to face him. "You okay?"

"Me— yeah, I'm fine. I wanted to clear the air with us. I didn't want you to go to sleep mad at me."

"I'm sorry about earlier, Charlie. You didn't do anything."

"Well, I feel bad I didn't warn you about the tryouts, but it was all last minute, and I had no idea that was Hannah's character's name or that you'd think for one second we'd replace you. I never would, you know."

Sara smiled at him. "No, it's fine. Don't worry about it. It's my issue, and I'm working it out. We're okay." She squeezed his hand.

The warmth of her hand in his made his entire body heat. "I wanted to ask you something before all this, and I hope my timing isn't horrid."

The light above the seat dimmed as the captain turned the cabin lights off.

Her smile brightened. "Your timing is awesome!"

His palms sweat as he spoke in a nervous rush. "You know our last game is Friday, and win or lose, there's a big dance after, and I hoped you'd be my date?"

The smile on her face froze and her eyes widened. "Um— sure, yeah, okay—" a pause followed while she stared at their clasped hands. "Like a real date?"

The way she hesitated and glanced away left him uncertain. In one of the bravest moments of his life, he threw caution to the wind and leaned closer. "Yes, a real date. I'll pick you up and everything."

A smile lit her eyes, and his heart soared.

"Yeah, your dad will love that. I'll get a ride to Stasia's. We can meet there."

"Whatever you want." Elated she'd agreed to go on a real date with him, he grinned broadly at her before dialing it back to a normal smile. Maybe he should bring flowers. Stasia would know. He'd ask later.

This was the first time he'd ever asked a girl out, and he wasn't sure if he could kiss her now or not. Before he could work up the courage, she laid her head back on the window.

At parties or after games he'd kissed other girls, but none had meant a thing to him. No matter who he was with his thoughts always went to Sara. What Sara thought mattered to him.

He hoped he could kiss her goodnight soon and introduce her to his friends as his girlfriend. The thought of being able to touch her hair and hold her close made his throat dry. A wave of heat passed through him and he leaned back in his seat, trying to still his whirling thoughts about everything he wanted to do with her. The next thing he knew she was leaning over him, handing her pillow and blanket to the flight attendant.

"Sorry, did I wake you?"

Her smile made his heart pound.

"I don't think so; I just woke up. What time is it?"

"A little after midnight."

Charlie tried to stretch in the cramped airline seat and couldn't manage it. "An hour? Man, I feel like I slept all night this way. My neck has a serious crick in it."

"No, more like eight hours. You're forgetting the time difference. We're fourteen hours ahead of where we were."

Stasia's messy brown hair peeped from the gray airline blanket. She lay on her side facing away from him in a fully reclined seat with the blanket covering her face. The tips of Hawk's combat boots peeked from his blanket. He was still curled in a tight ball. Quiet clicking showed Oz awake and at his keyboard.

"Man, I hate to wake them, but I need a bathroom break badly."

"Me too." Sara leaned over him and

poked Stasia.

His breath caught when her breast brushed his arm. *Jesus, get a grip,* he told himself and tried to think of something else before she noticed the effect she had on him.

"Are you mumbling timing sequences?" Sara glanced up, blue eyes sparkling.

"Yeah, I really gotta go."

Not waiting for his friends to wake, he climbed over them. Stasia woke startled. He mumbled an apology and hurried to the restroom. The cold water felt good on his burning cheeks. The small mirror over the sink showed his hair sticking up.

"Great," he murmured as he smoothed his hair down with his fingers. "I probably snored too and drooled. I probably drooled all over."

A disposable towel made a make-do toothbrush after he washed his face again. A quick search in his jeans pockets revealed a piece of gum, which he chewed energetically before spitting out. *Not bad,* he decided. The face in the mirror appeared almost normal now.

Hawk passed him in the narrow aisle on

the way back to his seat.

Sara was back already with her laptop on her tray table and her headset plugged in. She gave him a shy smile when he sat but returned her attention to her laptop. A small clip held her freshly brushed, long blonde hair from her face. The thought of curling his fingers in her thick, wavy hair and pulling her closer for a kiss, almost made him moan aloud.

Friday, he could wait until Friday. With another mental smack to keep his mind on the game, he opened his laptop.

Soon, everyone was awake and ready to practice.

They couldn't connect to the game server, but they'd downloaded files on the bosses they expected to see in the tournament and went over each one. Charlie listed the different special abilities they might encounter and the abilities and strategies used to counter them.

The stewardess walked by and offered muffins and juice, which they accepted. They put the laptops away and took out their notebooks.

"Okay, a few more things before the finger exercises," Charlie said as he handed everyone a sheet of paper. "Traditionally, the Asian tournaments finish with a dragon. Even if it doesn't end with one, we're sure to face one. These printouts show the safe spots. Last year's dragon almost killed us, so a quick recap. Dragons always have a damaging breath. They can stomp you flat or use their tails to knock you over. Anyone bitten receives a ninety percent health loss and will be poisoned. The key here is timing. A line-of-sight strategy is best; kiting is second best. No other options exist. Death throes can kill us if we're too close when it dies. Let's not be noob here. If possible, save a defensive cooldown for the kill. While it would still count as a win if he dies and kills us, I want to win in style."

Charlie flipped a page in his notebook. "Okay, now for strategies. Let's cover the PVE one's first. We enter in our standard formation every time. Hawk accesses the line-of-sight for the damage dealers. Oz, you decide what the secondary targets and CC are. Sara calls for any positioning, and as always, the healer rules, if she says move somewhere— go. I'll call out for damage on the boss, and Stasia is on special timers. If she tells you to do something, do it. She'll be watching for timers, don't be lazy, watch too, but that's her priority. When we enter, she'll scout and see if any traps or levers need to be pulled."

Charlie sorted papers, searching for the printout he'd made on the Magical Locate spell.

"Our bank account is now completely empty." He handed a copy of the printout to each of them. "We had just enough gold to buy Oz the Magical Locate spell. This printout lists what it can find. There isn't much data out there. That spell is so expensive not many people have it. Oz will now run a locate as soon we enter to find our objective, but keep in mind just because something is south of us doesn't mean the entrance is south."

Oz grinned and waved the paper at them. "This spell should be really helpful. I can hunt for almost anything. There's a drop-down list, tunnel entrances and exits, trap doors, all sorts of things. I can even type in the name of something to search for it. I've already made some macro's and keybindings for it."

Charlie handed out another paper, this one with pictures of monsters and men labeled with their targeting system. "Targeting remains the same. Stasia always targets the left CC, Hawk the right, Sara middle. T-one is the first person on the left, T-two the second and so on, the same as always. Name the spell first, then the timer, not the other way around. Tick and tock signify cooldowns on and reset. A simple alert of mine is enough when we're keeping something silenced or interrupting a spell. You can also announce your CC like that— T-one, mine, CC, only state the spell if you have to. As for CC timers—

"I'm sorry," the stewardess interrupted, "I couldn't help overhear you and I had to ask what a CC is?"

"It's shorthand for crowd control. CC means a spell that lets you control an object so it causes no harm so you can fight something else and come back to it later.

Oz's main CC is a sheep; he turns his enemies into sheep that wander around harmlessly."

"Oh, that sounds fun. What game is this?"

"UBM, Ultimate Battle Magic, we're on our way to play in a tournament." Charlie showed her the printout of the tournament flyer.

"It sounds like fun. I'll let you return to your strategy session." The stewardess headed down the aisle.

"Where was I? Oh yeah, okay, CC timers, call them out the same as always."

Charlie turned another page. "Okay, spells with long cooldowns are your business. Use them as you deem appropriate unless we're running a specific scenario. Do I need to read the list or are we sure of our jobs in all scenarios?"

"Read the list, but not the description unless one of us asks for clarification. Most of those we could do in our sleep," Sara said and leaned over his arm to see the list.

Charlie cleared his throat. *Mind in the game,* he told himself, trying to ignore the heat from her body. "Stop me if you have questions, kite, stall, hide, short-stack, Leroy, sacrifice—"

Sara tapped the paper. "Stop on sacrifice; is that me or you?"

"Yeah, we need to clarify this, it could go either way. The strategy calls for me to give you my invincible spell and you tank as long as you can, going through your power shield, then Hawk puts a taunt on your death angel. At this point, you're dead, the sacrifice, and healing or fighting as an angel, but we could do sacrifice the other way. We could hit me with all cooldowns, then you switch to damage, sacrificing me for a damage boost, which we've called a sacrifice in the past. Should we change the name or is sacrifice Sara, sacrifice Chief, good enough?"

"Good enough. Carry on."

"Okay, let's see— stampede, tag, free-for-all, relay."

"Stop," Stasia said. "Relay is Oz ninety percent of the time, but it could be any of us. I propose we put it with a first name. That's a no-brainer, but let's be clear. If Chief shouts Oz relay Stasia, you bring the mobs to me.

That doesn't mean I take them to Oz."

A quick recap followed of their common terms. Charlie flipped the last page of his notebook. "Okay, resurrections. The usual rules apply. I call it. If, for some reason, I can't call it, I fell off a cliff, or into a well and can't see the fight, Sara calls it, then Oz, Stasia, and Hawk. But, if you think I'm wrong, say so immediately. I'll trust your judgment. I don't want to hear, oh, you should've rezed me and we wouldn't have wiped. If you know something I don't, call it out. But don't call because you want in on the kill, we all want that. Only call for a strategic advantage."

"Now, we have four resurrections available to us. We have Sara's, and if I steal it before she dies, I have hers too. Then we have mine, and if Hawk can find plants, we have his. The timer on Hawk's is three hours, so we only have his once. Sara can do it as often as she wants, but game rules only let her cast it once in combat. Mine is a thirty-minute cooldown, and it's a ten-second channel. Interruptions will ruin the cast. If I'm tanking, my rez is out. In effect, we're limited to two per fight unless we're fighting one enemy and can let it chase Stasia while I rez. Spell-Steal has a three-minute cooldown and a three-minute duration, so I have to steal it and use it within three minutes of her dying, but she knows to tell me if she's going to die. Everyone will be carrying an extra stack of sun-juice in case Sara needs it. Any questions about resurrections?"

Hawk rose his hand. "Not a question, but a comment. Since the last game patch, Oz can disguise himself as a tree and I can use him if I sit at his feet. We tried it. It works."

"Okay, but the cooldown still sucks."

Charlie flipped through his notes again. "I think we've covered everything. Our gear is ready to go, and we have flasks and potions. For the PVE portion we can use whatever we want, but the PVP part we can only use what we're supplied with."

He was leery of bringing up PVP after the fiasco of last evening but boldly pressed on. "No style kills. Straight up kill our opponents as fast as you can. Make sure our group buffs are on with my pain management first, so it's the last one dispelled. Next is Hawk's Endure Elements, and Sara's Sunrays, then Oz's intelligence, and Stasia's quick. So, when we enter the waiting area, I'll say go, and we start buffing. Be paying attention so they're in the correct order. The only thing we need to do is practice targeting. I printed out these keyboards. They're regulation size and exact duplicate. Let's call targets and see how we do." Charlie handed them out.

The stewardess appeared and pointed to the no electronics light.

"We're landing already?" Charlie asked in surprise.

"No, there's a storm, and the captain wants all devices off. I see yours are away. Are the headsets plugged in?"

Everyone showed the dangling ends. "You guys are the only ones I saw awake but I better check." She headed down the aisle, looking for anyone using an electronic device.

Charlie continued to call out targets quietly and inspected them hit buttons. Everyone was doing fine. The practice was probably unnecessary. A sudden lurch and ding made him glance up as the seatbelt light lit. The cabin lights lit as he buckled his seatbelt. Stasia's seatbelt buckled next to his, so he helped her.

The stewardess leaned over the still sleeping passengers in front of them and gazed out the window. "This is some storm we're having. We're almost there though."

Charlie glanced over at Oz who was handing his soda to Hawk when Sara gripped his arm.

"Oh, my God— the wing is on fire!"

The window shattered and the stewardess and Sara screamed at the same time.

Time moved in slow motion as Charlie turned to Sara and felt the wind from the broken window. A truck hit him, a shattering impact, lighting his bones on fire. The fire froze him in place unable to move or call out. Intense heat grew until he passed out; his last thought was he wished he'd sat by the window to block this from Sara who was hit first.

- 5 -

THE PLANE CRASH

The stewardess stared out the window, screamed and jerked upright. Broken glass flew in glittering shards as the girl sitting in the window seat screamed. One hand went up to block her face, the other clutched the boy beside her.

A blue bolt of lightning hit the girl and traveled through her, lighting her like a neon sign. The lightning hit the boy beside her, then the girl next to him. Before the stewardess could blink, it hit the boy beside the girl and leaped from his hand to the boy offering him a can of soda. The lightning traveled through the can, causing the can to glow.

The boy holding the can shone with a blue light as the lightning arced from his head into the ceiling where it built up brighter and brighter. Sudden screams sounded as the woman beside the boy woke. More screams echoed in the cabin as people woke and noticed the glowing children.

The five children continued to glow with a blue light. The same light swirled around the wing of the plane. A purplish-blue flame appeared and covered them, and the smell of ozone filled the cabin. The blue flames didn't appear to burn even though they sizzled and cracked. The woman seated beside the boy was crying, and the passenger beside her yanked her reaching hand away. Passengers on the other side of her unbuckled and ducked away.

One man pulled the crying woman with him. "Calm down, it isn't fire!" he bellowed as he dragged the protesting woman. "Saint Elmo's fire won't burn us."

At the front of the plane, a steward pushed the intercom and told everyone to remain calm and to take crash positions. The other flight attendant ran to the pilot's door, banged on it, and picked up the phone.

The stewardess by the kids warned people away from touching them. When she glanced back out the window, black smoke billowed and flames shot from the wing. Blue light still swirled around it. A sudden brilliant flash of light dazzled her followed by a loud squeal and shriek of tearing metal as the lightning leading from the boy's head pushed through the ceiling of the plane, making a large hole.

The blue Saint Elmo's fire on the children rippled across the cabin, coating everyone before dissipating. The screaming in the cabin intensified, heard over the shrieking of the wind through the holes in the hull. Blue light flickered and pulsed as it traveled through the window over the children and into the ceiling. The stewardess couldn't tell if the lightning was disappearing or going in a circle through the children, around the top of the plane, over the wing, and through them again.

Wind whipped through the cabin, sucking small pieces of debris into the two holes. Passengers shrieked and shouted as the emergency oxygen deployed from the ceiling, and a loud, rumbling hum filled the cabin. A sudden lurch as the plane dove at a sharp angle caused the stewardess to grab a seat back, and the man in the seat grabbed her. The screams quieted as the plane leveled out, and she stared out the window.

The blue-white glow still surrounded the wing. Black smoke still billowed in long wisps, but no fire was visible. The steward in the rear of the plane strapped the passengers that had sat by the children into the jump seats in the back. She glanced around wildly searching for something, anything, she could use to move the children from the path of the electricity.

Another flash of light caused more screams as the bolt of lightning disappeared through the roof with another blinding flash. When the glow surrounding them passed, the children slumped over unconscious or dead, she didn't know which.

The stewardess approached cautiously and touched one with the back of her hand; feeling no tingles, she felt for a pulse. *This one was breathing,* she thought in relief. She felt the next; she was breathing, so was the next one. The girl who sat in the window seat had no pulse. The stewardess unstrapped her and yanked her into the aisle where she performed CPR.

"Can I help?" The man in the seat next to her had already unbuckled his seatbelt. "I'm a paramedic."

"Can you take over? I want to check the other child."

The paramedic knelt on the floor between the seats and began CPR on the girl.

The stewardess checked on the boy still clutching the soda can, expecting him to be dead. The lightning had exited through the top of his head. No burns marked him, but he had no pulse. She called for help and another flight attendant assisted her. The two women lifted him, laid the boy in the aisle and started CPR.

The captain's voice issued from the intercom. "I've declared an air emergency and have clearance to land at Camp Foster on Okinawa." A few people yelled for silence, unable to hear the captain over the crying and still whistling wind, and the cabin became quieter.

A crackle of static preceded the next announcement. "The right-side engines are out and a fire is burning inside the right-side wing. Passengers seated on the right side of the plane will evacuate first using the doors on the left side of the plane. Please, remain calm. Your flight attendants will direct the disembarkation."

The plane turned steeply, and passengers began screaming again.

The pilot said, "This is a controlled turn. Don't be alarmed. I have full confidence we can land safely. Please stay seated and buckled in."

The screaming died down as the pilot spoke.

The paramedic performing CPR on Sara had stopped. "She's breathing. How's the boy?" he asked as he climbed over the seat to reach them. "Let me check him. Go make sure everyone is buckled in."

He took over doing CPR, and the stewardess stood and hurried down the aisle, making sure everyone was securely fastened with an oxygen mask in place.

When she reached the galley, she grabbed a tray and a roll of duct-tape, hurried back to the broken window, and taped the tray firmly over the hole. The steward from the front approached, holding two trays and another roll of tape. He climbed on the seat and taped the trays over the hole in the ceiling. The cabin became calmer as the wind stopped whistling through the holes.

The captain spoke on the intercom. "We're preparing to land. Expect a jolt as we dump our fuel and lower the landing gear."

Two minutes later, the expected jolts hit. The intercom crackled to life again. "The landing gear on the right side is malfunctioning, so we'll be performing a belly landing. Expect loud noises. The possibility exists that the plane swerves wildly. Emergency vehicles are standing by. This is scary, but we have the situation under control. We expect to land in eight minutes."

Sobs and crying sounded over the sound of the straining engines as the plane continued to dive. Using the seat backs, the stewardess pulled herself back to the children. The paramedic had stopped CPR, and the stewardess was relieved to find the boy breathing on his own. Two other passengers leaned down and kept the girl from tumbling down the aisle while she and the paramedic buckled the boy into the nearby seat. They lifted the girl together, straining against the pull of gravity, as the plane continued its rapid descent.

The paramedic sat between the two unconscious children checking their pulses. Emergency lighting tinted the cabin red, suffusing their pallid faces with false color. The stewardess buckled herself into the seat near them. Pressure built in her ears at the rapid descent. The plane leveled off to a more normal landing approach, making her ears pop painfully and the sounds in the cabin became clearer.

Prayers grew louder when the pilot announced the imminent landing. A rough jerk and the sound of metal tearing boomed through the plane as it landed and swerved, tipping to one side. Screams echoed through the cabin as the plane vibrated. A loud screech followed by the sound of metal shredding reverberated in the plane as it veered first to the left, then the right. The plane lurched to a full stop, tilted to the left, making the floor of the plane uneven. The flight attendants opened the left-hand doors and manned the emergency exits in moments.

With a minimum of pushing and shoving, the passengers disembarked. Two of the stewards forced the crying woman who had sat beside the children to leave. The paramedic stayed with the stewardess. He unbuckled the boy and carried him to the slide in the emergency exit.

Emergency personnel waited at the bottom as he slid him out. Two firefighters entered the plane from a different entrance, and the stewardess pointed out the children unconscious in their seats. The firefighters each took one child and left, carrying them to the exits and out. Four more firefighters entered as the stewardess and the paramedic from the plane carried the girl to the doorway where they slide her to the waiting paramedics.

"You go." The stewardess hugged the

paramedic. "I'll make sure the last child exits. Thank you, you saved their lives."

She turned back to make sure the last boy got off the plane. Thick black smoke curled around the plane and crept into the cabin as she hurried to him. Two firefighters carried him already. The firefighter motioned her to leave. Instead, she went right up to him.

"I haven't checked the plane. I don't know if everyone's off!" she yelled, wanting to assure he heard with his gear on. Black smoke now half-filled the cabin. Her eyes watered uncontrollably as she coughed.

The firefighter turned her and pushed her toward the nearest exit. "We'll check; you go!" he hollered.

She gave him a quick nod and ran to the closest slide. More firefighters grabbed her arms and rushed her away once her feet hit the ground. The plane had landed on an American base. Everyone wore a military uniform. She should've realized sooner when the firefighter spoke English to her, not Japanese. Emergency personal waved the passengers to buses that rushed away.

A representative from the airlines spoke

to the employees and took written and video reports from them. When she asked how the children were, no one knew.

- 6 -

AFTER THE LIGHTNING

Charlie woke with a blinding headache and a raging thirst.

"Oh, thank God! Charles, can you hear me?"

A bolt of pain shot through his head when his mother spoke.

"What happened?" The dry cracking of his voice surprised him.

His mother handed him a glass with a straw. The hospital room registered, and he remembered Sara's scream and the terrible heat.

"Oh God, Mom, is Sara all right?"

"Yes, we think so. Well, we hope so

anyway. There's no physical damage except a small burn on her hand, but she's still unconscious. Don't panic. You were unconscious too until a few moments ago. You scared the heck out of me! How are you feeling?"

"My head hurts, but other than that, I'm fine. Is everybody else okay?"

"Well, no. Everybody got hit with lightning. You've been out cold for almost forty minutes now. If you're okay by yourself a few minutes I'll go check on everyone."

Charlie nodded.

A nurse entered Charlie's cubicle as she left.

The room Sara occupied was still crowded with nurses. Stasia and Hawk were awake, and Mary spoke to both briefly before checking on Oz.

Oz was just regaining consciousness. The nurses kept her waiting in the hallway while they checked him over. Finally, they let her go in.

"Holy cow." Pale and shaky, he lifted a hand to his forehead and winced. "Man, my head. What the heck happened?"

After telling him what had occurred, she checked Sara again. A flurry of activity ensued in her cubicle, and the nurses kept her out. Two doctors entered at a run.

Mary bit her nails while she waited.

Finally, a doctor approached. "Miss Mitchel is conscious with a headache but no sign of concussion or any other injury. Minor arrhythmia presented for a moment, but that's nothing to be alarmed at. It straightened out nicely. All tests indicate they have no injuries. In fact, we'll monitor their vital signs a few more hours, and if they look good, they can go."

"Oh, thank God. I was so worried. May I see her?"

The doctor nodded and waved her into the room.

Machines hummed quietly around Sara, the steady lights a reassurance. "The IV is fluids for the shock. Headache is to be expected and should subside in a day or so." The doctor made a note on the clipboard at the foot of Sara's bed.

"How are you, honey?" Mary uneasily eyed the doctor.

"I'm okay, is everybody else okay?" Loose tangles of hair covered Sara's face as she pushed herself up.

"Everyone is fine, just headaches. The doctors think you can be discharged tonight."

"What happened?"

Mary told her about the plane crash landing.

Sara pushed the mass of blond hair behind her ears, rubbed her forehead, and winced. "I don't remember any of that, just the bright light and a feeling like fire in my bones. What about our luggage and our game? Can we still play?"

"The luggage is being sent to the hotel. As for playing— I guess, if you're up to it. Let's not worry about that now. Rest and call your father. I'm sure he'll be worried."

Sara frowned at the hospital gown she wore. "Where are my clothes? My phone was in my pocket."

"The nurses cut your clothes off and your phones are fried. You can use mine. Your dad's number is in my phone book."

Mary handed her the phone. Sara nodded and reluctantly called her father.

"Yes, Mrs. Hayes, I hope Sara isn't causing any problems." Her father answered the phone sounding annoyed, but that's how he always sounded.

"It's me, Sara. I'm calling to let you know I'm okay. Our plane had a small accident. We're okay, but my phone was ruined."

Silence filled the line a moment. He cleared his throat. "I see. Do you need anything?"

"No, I don't think so. Our bags are being sent directly to the hotel."

"I'll take care of this. Have Mrs. Hayes call me. Sign nothing. My lawyer will be in touch. Will you return at the scheduled time?"

"I think so. We still want to play."

"Fine, thank you for informing me. I'll have the lawyer call Mrs. Hayes— I'll inform your stepmother."

Dial tone ended the conversation.

Sara's eyes filled with tears and a deep sighed escaped her as she hung up.

Mary gave Sara a quick hug and a sympathetic glance before returning to Charlie's cubicle.

"Everyone is awake and doing well. I spoke with the doctor and he thinks you can be released later today," Mary said.

"Will we make the game?"

Mary laughed and patted his hand. "Sara asked that too. Let's see how everyone is feeling in a few hours. The luggage shipped to the hotel. Flights out of here might be hard to find. This is a military airbase, not a civilian one."

"Find us a ride as soon as you can. The first game is at ten tomorrow but check in is at nine."

"I'll do what I can." After kissing her son's cheek, Mary brought the phone to Stasia but found her on one already. "Is that your mom?" she whispered.

Stasia nodded agreement and held up a finger. "Mrs. H is here now. You can speak with her. Yes, I'm sure we're fine. Okay, Mom, I love you too." She held the phone out to Mary.

"Yes, Camila, the doctor says they're fine – very scary, yes – No, they still want to play. I'm working on getting them there. The doctors are releasing them in a few hours.

Sara's father is sending a lawyer and said he'll handle everything and we're not to sign anything. Of course, I'll let you know immediately. It's no problem at all." Mary handed the phone back to Stasia. "I'm going to check Oz again and then see what I can do about finding a ride to the hotel. I'll return when I can."

Stasia nodded and resumed speaking to her mother. "Yes, they tell me Hawk is fine too..."

Oz sat up in bed with a glass of water. After informing him of everyone else's condition, and assuring him everybody still wanted to play, she offered him her phone, which he accepted to call his father. No one answered, so he left a voice mail with a promise to call later.

"I'll see if I can book a flight for this evening. You rest." Mary took her phone back, went into the hall, and called the airline to find out how the passengers from their flight were continuing to their destinations and then called Sara's father.

Nurses smiled and greeted her as she returned to Charlie's cubicle.

"The airline must fear lawsuits. They're sending a private plane for us and an escort to get us to it. I never heard of this kind of service."

"Did Mr. Mitchel call them?"

Mary shrugged. "I don't think so, but that would sure explain the service, wouldn't it?"

Charlie nodded and gave her a matching shrug. "I'm just glad we'll make it on time. Is there any word on our laptops or more importantly, our mice?"

"Nothing specific. The airline said that your bags will be sent to the hotel. Won't the tournament have computers for you to use anyway?"

"Yeah, but we can use our own mice. Mom, can you find somewhere selling Razor Naga mice? If we can't use ours, we'll need new ones."

"Where would I find that?"

"There's a where to buy section on the website. Could you find an internet cafe or something?"

"I'll do my best, but no promises. The first thing I need to buy you guys is clothes. The only things not cut off were your jacket and shoes. I'll see about replacing your clothes while you rest."

"Sure, and thanks, Mom. What time is it anyway?"

Mary glanced at her watch. "Almost three in the morning. You guys will have one heck of a case of jet lag. I need to call your father and get your clothes and the mice. Stay in bed and rest." Before leaving, she kissed his cheek.

After a talk with the on-duty nurse, she had their old clothes in a bag and the name of a shop nearby to purchase new ones when it opened at nine. The nurse used her smartphone and found a store in Tokyo that sold the gaming mouse. Google maps located it for her; it wasn't too far from the hotel. If they needed to buy new mice, they could. Mary thanked the nurse and went to phone her husband.

"Hi, hon," he said cheerfully when he answered the phone. "I was expecting your call. Are you checked in at the hotel?"

"Not exactly. We had a slight delay. Let me start by saying everyone is okay."

"What happened?"

She heard him move his phone and pictured him sitting up straighter with the look on his face he got when one of the boys called late at night. "Our plane was in a bad storm and sort of crashed."

"What— the plane crashed? As in, it fell out of the air?"

"Well, it glided out of the air, but yes." She told him what happened.

"And everyone is okay now?"

"Yes, the doctors will release them this afternoon. I'm telling you, John… that was the most terrifying experience I've ever had. I thought they were all dead." Mary cried quietly in reaction.

"Honey, should I come there? If you need me, I'll get on the next plane."

"No, no, we're fine. I'm fine. It was scary, but they're okay now. All they care about is not missing the game." Mary wiped her eyes with the back of her hand and then rummaged in her purse for a tissue.

"Call me when you reach the hotel, no matter what time it is. Thank God, you're all okay. I love you, sweetheart."

"I love you too. I'll call when we arrive at

the hotel." After she hung up the phone, she took a minute to compose herself before going to tell the kids that everything was in hand.

They left the hospital at three that afternoon. The doctors discharged them at noon, but their escort hadn't arrived yet. While they waited in the lobby, they discussed the abilities they expected from the different creatures they would fight.

Stasia was explaining the difference between dire beasts and regular beasts to Mary when their escort showed up.

TOURNEY

Charlie took a deep breath, and boarded the plane, taking the window seat this time.

The plane arrived without incident. To his relief, their laptop bags waited at the hotel when they checked in. After unpacking and hooking up the computers, everything worked fine. The laptop bags had a funny scent, but the same weird smell permeated everything from the plane.

Stasia and Sara headed to the shop in the lobby for perfume to cover the odor on their clothes and returned with body spray for everyone. After a light dinner, right next door, they went to bed early. Charlie's head still hurt, and he suspected that headache still plagued everyone.

The sun had been up for an hour when they met in the girl's room. No one felt like eating. Everyone except Mary was queasy. Stasia did her hair and makeup, then Sara's, and sprayed them both with the body spray.

"The smell is much less noticeable now, isn't it?"

Mary obligingly sniffed them. "The perfume worked. I don't smell it anymore. Does anyone want breakfast before we go?"

"Water is fine. I'm too nervous to eat," Stasia said as she took one of the complimentary waters off the small table in the room and handed one to Sara.

Charlie took a Tylenol and gave the bottle to Sara who took two and passed the bottle on. Mary escorted them to the convention center with their gear. When they entered, a photographer took a group shot, a few posed pictures, individual pictures, and a few pictures of the girls together.

The pictures of the girls would make the cover of most of the video game magazines, Charlie thought and exchanged a grin with Oz. The girls looked good together, happy and excited. Charlie didn't blame them for using the girls on the covers. Sara was convinced they used her photo because of her mom, and while that might be true, he was certain they'd still use them even if her mother wasn't famous.

Sara's mother hung a shadow over her that her stepmother darkened with constant unflattering comparison— she was too tall, too thin, too undeveloped, too blond. To Charlie's eyes, Sara was perfect, exactly the right height and shape.

Charlie frowned when Sara caught him staring and turned away, blushing and tugging her sweatshirt closed. He wanted to say something encouraging but was afraid to make her feel more self-conscious. *I'll love her so much she'll never doubt how beautiful she is*, he thought and pushed through the crowd to reach her side. She took his hand and let him clear a path for them to a small room where a monitor waited with five computers hooked up. People in the hallways cheered as they passed.

Camera crews filmed Stasia and Sara entering, and Team Valor's name showed up on the big screen in the main hall of the convention center. Charlie grinned at Oz and slapped his back as he ruffled Hawk's hair and slung an arm over his shoulder.

The computers supplied by the tournament ran the loading screen for the game. The monitor took their laptop bags and locked them in a cabinet before hooking up each mouse to run a test program. Once satisfied they contained no illegal mods, he let them log in and handed them headsets. Anyone who wanted to could listen to them play on a private channel. Their screens showed on displays inside the convention hall and streamed live on the web.

When they were ready to play, the monitor cleared his throat to gather attention. "Okay, we're playing this by tourney rules, which means no swearing or foul language. Too many infractions disqualify you. The timer starts once the game master ports you to the first location. Take breaks whenever you wish, but the timer doesn't stop. There's a bathroom through that door there." He pointed out the restroom.

"There are twenty scenarios. One of you will click the portal at the end of a scenario to transport everybody to the next one. Every dead character at the end of a scenario subtracts one point. Each live character adds one point. If you wish to pass on a scenario, everyone must type Team Valor gives up and click the portal. Skipped scenarios result in a loss of twenty points. Passed scenarios gain one hundred points. The total allotted time is five hours with two fifteen-minute breaks. The in-game clock will begin counting down the moment your characters materialize. Each scenario has a different amount of time allotted to it before it's a fail. Unused time adds to your score, but you can also use that time to retry a failed scenario. Do you have any questions?"

No one did.

The monitor took out his phone and made a call. "Team Valor is taking the field."

A second later the crowd roared as the announcer officially pronounced them ready to play.

"Okay, team, let's go. Hawk, don't forget to cast the No-See-Um when we enter to give us time to pick our targets." Charlie grinned in excitement. They lined up their characters, and Charlie clicked the portal teleporting them into a dark cave. Hawk cast his No-See-Um, while Oz cast Magical Locate.

"Five bats incoming, Chief," Hawk warned.

"Okay, Sara, you know what to do."

Charlie smiled at Sara. Seraphim lifted her glowing hands in the air and the fight was on. For three hours, they fought steadily, using the bathrooms during their breaks and turning down food.

"Sorry, I need a bathroom break." Stasia rose and ran to the bathroom.

Charlie's stomach gurgled as well. When she exited the bathroom, Sara ran in. By the time everyone used the facilities it had cost them eight minutes.

"We picked up a stomach bug." Charlie glanced a Hawk as Hawk's stomach rumbled. "Play through it. We're almost done— be the character. I'm not Charlie who wants to be sick; I'm Chief, a mighty warrior who doesn't feel pain." The wan grin he gave Hawk got a grimace in reply.

"Yeah, okay, I'm Hawkeye, the most feared ranger in the world. I never miss what I shoot at and my healing aura means I'm never ever sick! Let's kill these buggers."

They returned to the battle. All of Charlie's concentration was on the fight, calling for attacks, sending his team to new positions, assuring the mobs attacked him and not the others, and clicking the portal sending them to their next battle. The fights blurred, his entire being focused on clicking the next portal, blocking out how awful he felt. Charlie clicked the portal again, and they materialized in a barren stretch of desert. The only thing in sight was a mound of light brown sand.

"Where to Oz?" he asked.

"Straight ahead on the boss, but I don't know, there could be adds under the sand."

"Stasia, relay Oz. Do a perimeter run. Bring whatever pops out back here."

Stasia hit her sprint and ran around the room. Nothing attacked her.

"A dragon is in front of us." Hawk was busy at his keyboard. "No other enemies remain in my range except one dragon."

"Okay, this is the dragon scenario. There's no cover. Let's make it show itself. Take your kiting positions." Charlie yelled his battle-cry, which doubled his stats for thirty seconds and forced enemies to attack him and cast Valorous Leap, landing twenty-five feet from where he started in range of the dragon.

A giant red dragon emerged from the sand breathing fire. Dark-red wings swept clouds of dust over them, temporarily obscuring vision. Charlie heard the fans yelling in the other room but blocked it out. All his focus was on being Chief the warrior, not Charlie with the gurgling stomach and aching head.

The dragon was fast. Oz hit it with freezing rain and then dropped his Frost Field, making a cold area to slow it, allowing Charlie to race ahead, but the rain caused little damage. Oz needed to cast damaging abilities to make the timer. A gout of fire from the dragon's mouth nearly got him, but Sara pulled him to her side using her Protective Companion spell. The dragon stood on its hind legs, using its front ones to paw at him as it reared its head and sent a jet of fire after him.

Stasia cast Precognition and said, "The dragon bites in one minute, twelve seconds." Then she cast Waylay and appeared by its back leg going full out on it, but she had to keep chasing it as it chased Charlie, which lowered the damage she did.

Charlie was worried. The dragon was doing incredible damage to him and he wasn't even taking full hits. The dragon didn't have many hit points but it ran faster than normal and did more damage with every attack. This would be a wipe unless two people slowed it and probably a tournament loss because they wouldn't make the timer. Some of the time would need to be used redoing this, plus twenty points for a skipped scenario. If he didn't decide quickly, it would be twenty-five points when the dragon killed them all in addition to the wasted time.

"Sacrifice me," Sara said.

Immediately, he cast invincible on her and stole her resurrection spell, as she cast her heal-over-time spells on herself and used her strongest shield.

Hawk forced the dragon to attack her with his taunt.

All five of them attacked the dragon.

Sara used her staff, casting a wave of darkness over the dragon, and started to smite while it clawed her ineffectually.

Meanwhile, Charlie switched his stance, dropped his shield, drew his other sword, and initiated full combat mode, doubling his damage.

Sara died and with precision timing Hawk instantly forced the dragon onto her death angel with a taunt.

"Fifteen seconds until my angel is gone," Sara warned. "Rez is a three-second cast, be at least that far from it."

Hawk leapt away, going to his maximum range. Charlie intercepted him and used Sara's own resurrection on her. The yellow glow of the resurrection spell was still fading when he bounded away from everyone, taunting the dragon as he ran, making it chase him, giving Sara time to cast a heal on herself.

Hawk forced the dragon to attack Sara

again.

When she rose, she cast Immortality, a spell with a fifteen-minute cooldown that healed her to full health and made her immune from harm for five seconds, and she lived through two hits before dying. Once again, she became an angel and attacked with smite.

Hawk forced the dragon onto her death angel again, and everyone pummeled the dragon for another minute.

"Eight seconds," Sara warned.

Charlie glanced at the dragons remaining hit points and said. "It'll be close. We need a few lucky crits to proc to make the timer. My resurrection spell this time. I'll need ten seconds. Hawk, set the dragon on Stasia. She can sprint away and use evasion until Sara is alive again and your taunt cooldown is up."

The attack went as planned and all five of them got another minute of damage on the dragon. Charlie considered the dragon's remaining life. "Okay, Hawk, use tree rez near Oz. Sara can only be rezzed once more until we hit the rez timer—"

"No," Stasia interrupted. "Hawk, rez Sara

after it's away from her, so death throes won't kill her. Chief, taunt it away. The dragon will die, I guarantee it. My big hit is coming up, with all my DOTs procing."

Hawk leapt towards Oz, while Oz used Wink to meet him, and standing side-by-side, they kept up their damage rotations. Sara's angel disappeared right as Hawk sat to cast resurrection beside Oz who'd turned himself into a tree. Hawk jumped up and continued to fight. Sara rose from the dead and cast heals on Chief as he ran from the dragon snapping at his heels.

"Death throes!" Stasia sprinted away as the dragon convulsed madly, but this time the scales on its back grew redder and shinier. "Steam is coming from it. I think it's going to explode," Stasia hollered.

"To me!" Sara planted her staff, pulled Chief to her side, and threw a mirrored shield over them as Oz cast freezing rain. A wave of fire passed over, leaving them unhurt and the dragon dead on the ground.

The team was alive, and the dragon dead. The split-second timing used passing agro and resurrections had saved them. Charlie turned and high-fived Hawk as Sara ran to the bathroom and threw up.

"Hurry up." Stasia leaned against the bathroom door and grimaced. Sweat trickled down the side of her white, pasty face. She pushed into the room and was ill. Charlie moaned and slapped his hand over his mouth as Hawk gagged and Oz grimaced and headed to the garbage can.

"Two bathrooms are across the hall." The game monitor opened the door and pointed out the bathrooms. "That was the last scenario. I'm pretty sure you set a time record. Go ahead if you need to." Charlie nodded gratefully and headed to the bathroom, followed by Oz and Hawk.

Fifteen minutes later, they were back in the small room. "Let's go to the hotel. We can see our score later. I want to lie down." Sara's voice trembled and she swallowed heavily.

The monitor hailed them a cab.

Mary was surprised to see them and then

concerned they were so sick. The kids had cold chills, followed by vomiting and diarrhea, which kept them running for the bathrooms. She called the front desk and had medicine and ginger ale sent to the room.

"Man, we have one more day of competition; I don't know if I can do it." Sara peered at Charlie unhappily from beneath her covers when he entered the room to check on them.

"Do your best." Charlie wasn't sure he could do it either, but his job was to motivate them. "A little rest and we'll be good as new. Think about the game. Try to put this out of your mind. Remember, you're Seraphim, a warrior priestess who kicks butt with her magic staff. You heal your comrades and smite your enemies. And, you're not Stasia, you're Stasis the rogue. Rogues don't get sick, they get even. Picture us defeating our foes and winning the game."

Charlie touched their foreheads, their eyes were closed, faces scrunched in misery. They were cool with no indication of fever, and he thought that was a good sign. He wanted to kiss Sara's forehead but didn't quite dare. He smoothed her hair back before leaving her to sleep if she could.

Back in his room, the boys were as miserable. The same speech he'd given the girls got the same wretched look. The gurgling of his stomach was echoed by theirs and with a grimace he curled up in his own bed.

"Right." Oz closed his eyes. "I'm a mage."

Hawk mumbled spell timers. Charlie did the same until he fell asleep. Pain in his gut woke him in the middle of the night and he was ill again.

As he exited the bathroom, his mother entered the room. "The girls are still sick too. Are you feeling worse?"

"No, are the girls?"

"No, but they probably wouldn't admit it anyway. Does your head still hurt?"

"Yes, but the Tylenol helps. Don't worry, Mom, it's a flu. We'll be fine."

Mary ran a hand over his forehead and kissed his brow. "Can I get you anything?"

"No, don't let us oversleep and miss our games."

"The alarm is set. Don't worry about oversleeping. Get some rest."

When she left, Oz raced to the bathroom. All night, someone was in the bathroom being sick. In the morning, they were a wan, pasty bunch.

Stasia tried to fix Sara and herself up with makeup but gave up, unable to hide the dark circles and pasty skin. Both girls wore their hair in ponytails and put on heavy pullover sweatshirts.

"Are you guys sure you're up for this?" Mary eyed them doubtfully. The kids looked horrible. Purplish crescents under their eyes were the only color in their pallid, white faces.

"Yes, today is easier. We'll have time to rest between fights." Afraid his mother would make them stay in bed, Charlie tried to sound energized. "Thirty matches and we're done."

The trip to the convention center seemed to take twice as long as it had yesterday. The car ride made him feel worse. Noise echoed painfully in his head. By their winces when the crowd cheered them on arrival everyone still had headaches.

After checking them in, the monitor eyed them dubiously. "You guys don't look so good." He called on his cell phone and got them water bottles. Another call got him two blankets, which he handed to Charlie. Charlie thanked him, and they huddled together on the floor while waiting for their first contest. Sara sat on one side of him with Oz on the other. Despite being miserably sick, he was almost happy. Sara lay with her head on his chest and her arm around him.

"The first fight starts in three minutes. Your opponents are taking the field," the monitor warned them. "You should be home in bed! Crazy gamers, you'd play on your deathbeds," he mumbled as he turned away.

In minutes, they were deeply involved in the fight, paying no attention to anything else. The monitor made another call. "Look, these kids are playing their hearts out. Do me a favor and set up their fights quickly. Yes, I realize it'll be out of order, but so what. These guys are really sick. Yeah, okay, thanks. I owe you one."

Charlie gave him a grateful smile. His

smile faded as Oz ran to the bathroom to vomit, but when he returned he played brilliantly, with complete focus. The team followed Charlie's one-word commands and worked together flawlessly executing beautifully timed moves. So far, they'd won every match and had six remaining. After winning the next three, they hit a delay. The last team they had to face wasn't ready yet, still busy fighting another team. None of them moved, sitting at the keyboards still as statues their eyes closed and hands in their laps.

"Are you guys okay— should I call for medical help?" the monitor asked, sounding freaked out.

"No, were fine," they said in unison.

Charlie leaned forward and ran his fingers over the keypad. "Okay, guys, one more set and we can leave. Heads in the game. Sara, drink some water— at least a sip. We can go lay down in a few more minutes."

Twenty minutes later their rivals we're finally ready to play. Charlie had to wake Sara and Oz. Both moaned and clutched their heads as they sat.

"Okay, guys, let's kill them fast and get out of here. Be the character! Go get 'um!"

Every time he said tick, Sara was on it, she never missed. The ticks and tocks were right on the money. They won all three matches in nineteen minutes, ten of which they spent waiting for the other team. Each team could take a five-minute break between matches, and every team had three chances to beat their opponents. Everyone received the same gear. Skill, not item level, would ensure victory.

After their last match, they sat still until the monitor told them, they'd finished.

"I lost track, I was too busy being Chief. Let's go," he said in a combination of relief and worry.

A burning sensation had spread throughout his body and his bones ached. He was exhausted; he'd never been so tired in his life. While waiting for the taxi, they huddled together under the blanket. Sara felt flaming hot to him, and he was sure she now had a fever.

"How'd you do?" his mother asked when they entered.

"I don't know," Charlie, admitted, "I forgot to ask, but we did our best that's what counts."

Mary was seriously concerned. If they hadn't even asked how they'd done they must be much sicker than they let on. The front desk sent up a doctor when she called. Huddled together on Sara's bed both girls were feverish and hard to wake. The doctor arrived and after a quick exam called an ambulance. After checking the boys, he called for another.

"The children are extremely ill; they're dehydrated, and some tests are in order." The doctor felt her forehead. "You look a bit pale too. Are you quite alright?"

She admitted to a headache and mild diarrhea, and he prescribed plenty of fluids and bed rest.

The ambulances arrived and took them to a local hospital. The fact they didn't protest alarmed her even more. By eight that night, she was frightened. All the kids had spiked high temperatures and were unresponsive. The CDC was called in. Mary phoned John, and he promised to call their parents and head there on the first available plane.

The doctor, a Japanese man with short black hair and large glasses, spoke with her outside the room.

"The symptoms they're displaying are worrisome, and we're running tests now. Since you've developed a headache and diarrhea too we're going to quarantine them as a precaution. The blood work should be back any time now and we'll know more than. Please stay here until I receive the test results. I don't want to admit you, but I don't want you possibly spreading whatever this is."

Fifteen minutes later she was startled when people encased in white and yellow plastic body suits showed up with stretchers that resembled giant glass coffins. The doctor she'd spoken with earlier approached her wearing a bulky plastic suit.

"Well, we have something of a situation here. Somehow, you've been exposed to radiation. The children are being medevacked back to Camp Foster by helicopter. The facilities there are top notch and they have the equipment to keep them isolated and deal with the radiation. We'll need a complete list of everyone they've met with and everywhere they've been, and I'm afraid you must be admitted."

Mary was shocked speechless. She finally got her thoughts together to ask a question. "Will they be okay?"

"I'm afraid I can't answer that. The doctors at the base will have a better idea."

The doctor's words seemed to be coming from far away. Her hands shook, and she sat with a thump in the nearest chair.

"Would you come with us, please?" The doctor gestured for her to follow the nurse.

The nurse had to help her rise. In a daze, she was escorted to a room where she was asked to don a suit like theirs. "I need to call my husband first. I'll only be a minute."

The nurse nodded and left the room.

"I've got a flight Tuesday morning," John said when he answered the phone.

She started crying.

"Jesus, Mary, what is it?" Between sobs

she told him what she knew. "Dear God, how did that happen?"

"I have no idea." Her voice cracked in distress and she had to take a minute to compose herself before she spoke. "It must've happened on the plane. I have to go. The doctor wants me in a suit too. They think I've been exposed."

"I can't get there any sooner. I'll notify the other parents. Let me know when you hear anything at all."

"I love you," Mary sobbed.

"I love you too, honey, and I'll be there as soon as I can."

- 8 -

DYING FROM RADIATION

Charlie slowly became aware of his surroundings. A fiery ache pulsated deep in his bones, and his entire body felt like it burned.

Without opening his eyes, he knew where he was; he didn't need the hospital smell or the quiet beeps and hums to inform him. The sheet felt vise-tight around him, but the effort to loosen it hurt too much. A sharp pain shot through his hand, radiating through his body when his mother's gloved hand touched his. The agony was almost enough to rouse him to moan. Blackness covered his vision and he faded back into unconsciousness.

An indeterminate amount of time later he became aware of people nearby speaking in loud, angry voices. The word Sara registered, and he made a herculean effort to focus on the voice. Sara's father spoke in a clipped tone to someone.

"No, we have to move the meeting back at least three hours—"

A nurse interrupted him, "Sir, I'm sorry, sir, but no cell phones or electronic devices at all in this area. I have to insist you power it down immediately."

"Yes, yes, one moment." Her father sounded impatient. "This isn't a good time. I need to call you back, but I'll definitely be at the meeting. The board will tolerate no more delays on this project. What— yes— thank you. I'm at the hospital now making arrangements. The doctors say it won't be long now. No, no need to reschedule."

The nurse interrupted again, this time more forcefully, her voice angry. "If you don't hang up this instant, I'm calling security; you're endangering my patients with that device."

"I'll get back to you," Sara's father said, and Charlie heard loud footsteps and a squeaky wheel. Mr. Mitchel spoke again. "Arrangements have been made for the body to be moved to Oak Hill upon death. I've arranged for lead-lined caskets and special transport. Contact my assistant to work out the details. I'll be sure to inform your supervisor on your unhelpful attitude. Good day."

A door open and slammed closed and his mother whisper, "What an ass."

This was the first time he'd ever heard his mother swear, and he wanted to laugh. Then the full import of what Mr. Mitchel had said sank in. Sara was dying if not already dead. Jesus, how could this be happening?

This must be a dream. He couldn't bear the thought of Sara dying. The monitors beeped faster as the pain in his chest grew and his mother touch his hand again, a sharp stab of agony.

The hurt in his mother's voice made him want to cry and he wished he could comfort her. "Don't worry about her idiot father. Sara won't be alone. I'll be with her. Fight this, son! Dad is coming." Small sounds told him his mother was crying. "None of you will be alone. I'll be there."

A nurse fussed over him. He lost consciousness again when she leaned across his arm, the pain was excruciating.

Some time later, he became aware again. A doctor stood right beside him, speaking to his mother. "I'm sorry, Mrs. Hayes, Charles is in a deep coma now. We don't expect him to wake again. Sara is the only one who remains conscious. Ma'am, I'm truly sorry. To lose both your sons, well, I'm so sorry."

A nurse fussed at his side; the pain was distant now behind a wall of fog. His fever raged, his thoughts jumbled and he couldn't remember where he was. No, he knew, he was at the tournament.

Sara, he thought to himself, *Sara is alone. If she dies, it's my fault. My strategies got her killed. I should be with her; it's my job to protect her. I'm the tank— she can't die— we need a new strategy.*

With all his might, he tried to say they needed a new strategy. If you weren't winning the game, you needed a new plan. The healer dying means the tank goofed somewhere. Thoughts whirled frantically in his head. Sara needed him. He had to reach her. As unconsciousness took him, he muttered, "New strategy."

His mother leaned over him crying, "What— Charles, please wake up! I love you. Dad's on his way here. Wait, please, Charles, he needs to see you— to speak to you again!"

Major Elizabeth Harris, the nurse in charge, gently led Mary away. "I'm so, so, sorry. Come with me. You need to take better care of yourself. You haven't rested a moment since the children arrived. Let me bring you some coffee at least."

"I can't leave them. They shouldn't be alone when—"

"Take a few minutes for yourself, please. The nurses will be with them," Liz assured her. "Clean up and eat something. The monitors will notify you if anything changes. Come, take a rest."

Mary wiped at her nose and made a frustrated sound when she touched the helmet instead. The radiation suit made such simple things impossible. She went with the nurse.

"When your husband arrives I'll come get you, or if there are any changes."

Mary entered the bathroom, and Liz returned to her patients.

Nothing had changed. Four had lapsed into deep comas. One was in and out of consciousness. Tears sprang to her eyes— she pulled herself together and administered the pain medication to them, gently coating the weeping sores with lotion, then checking the fluid levels of the IV's before informing the other nurse she was going for lunch and would return in thirty minutes.

She'd already been on shift for five hours and expected to be on duty for at least five more— unless the end arrived sooner. The children's parents would be arriving within the next few hours, and she planned to stay on duty and assure they got a chance to say goodbye.

Decontamination took the usual five minutes before she could safely remove her suit. A quick check of Charlie's mother showed her dozing in the chair in the room next door, her food untouched. Tiptoeing out, she headed to the cafeteria with a quick stop to tell the nurse at the desk that Mrs. Hayes dozed next door and to buzz her in the cafeteria if anything changed.

The nurses at the station near the elevators glanced up, their eyes sad when she approached.

"No change," she said and exchanged unhappy nods with them. Everyone knew the news wouldn't be good and soon. "Any word on when the other parents arrive?"

"Within the next three hours," one of the nurses said. "Sara Mitchel's stepmother arrived yesterday, followed by her hoard of paparazzi. She didn't come in?"

"No, she entered the ward, but declined to wear a suit." Liz had never seen parents as heartless as Sara's. Even the drunken abusers made more of an effort. The interview Tara Leland Mitchel had given on television, of a grief-stricken mother, had been academy award winning when Liz knew she hadn't even seen Sara.

The nurse at the desk gave a small shrug.

"Maybe she's claustrophobic."

"Maybe," Liz agreed and continued to the elevator. *Tara was just a cold woman*, Liz thought as she stepped into the elevator. The only use she had for that sick child was publicity. She was milking it for all she was worth, doing news spots and talk shows. It broke Liz's heart to see pictures of a smiling, healthy Sara at a track meet or dance recital.

The other parents might be in time. Their children were fighting hard in there. After a quick meal, she headed back to her patients. A man in the hallway outside of the isolation wards, wearing a dark-blue business suit, spoke on a cell phone, checking his watch, waiting impatiently for Sara to die so he could get on with his day. While Mrs. Hayes made the rounds, talking to each of them, reading to them, or sitting with them, he hadn't visited once.

Visitors probably made no difference at this point. The children were too far gone to notice anything, but still, the utter disregard that man showed for a child in his care. Her lip curled farther as she thought of the heartless parent who'd left his child to die alone. *Not on my watch,* she would ensure that didn't happen. Her shoulders straightened in determination, *nurses monitored them continuously.*

As she thought that, she spied her colleague. Nurse Young was already outside of the decontamination room. He shouldn't have been. He shouldn't leave until Liz was suited up. It took five minutes to suit up properly. *If something happened while no one was suited, well...* the alarms sounded.

- 9 -

REALIZATION

"Damn it!" Liz yelled and ran to the prep room. "Get that suit back on now!"

Both nurses fumbled with the suits, putting them on as fast as they could with hands made clumsy by haste.

"You're on report! Why the hell did you leave them alone?" Liz slammed her helmet on, not waiting for a reply. A fine mist and an ultraviolet light and blower kicked in as she counted the seconds in her head. "Come on, come on," she said, staring at the light over the door, willing it to turn green as more sirens blared and someone screamed.

Jesus, that had to be Sara, Liz thought. She

was the only one conscious enough to scream. The children had been quiet through the entire ordeal to this point. *What would cause those screams?* A bright yellow light startled her when she jerked the door open. The screaming stopped and was replaced by sobbing and a confusing babble of voices.

To her shock, Charlie was out of bed, leaning over Anastasia, saying something she couldn't hear to the sobbing girl. Oliver sat up, pulling off his stomach tube, while Sebastian gagged and yanked out his own throat tube. Every alarm in the place shrieked. Liz hit the intercom button. "Get me help in here, stat! Call the doctors and keep Mrs. Hayes out. No one comes in here except us! Doctors and nurses only."

Not bothering to answer the nurse on the intercom jabbering questions, she went to check on Anastasia who still sobbed. Sebastian was gagging, she assumed from removing the trach tube. A flash of light startled her. Sebastian saying thanks startled her even more. When she whirled to face him, he was lying down now. His eyes were closed, his face white under the red, scaly skin. The monitor above him read flat lined with all alarms blaring, but his chest rose and fell.

The other nurse entered, eyed the pandemonium in the room, and quickly went to the monitors and started shutting them off. "What's going on in here?"

"This was your watch! You tell me! I was on a break," Liz said as she tried to replace a blood pressure monitor on Sebastian. "Why did you leave them alone?"

"The leg of my suit ripped on the edge of Charles's bed and I had to go out quickly. They appeared to be unconscious. Charles was restless, but not awake. I was only gone minutes," Nurse Young said as he reattached the monitors on Sebastian.

"Check Oz. I'm okay. I don't need help." Hawk's voice was dry and cracked.

"I will, sweetie. We'll help everyone, but you have to let us. Let me clip this to your finger. It won't hurt."

"The hell it won't!" Hawk yanked his hand away and flexed his fingers. He examined them in surprise, then glanced at Oz lying next to him. "Jesus, we look like the walking dead."

He held his hand out to the nurse and gritted his teeth as she reapplied the monitor. His expression changed from dread to relief when the small, finger monitor was in place.

"Yeah, that don't hurt now." He turned a grinning face to Sara. "Thank you, Sara— Jesus, Sara, pray for the love of God!"

Liz also turned to Sara. Every alarm hooked to her blared. All leads were still hooked up. She was failing badly.

Stasia let out a piercing shriek as Liz headed to Sara and Charlie hollered, "Please, we need you here right now."

Liz heard Sara mumbling a Hail Mary as both nurses turned to Charlie. When Sara muttered amen another flash of light lit the room. The monitors above her quieted and her eyes closed. The white sheet covering her rose and fell with her breathing.

"Jesus Christ, I got her. You check the other one!" Nurse Young said and hurried to Anastasia's side.

Liz ignored the monitors, unsure what ones worked. Sara's pulse was nice and steady when she performed a quick check, and she sighed in relief. One by one, she reattached the monitors and checked the results. "Respiration right where it should be, let me check—" she broke off as another voice broke in.

"What's going on here? Nurse Howin sent me an urgent page. Both of you, report to my office after we straighten this out!" Doctor Allen sounded pissed. Liz knew heads would roll, probably hers. *Damn Nurse Young for leaving them alone.*

"What the hell happened?" the doctor asked.

The children were clearly much better. How that was possible when they were hours if not minutes from death, she had no idea.

Another doctor entered, and they worked together reattaching the patients to the monitors. within ten minutes the room was quiet again, all monitors back to beeping and humming quietly. The doctor questioned Charlie, who'd grudgingly gotten back into bed.

"Give me a full blood panel on all of them; urine samples, skin samples— the whole deal. Take scrapings from these sores here or should I say where those sores were." Doctor Allen beckoned to Doctor Hill. "This is bizarre. Look at these scabs. It looks like it healed instantly. There isn't a mark to show where we inserted the lung or stomach tubes." He turned to Liz. "Bring them food, no solids. If they can handle liquids, we'll add in solids later. Move them to a new suite but keep them in full quarantine. I don't know what this is or if it'll go as mysteriously as it arrived." He checked Charlie's vitals and reflexes. "How do you feel, young man? Do you have any pain or discomfort anywhere?"

"Itchy. I feel itchy, and hungry, and tired. But no, I don't hurt anywhere in particular just an all-over achiness."

The doctor turned to the room in general. "Do any of you have any pain or discomfort anywhere?"

Sara and Stasia both said they did and Oz and Sebastian mumbled they did too. The doctor went to Stasia's side. "Where exactly does it hurt, young lady?"

"Um," she pulled the doctor down to her and whispered to him.

He straightened and smiled. "Yes, well,

we'll see to that at once," he beckoned Liz over and held a whispered consultation with her.

She nodded and pulled the curtain around Stasia closed.

The doctor gazed thoughtfully at the others. "Yes, well, I think we can remove the catheters." He peered at the trach and stomach tubes on the floor. "It seems you've already removed all my hard work. Before I examine each of you individually, is anyone in any immediate distress?"

Doctor Hill spoke up. "Is anyone having any problems breathing, seeing, or hearing?"

Charlie shook his head, his gaze traveling his friends as they shook their heads no.

"Okay then, while I'm happy to hear it, does anyone have an explanation of what happened?"

"I woke up, sir," Charlie said before any of the others spoke. "I was suddenly stronger, err, better. I got up to check the others, and they were better too. Stasia was choking on the thing in her throat, so I yanked it out. I probably shouldn't have done that, but I panicked. When she screamed, the others got up too."

"And everyone decided to remove the medical equipment you felt so chipper?"

"Well, yes." Oz grimaced. "And it wasn't fun, but it was choking me; I had to get it off."

"What he said." Hawk grinned at the doctor.

Sara nodded. Unexpectedly, she started crying. "Am I dead? Is this Heaven? Or—Hell? Please, don't let this be Hell! I was never bad enough for Hell!" Pale trembling hands rose to cover her face as she sobbed.

Charlie immediately rose, and disregarding the beeps and buzzes as the wires once more disconnected, went to her side where he leaned down and hugged her tightly. "This isn't Hell, and we aren't dead, I promise. This is a miracle. *You* are a miracle."

He put his head next to hers and whispered, "Don't say anything. We'll talk later in private. I don't know why or how this happened, but you are a miracle."

Sara still cried.

Charlie rested his head on hers. "It doesn't matter, everyone's fine. We're a team, and we're together. This isn't a dream; I promise you, we all lived."

Charlie's gaze traveled his friends again. They did resemble the walking dead. Rough, reddened skin had flaked off, leaving big patches, and Sara's hair stuck to his fingers as he rubbed her back. He tried to wipe it off unobtrusively. The long blond strands of hair caught in his fingers made her cry harder.

Stasia put a hand to her head and stared in horror at the handful of hair that detached. A loud sob tore from her, and she turned to her brother, "Jesus God, is this Hell?"

Sara cried harder.

"No, Stasia, we're fine." Hawk started pulling off wires to go to his sister.

"Stop right there, young man!" Nurse Young barked. "Doctor, some sedation might be in order here?"

"Yes, by all means." He turned to Liz. "Nurse Harris."

Hawk again started removing his monitors to go comfort his sister.

"Okay, fine," the doctor said loudly. "The pills are mild, and you don't have to take it, but it's one small pill to help you be calm while we sort this out. Stay in those beds. I mean it!" The doctor glared at Hawk.

Liz approached Sara with a small pill she took from a nearby locked cabinet and handed her a cup of water.

Sara leaned away from Liz.

"Take it. The sedatives will help you," Charlie commanded. "Do what the doctor says. This was a shock. Take that, and I'll look after Stasia. Everyone is okay." Charlie watched her take the pill. "I'm here. You aren't alone. This isn't Hell. It's not Heaven either; it's a hospital. As soon as I check on Stasia, I'll return."

Charlie stepped to Stasia's side, hugged her, and whispered in her ear. The tears stopped, and she held his hand tight while she took the small pill.

Charlie turned to the boys. "Take it. Do what the doctors say. This is team business. We'll work it out. Everyone is okay. We'll stay together. Sara will be fine. Let's take a minute and catch our breath."

"My hair and skin are falling off," Stasia said, still crying. The hand holding a hank of her long, dark hair shook. "That doesn't feel fine. She needs to pray harder."

Charlie nodded and kissed her cheek. "She will, just not right this second. We'll set a new trend. Bald is the new cool—"

The doctor interrupted, "In my experience people who've undergone radiation and experience hair loss have it grow in thicker than before. I don't believe you'll be bald long."

Oz ran a hand over his head and wiped off the hair clinging to his fingers on the sheet with a grimace of distaste. "It'll grow back?"

"Ninety percent of the time it does," the doctor agreed.

"This isn't a dream? This feels like a dream." Sara sounded scared when she turned to him, her bright-blue eyes huge, swimming in tears, surrounded by dark circles and patchy red skin smeared in shiny cream.

Charlie took her hand and kissed her temple.

Doctor Allen glanced up from a chart at the foot of Oz's bed. "I assure you, you are in fact alive, very alive, more than you were one hour ago. Your friend is correct; it's been a miracle."

"How long will we be here?" Oz said, still trying to wipe off the hair sticking to his fingers.

"That I don't know." The doctor rubbed his chin thoughtfully. "Until we're sure you aren't contagious or emitting harmful radiation, we can't release you. Once we prepare a new suite, we'll move you to a different isolation ward. This room needs to be decontaminated. If somehow you miraculously recovered from the radiation that doesn't mean it's gone, it could be here. Well, we know it's here, it's just not inside you."

The doctor pointed to a meter over the door. "That tells us there's radiation in this room. We need you out of here in suits, pronto."

THE GOOD AND THE BAD

Liz took the blood and skin samples the doctor had requested and had a tray ready when the Hazmat suits arrived. After helping the kids don the suits, she ushered them into the decontamination chamber. They stood in the chamber for two cycles before being escorted into a room identical to the one they'd vacated.

Five beds placed close together were separated from the hallway by a wall of windows with drawn blinds. Two small bathrooms leading to the showers were along one wall and a long narrow window that showed late morning sunshine was across from the door they entered. Three metal chairs stood against the wall and monitors on rolling stands stood between each bed, leaving little floor space.

Liz helped them remove the bulky radiation suits. "I want everyone to shower using the blue soap followed by the white one. Let the blower dry you and dress in the clothes provided. I'll be checking each of you for radiation as you exit. If you check clear, we'll stay here, but if you don't, we'll do this again and see if we can wash any residue away.

"The shower is on a timer. There's a hand-held water wand to reach any hard to reach areas. Make sure you do the soles of your feet and behind your ears. Use the brush provided to scrub your backs. Don't be alarmed at the dead skin that comes off and loosing hair. I'm sorry, sweeties, but it's all going to fall out."

As Liz spoke Sara flicked her fingers and winked at Charlie. He grinned back as she cast dispel and a renew on all of them one at a time. Nurse Harris didn't appear to notice a thing. Even looking for it, the small spark of light that flit from Sara's fingertips to each of them was hard to see in the well-lit room.

"If you want to neaten up the patches that linger, I'll have a razor handy. Three shower stalls are through those doors. Boys, you go first. Pull the cord if you need help, and Nurse Young will come help you. We can't remove our suits yet, but soon I'm sure. Go ahead. I'll be right out here with the girls."

The three boys trooped into the shower. The loud buzz of a razor blocked the sound of conversation as Charlie stepped into the shower. The girls must've decided to shave off the patches of long hair they had left. Stasia would be heartbroken, losing her hair would be hard on her.

He wasn't sure what Sara's reaction would be. She never fussed with her hair, preferring a quick ponytail or messy bun. But, he supposed, for any girl the loss of their hair would be a bigger blow than for a guy.

For himself, he didn't mind. He often wore a crew cut in the summer and kept his hair short the rest of the time. Oz and Hawk would be upset too. Oz was vain about his shoulder-length blond hair and Hawk had been mimicking the style. Charlie was just grateful they were alive, to hell with their hair.

He soaped diligently while he pondered the idea this was a crazy fever dream. This wasn't Hell and was unlikely to be Heaven, although that was a distant possibility. *Sara couldn't be in Hell, ergo, this wasn't it. But, Heaven, yeah, she could be there. Would there be soap this smelly in Heaven though? Holy Christ this stuff was rank.* At the buzzer, he gratefully switched soaps.

The big flakes of skin and all the hair swirling down the drain freaked him out, so he tried not to see it. When it all seemed to have come loose with no new patches falling off, he sighed in relief. The buzzer sounded, and he stood under the clean water trying to decide what they should do now. They would all probably be debating that. The nature of the miracle, while clear to him, was so outside of his previous reality he almost believed this was, in fact, Heaven or a fever dream.

The water turned off and blowers turned on, drying him in moments, but he remained still until the blower turned off. When he exited the shower, he found someone had removed his bio suit and replaced it with a pair of white sweatpants, white shirt, white boxers, and a white sweatshirt. Under the clothes, he found white socks and slippers.

The girls weren't in the main room, and he was grateful when he gazed in a mirror hanging over a small sink.

"Jesus Christ, I'm a hot mess."

Weird clumps of hair stuck up randomly in spots on his mostly bald head. The skin on his face and arms was patchy; white in spots, red in others, with scabby brown patches, and a few tan spots here and there.

Oz and Hawk entered the room. They looked like him and judging by their horrified expressions when they saw him were unaware of it. He gestured to the mirror and turned away, giving them privacy.

"Holy shit!" Oz exclaimed at the sight of himself.

Followed by a mournful Hawk. "We won't make the cover of Video Gamer looking like this, that's for sure."

"The covers shot already." Oz sounded disgusted. "And you wouldn't make it anyway; they always use the girls."

"Oh man, Stasia will freak. I hope they have more pills for her." Hawk turned to Charlie. "Hey, Chief, can Sara fix this, you think?"

"I'm sure she can't, but she saved our lives, so let's not be nitpicky. It's just hair. I for one am going to shave off the rest as soon as I can."

"Yeah, me too, this is freakish. Where is everyone? I thought they wanted to see if we're still radioactive." Oz lifted the blind on the window behind the bed and peeked out.

The showers were going. The girls would be washing up. Charlie shrugged and headed to the call button when Nurse Young showed up, still suited, and carrying a small box that he ran over each of them individually. After smacking the box a few times, he frowned at the results and redid it.

"To be sure, I'm getting another machine. This one says there's no radiation. I don't see how that's possible. Please get into the beds, you need to rest."

Charlie obligingly got into bed. Hawk got in the one beside him, and Oz took the one nearest the door.

Oz fiddled with the sheet covering his legs. "This sucks. We'll be poked and prodded until we're bored to death."

"I'm already bored to death," Hawk complained.

"Not a word to anyone until we have a chance to talk. We don't want them to take her." Charlie met their eyes, ensuring they agreed.

"As if we would." Hawk flopped back on his bed and stared at the ceiling. "We heard you, it's team business. Besides, I don't think she's the only one."

"She isn't; I'm sure of that. But, let's talk later when we're out of here."

Nurse Young returned and reran the tests. "Beats me, boys, but you're all clear. Let me help you clean up," he offered, holding out an electric razor. "Your parents are here and excited to see you. We'll allow visits for a short time, but you need to rest, and we have more tests to do. The doctors have a full exam scheduled."

Oz went first.

The nurse spread a gown over him and carefully shaved his head. He gestured to a tube of ointment on the counter. "Try that, it should help with the itching of your dead skin, but only time will make this blotchiness disappear."

"How much time?" Hawk asked as Nurse Young shaved his head.

"Well, it differs for everyone but a few weeks at least, maybe as much as a year. But most likely two months tops," Nurse Young added hurriedly as Hawk groaned in dismay. "Besides, you can use a cover-up, and no one will notice it."

"Makeup." Hawk dropped the tube of ointment Oz handed him. "I'm not wearing makeup, no way!"

"No one will make you, but men wear foundation all the time." Nurse Young removed the towel from Hawk's neck. "Every actor on Earth wears it but suit yourself."

After rinsing the razor quickly, he gestured for Charlie to take a seat. He was almost done with Charlie's head when the girls entered wearing the white clothes. They went right to the two empty beds without glancing up and huddled under the covers.

Hawk hugged his sister. "Matching haircuts," he said cheerfully, then glanced at Charlie in dismay as his sister cried on his shoulder. "Aw, Sis, come on, don't cry. It's just hair. It'll grow back, and our skin should be fine in a few weeks, and Nurse Young says there's makeup to cover it anyways."

Charlie didn't hear the answer, if any, that she made. He knew she was crying, but she was doing it quietly. He thanked Nurse Young for the haircut and gestured to the girls. "Should I go talk to them or give them their space?"

"You know them better than I do. Do what feels right even if it's hard," Nurse Young whispered back.

Charlie nodded, swallowed heavily, straightened his shoulders and ran his hand over his newly shaved head, smiled ruefully at the nurse, and went to speak with the girls.

"This is bad, there's no denying that." Charlie took their hands. "We'll get better now though, and that's good. This ugliness is temporary, and honestly, after the patchiness fades or we cover it, it isn't that bad. You have very attractive heads."

Oz rolled his eyes when Charlie glanced at him. Charlie glared back and turned to the girls again. "We've been given a miracle. Let's keep that in mind and not wallow on what we lost. We've all gained far more. Let's put a brave face on it for our parents, cooperate with the doctors, and return home as soon as we can." He leaned over to kiss Stasia's cheek, and then Sara's, and ran a hand lightly over her head. "Nothing's changed about how we feel for you guys. This doesn't matter, we're still a team."

He sighed unhappily; his speech had no effect. They both still looked miserable. He climbed into his bed suddenly exhausted.

- 11 -

MIA

Oz's mother entered wearing a bulky bio-hazard suit and embraced her son awkwardly. After greeting everyone, she stood by Oz's bed and clumsily patted his hand.

"Once everybody else visits their kids, your father will be in," she said.

The seat at the foot of Oz's bed was positioned poorly for conversation, but she sat there anyway and fiddled with the suit, not up to making small talk. A relieved expression crossed her face when Camila arrived.

Camila went directly to Hawk and hugged him. "Only two extra suits are available right now, we need to be quick, but we can come again tomorrow, and you might be out of quarantine in a few days. Sorry I took so long to arrive. I had a hard time rounding up the money."

"No problem, Mom. We knew you'd come as soon as you could." Hawk hugged his mother, suit and all, and she turned to her daughter.

"Oh, sweetie, your beautiful hair!"

Stasia burst into tears in her mother's arms.

Hawk sat next to his weeping sister, rubbing her back as she cried. "The doctor says it'll grow back."

Oz's mother turned to him after observing the reunion. "Has anyone said anything about the cause, or well, anything?"

"No, they think it's from the plane, but they have no idea really." Oz shrugged.

"Are you better now, though?" Oz's mother asked as she stared at the Moraleses.

Camila turned to hear the answer, her grip tightening on her daughter.

"Well, I'm not sure what's going on, but we feel a lot better, and the doctors think we're recovered," Hawk said.

"The commotion when we arrived, well, we thought you'd died. Don't ever do that again," Oz's mother said as she hugged him. "If you're better now, I'm going to head home tomorrow." She tittered nervously. "Work, ya know. Your father will be staying— he'll be in shortly. Feel better," she called over her shoulder as she fled the room.

Oz's father ambled in a few minutes later.

Frankly, Charlie was amazed the suit fit him.

"Been causing trouble I see, boy." The suit bulged alarmingly when he leaned over to give his son a hug. "Glad to find you're doing better. We thought you died on us. This place is a circus. I have half a mind to sue."

"Mom says she can't stay long. Charlie's mother can escort me home if you have to go home too," Oz said.

"We'll see, boy. I'm not sure what the plans are. The airlines reimbursing our tickets, so that ain't nothing to worry about, but I can't miss much more work this year." He patted his son with his gloved hand and stared at it curiously. "This is sure some rig they got us in. I'm glad you're recovering, but how I'm going to pay for all this...." He trailed off uneasily and slapped his son lightly on the back. "There's a waiting list for this here rig. First thing tomorrow, I'll return." He looked the others over as he stood. "You all look like a bad day at the beach." He chuckled at his own joke, his voice sounding tinny and far away in the helmet.

Mrs. Morales followed him out, promising to come back soon.

Fifteen minutes later, Charlie's parents arrived together, and his father headed straight to him. After hugging him tightly a moment, he went to Oz and hugged him as tightly. The rest of them received quick hugs before he returned to Charlie.

Mary spoke to Sara, "Your father was unavoidable detained, sweetheart. Mr. Ramos is here to watch over you and asked me to find out if you need anything."

"Thanks, Mrs. H. I'll need clothes, I guess. Ours were destroyed. Could you ask him to send clothes and toiletries and a new credit card for my ticket home?"

Mary patted her hand, the suit making a thumping sound. "Don't worry about a thing; I'll take care of it. Does he know your sizes?"

"Have him call my housekeeper. She can tell him or send something overnight."

Mary patted her hand again. "I'm staying until everyone is released and I'll make sure you get home safe. You won't be alone here, I promise."

Charlie was aware his father was silently crying. He hugged him tighter before sitting back and smiling at him. "As you can see, the news of our demise was premature. We seem to be healing up quickly."

His father cleared his throat; his gruff voice thickened with tears. "Son, I've never been as relieved in my life. When I arrived and heard the commotion...." He stopped and cleared his throat again and tried to wipe his face but couldn't through the helmet. "I thought you died. To lose both of you..."

"John!" His mother said sharply, interrupting him.

His father stopped speaking and hugged him again. A chill settled over Charlie and he remembered a barely heard conversation.

"Where's Richard? Why didn't he come too? Oh, my God, did something happen to him?" Charlie's voice rose and cracked.

His mother turned her head away.

His father sobbed aloud, slumped, then cleared his throat, and straightened, holding Charlie's hand in his.

The blood drained from Charlie's face, leaving him light-headed.

"We don't..." A shuddering breath traveled through his father. "We don't know. ISIS attacked his transport. A telegram arrived informing us he was MIA— his entire squad is MIA. The convoy was wiped out completely."

"Is my brother dead?" The shrillness of his own voice startled him. Cold dread filled him. He rubbed his face and took a deep breath. Stasia made a noise between a whispered scream and a sob that rose the small hairs on Charlie's arm.

"No!" His mother laid her gloved hand on his arm. "He's missing! Not dead— missing!"

"Mary, we both know that's false hope," his father said sadly.

"No, they're missing, and there's no such thing as false hopes. Our son is miraculously healed. Look at him, he was in a coma, almost dead, they all were. He hasn't spoken in two days, and he's talking now. Have faith, please, John, have faith." Mary put a comforting hand on her husband's shoulder.

"Yes, miracles exist." Charlie's father took a deep breath and gripped his son's hand clumsily through the gloves. "There's hope. We won't give up. This has been the worst week of my life. Hell, the worst week of anyone's life! Words can't express how grateful I am you're doing better. That I can speak to you again and see you smile." John gazed at the others as tears trailed over his cheeks. "To see everyone doing so well is truly a miracle. I need to find a restroom to clean up. The doctors might not let me return tonight, but I'll return as soon as I can. Don't worry about Richard, he's a soldier, it's all he ever wanted to be. The military is searching. They'll find them. Have faith. You get well." John hugged everyone again before leaving.

"Now don't start," Mary said before he

spoke. "How could I tell you when you were dying right before my eyes? Until I hear conclusively they've found his body, I'll have faith. Please, everybody, get better. Try not to worry, just get well."

The suit crinkled as she hugged him again. "Tomorrow I'll bring the letter they sent. Know that he wanted to be here for you and he would've been if fate hadn't interfered. I'm sorry you found out tonight. I didn't want to tell you until you were stronger. Please, please, don't let this disrupt your healing. Try to rest."

She gazed at him with such worried eyes he couldn't stay angry.

"I'll rest, Mom, and we'll get better, and they'll find Rick and send him home. It's our week for miracles. All things come in threes. We're due for one more miracle."

He winced because they had their three even if she didn't know it. *But, maybe that didn't count,* he thought with sudden hope. Maybe, surviving the lightning strike and the new gifts were the miracle and not their survival. Perhaps that was one miracle. If that was true, they had one more coming, and

Rick would come home soon.

A relieved smile lit his mother's face. "I'll bring books or something tomorrow. Everybody get some rest." After hugging everyone, she paused at the door. "Good night, Team Valor."

Stasia lay on the bed and pulled the light sheet up to her neck. "This place is stifling;" she said crossly. "I need McDonald's and real coffee. Your dad is right. This is the worst week ever! God, and now Rick!" She threw an arm over her eyes to hide the tears.

Sara sighed and closed her eyes. "I want to sunbathe in the hot Florida sun with a good book."

Charlie sat with a thump in the chair beside her. "I wanted to go the playoff game and win it with my parents and Rick and all of you watching."

Tears filled his eyes; he closed them before they fell. Sara leaned over and hugged him.

"I want two things." Blue eyes shining brightly with repressed excitement, Oz stood in front of them and held up one finger. "First, I want to thank you all for helping me buy that last spell. It cost a lot of gold, but I think we can agree it was money well spent. And second," he held up a second finger and grinned triumphantly. "I want to Locate Rick."

Charlie sat up in sudden excitement and smiled at Oz. "Yes, I want that too."

Sara pulled away from Charlie, smiled brilliantly, and hugged Oz. "Yeah, I want to Locate him too."

"Well, duh, of course, we want to find him." Hawk turned from the window. "Why wouldn't we want to... oh!" A fierce grin crossed his face. He darted a quick glance around and glared at the intercom before peering back out the window. "Yes."

"I want to go shopping." Stasia eyes were closed, her hands clenched in the blankets. "We need some epic clothes. Your mom said there's some good shops. Let's plan our shopping expedition, or at least think about what we'll need. We need watches for sure."

"Tick," Charlie said his voice low and thoughtful.

"Tock," Sara replied as she took his hand and squeezed.

- 12 -

MAGICAL NEEDS

That night the nurses checked on them every three hours. Charlie woke when Sara asked the nurse for an extra blanket. The light by her bed went on as a nurse he didn't recognize examined her vitals and temperature.

"No fever, young lady, that's good. Your hands are chilly though. Let me bring you an extra blanket." The nurse spread another blanket over her. "Don't wait until we come in. Press the buttons anytime you need us."

When the nurse left, he hopped out of bed and dragged his monitor over to her. The skin on her hands and cheeks felt ice cold.

A pile of clean blankets sat in the nearby cabinet. He took one and covered them. Fine shivers wracked her.

"You okay?" he whispered, hoping he wouldn't disturb the others.

"I'm so cold. I can't get warm." She snuggled into his side.

No wonder she was cold, he thought, s*he must have lost twenty pounds this week*. Everyone had. Thin to start with, now her wrists were skeletal. Her once graceful fingers were bony claws clenched tight to the blanket. Bones formed hard lumps under his hand as he rubbed her back, trying to warm her.

"You need a sandwich. You're too skinny."

The reply she made was an indistinct murmur as she snuggled closer.

Her shivering gradually lessened, and she fell asleep. He didn't remember falling asleep; the nurse waking him surprised him.

"What's all this then?" The nurse turned the light on above the bed, rousing everyone. "There's to be no hanky-panky, young man. Get back in your own bed this instant!"

Charlie flipped the blanket back to show Sara cocooned in the other two. The nurse's hostile tone made Sara stare at him in dismay.

"Nothing's going on. I was trying to warm her up," he said indignantly.

The nurse harrumphed and gestured to his empty bed, sounding even angrier when she said, "Go! I'll take care of Miss Mitchel." With another disapproving glare at Charlie, she took Sara's temperature and felt her hands and feet. "You're cold, no doubt about it, not dangerously so, but if you become any colder, let us know at once. Get to sleep all of you!" The clipboards at the ends of their beds were marked decisively, and she marched out.

Charlie stared after her thoughtfully. A warrior's protective aura might have more consequences than he'd originally considered. He pursed his lips and leaned back on the bed, deep in thought.

After she'd left, Stasia rose and leaned over Sara. "Nurse friendly, huh? Move over." Using her blanket, she cuddled into Sara's side. "She can't protest about us. Jeez, you're an ice cube. No, it's cool, keep your feet on me, you need to warm up." Stasia rubbed her hands over Sara's back until they both fell asleep and woke when Liz arrived in the morning.

Liz didn't complain about the girls snuggled together, only asked if they were all right. The reading she got from the thermometer made her frown. "I'll return in one minute." When she returned, she carried an IV setup in her hands and used it on Sara. "The doctor ordered an IV for you. This will only take a moment. Breakfast this morning is another nutritional shake. If everyone handles that well, I'll serve yogurt and juice."

Charlie hoped for more; he was ravenous. "Thanks, but I'm starving. Can we get another one?"

The rest of his team asked for more except for Sara who drank hers and huddled under the covers, shivering.

Liz laughed and sent for more.

Doctor Allen arrived and pulled the privacy curtain around Sara's bed. Liz did the now usual check on their vitals. The doctor's voice was an indistinct murmur. Charlie glanced at Hawk who was closer. Hawk nodded and gave him a small smile.

Charlie released a breath he hadn't realized he held. "Food please, we're starving."

"Orange juice." Oz gave Hawk a pointed glance the nurse didn't see.

"Yes, orange juice, please." Hawk lifted an inquiring brow to Oz who nodded slightly. "Lots of it, everyone wants orange juice, please."

The nurse laughed and agreed. "I'll return in a few minutes with yogurt and orange juice."

"Florida orange juice if they have it, please." Oz glanced meaningfully at Sara's bed.

The doctor opened the curtain. "If her temperature doesn't rise in an hour, I'll order more tests. Keep me informed, nurse." Then he turned to the rest of them. "The blood work we took yesterday returned and looks better. So much better that more doctors want to examine you and take more samples if that's okay with you?"

"Sure," Charlie said immediately. "Any word on when we can go?"

"Not yet," Doctor Allen said. "Let's see what these new tests show first. I'll return in an hour. Eat, and shower if you like. There's fresh clothing in the bathroom. I'll order eggs and soft foods for lunch if the yogurt isn't a problem." The doctor gestured for Liz who followed him out.

"You okay, Sara?" Charlie hurried to Sara's side when the doctor left.

"Fine, just cold."

"A sun-priest needs sun-juice." Oz sighed in exasperation, "When a sun-priest is depleted to the point of impending death, or death, they need to drink sun-juice to restore their life force, water won't do it. Otherwise, she has to wait a forty-eight-hour cooldown. Her HP, spells and buffs will be half strength until the sun replenishes her. In the game, that takes two days of playing outside unless she goes to a Sun-temple, or another priest blesses her, or she drinks sun-juice. Sun-juice will replenish her instantly."

"OJ will help?" Charlie eyed Sara doubtfully.

"Couldn't hurt." Oz shrugged.

Hawk stretched his leg, rubbing his knee.

"Can you pray for me, Sara? My leg is almost completely better."

"I'll try. I don't know that many prayers actually." Sara wrinkled her brow and pursed her lips. "I'll attempt to do one just for you. Um— The Lord is my Shepard I shall not want, he makes me lie down in green pastures—"

Charlie laughed as he interrupted her. "I don't think you need to—" the door opened, and Liz entered carrying a tray.

"Sorry to interrupt your prayers. I brought you juice and yogurt."

"You heard us?" Charlie put his hand on Sara's shoulder protectively. If they suspected what she'd done, they would take her. *Over his dead body,* he thought. His grip tightened on Sara and his eyes narrowed.

"Well, yes. Cameras and intercoms monitor this room. Didn't you know?" Liz glanced up from the tray in her hand as she took a quick step backward.

"No, we didn't know." Charlie gritted his teeth, trying to remember how incriminating they'd been. *Not too bad,* he thought. *Just the sun-juice and that could be taken as weird,* he hoped. He took his yogurt and OJ from the tray, telling himself Liz was his friend.

"This room is monitored in lots of ways," Liz continued as she sidled past him. "Every spec of air in here is being monitored, light, temperature— every fluctuation. Soft conversation isn't audible, but talking as I'm doing now, and Sara's prayers, those are audible. Don't be embarrassed for praying; it's nice to see young people with faith." Liz turned to Hawk. "God hears everyone's prayers. You don't need someone else to pray for you, you can do it yourself."

"Yes, ma'am." Hawk stared at the floor, his ears turning red.

"Does anyone want a shower now?" Liz asked.

"After the tests are finished if you don't mind," Charlie said, and the others agreed.

"That's fine. Your parents are here and wish to visit for a few minutes, if you're up to it, that is."

"Sure, send them in." Charlie felt equal parts anticipation and dread. He wanted to see them but dreaded the letter they brought.

Liz turned to the intercom and told

whoever answered the Hayes could come in.

"I thought you said they're listening." Charlie frowned.

"They can listen but aren't always. The intercoms are at the desk and right outside the door where I heard you. To assure we're heard, we press the button to get attention."

Charlie sighed in relief. Maybe no one had overheard them calling Sara a sun-priest.

"Can I get another orange juice, please?" Sara still huddled in her blanket, but her face had more color now.

"Me too," the rest of them chorused.

"Sure, I'll return in a few minutes." Liz passed Charlie's parents as they entered.

His mother carried two shopping bags. His father clutched an envelope awkwardly in his gloved hands.

Mary hugged him, "Dad has the letter. These bags are for the others. I'll hand them out while you read it." After giving him another quick hug, she emptied the bag on Sara's bed. The team gathered around Sara's bed and his mother, allowing him privacy with his father.

Mary handed a black, knit hat to Oz. "I

brought caps. The doctors said you can wear them, and they've been decontaminated. This is a clean room. Everything we bring in, or out, goes through decontamination. Magazines are in the bag with a stack of news reports and an advance copy of Video Gamer."

Hawk picked up the magazines. The picture taken the first day of the tournament of Sara and Stasia had made the cover of Video Gamer.

"The cap might help you warm up, Sara." Mary handed an all-white, soft winter hat to Sara and one to Stasia. "I can bring wigs if you want."

"No, thank you," Sara said as Stasia shook her head. "Thank you for this, Mrs. H. We appreciate it."

"Once the quarantine is lifted, I can bring in cosmetics." She offered a notebook and pen to Stasia. "Make me a list of what you want and don't worry about the cost. Mr. Mitchel is generously footing the bill. He gave me a credit card for that express purpose. It was very kind of him, Sara."

"Yeah, that's him all right, Mr.

Generosity." Sara jammed the hat on her head. "I'm sure he has a team of lawyers preparing to sue someone right now for all of this." She hunkered down into the blankets and shivered. "If it isn't too much trouble, could you buy me a heavy robe? It's so cold in here."

"Sure, sweetie, I'll pick it up after this. I wanted to tell you, we, all the parents, agreed to more testing. We signed papers this morning. Doctor Allen said you gave permission already. You did, didn't you?"

"Yes." Stasia flopped back on her bed, sounding disgusted. "We agreed. We want to know what happened too. Have they said anything to you about the cause?"

"So far they think it's from that storm or whatever on the airplane. Only you guys were affected from the plane. A few people are sick, but they think it's from contact with you."

"Oh, my God, I didn't realize! Who else is sick?" Sara grabbed the arm of Mary's suit.

"No one seriously. In fact, I think they released everyone. I can check that though. The monitor in the game room, a maid at the hotel, and I was sick for one day myself. It seems you left bits of radiation lying around." She patted Sara's hand absently as she spoke. Oz and Hawk both moved closer. "The doctor said the dose was equivalent to one radiation treatment and we should have no ill effects. Don't worry about it, honey."

Sara sat back, looking relieved. "Is there any news on Rick?"

"No, nothing new, I'm afraid, but don't worry, I'm sure they'll find them."

Charlie spoke up, "No news is sometimes good news. There's too many missing, they must've been taken."

"That's what I think too, Charles. Your father spoke with the NCO where Richard trained. We received a letter from him. He said standard procedure is to notify next of kin when information becomes available. Colonel Bukner told Dad on the phone the search is ongoing, and he'd be happy to meet with us and answered questions, but we haven't done that yet. Dad wanted to be here in case— well, until you recovered."

"I'm headed there now," John said to his son. "Mom is staying here. She'll stay until you're all released, then we'll see. I had to see you before..." He stopped speaking and took a deep breath. "I needed to speak with you before I went. I'll see if I can find out anything more in person. We won't let them stop searching." The hazmat suit crinkled loudly when John hugged his son. "Promise me you'll get better, no relapses. You feel fine, right?" His brown eyes searched his son, seeking reassurance.

"I'm good, Dad. We all are." Charlie hugged his father, then stepped back. "Go; let us know what you find out right away. Don't worry about me— us."

Liz returned with an entire carton of orange juice, which she placed in the cabinet as unobtrusively as possible, giving the family space.

John took Oz aside, and keeping an arm around his shoulders, spoke to quiet for Charlie to hear, then hugged him before speaking to everyone. "I wish I could stay, but I need to go see what can be done for Rick. Once we're home, we'll have time to catch up. I want to hear everything about your trip. Take care of each other. I love you guys." After giving them all hugs, he embraced his wife and hurried from the room.

- 13 -

COOPERATION

Mary handed out the books she'd brought. "Your teachers are putting together homework packets, so you don't fall too far behind. Don't worry about school. I'm sure it won't be a problem for you to catch up."

She stood and looked them over. By her expression, Charlie knew they wouldn't like what she would say.

"The doctors might not have told you yet but you're banned from sports activities for at least one year. I'm sorry, Charles, but that means no more football and, Sara, no track or dance. Oz, no basketball either, I'm afraid.

The blood work showed a low blood-cell count. They'll perform bone density tests to check for existing problems and you'll be put on vitamins for a while too—"

Liz interrupted, "Even if the tests return good, no sports for one year. It's better to be safe than sorry."

Doctor Allen entered the room with four other doctors. "Good morning, everybody. Any warmer, Sara?" He checked the charts as he spoke.

"Yes, thanks."

"Any pain or discomfort anywhere?"

"No, I'm just achy."

"These doctors are here to observe if you have no objections. Everyone is interested in your illness and remarkable recovery."

"That's fine." Sara shrugged.

"Would you rather speak in private behind the curtain?"

"No, it doesn't matter."

Doctor Allen squinted at her chart and handed it to the man beside him; he scanned it and passed it on. "You were unconscious, or too ill to speak after the first day, but do you remember any of it? Any specific pains you couldn't communicate at the time?"

"Nothing specifically, everything hurt like I was burning. The slightest touch was agony, immense pressure that spread in waves."

"Does it still hurt now?" Doctor Allen asked as another asked when that stopped.

"No, I ache now, and that's less than yesterday, and the pain stopped almost instantly yesterday."

"Nurse Harris reported seeing a flash of light. Did you see anything?" Doctor Allen glanced up from the chart in his hand, appearing more interested in her answer.

"No, my eyes were closed. I thought I was dead, and that's why it didn't hurt anymore. I heard everyone talking over me and knew I was dying."

"That day you heard us?"

"Yes, I heard you every day, but I could've been dreaming. I'm not sure. I remember Mrs. H reading Don Quixote and telling me to fight and someone saying deep radiation burns and something about tissue trauma. When the nurse gave me a shot, it all floated away for a while."

"Interesting, you seem to be recalling

actual events while we thought you were unconscious." Doctor Allen took her chart back and flipped the pages. "This is a record of the tests we did, liver function, and blood cell counts; they dropped daily until yesterday morning. Those tests show imminent death. Sorry, Sara, I don't mean to freak you out. The tests in the afternoon display huge improvements. Nurse Harris will rerun them today. The tests are showing such improvement we're only keeping you isolated another day. Once you're in regular rooms, we want to run a few more tests, specifically, a CAT-scan, a spinal tap, and an ultrasound if the CAT-scan shows any problems. These examinations should be safe with minimal discomfort. Maybe a headache from the tap. We'll use a local anesthetic and a needle to remove a small amount of spinal fluid. These tests were done before, but you might not remember."

"Okay."

Doctor Allen turned to face the rest of them. "Everyone heard that?"

When they nodded, he continued, "We want to perform those same tests on everyone."

One of the other doctors asked if anyone remembered anything different from Sara.

"No," Charlie said. "That was a good description. It felt like I was burning. The sheet was so tight my feet throbbed in agony. The effort to move, or even open my eyes was intense."

"Yeah," Oz agreed, "Exactly like that. The cord under my arm felt like it would sever it. Normally, I wouldn't even notice."

"Everything hurt," Hawk nodded in agreement. "The slightest touch was magnified a million times."

"Do you remember the light?" Doctor Allen asked.

Oz nodded. "Yes, I saw a bright flash, but didn't know what it was or if I imagined it."

"My eyes were closed, so I didn't see it." Hawk rubbed his bad knee, staring fixedly at the blanket covering him, keeping his gaze from Sara.

"I saw it." Charlie met the doctor's eye, "A bright flash of light. I thought a lightbulb exploded, but I was distracted at the time.

Stasia was freaking out." Charlie turned to Stasia. "I never apologized for that, I'm really sorry. I didn't mean to hurt you; I panicked."

"It's all good— no worries." Stasia took Sara's hand. "Is Sara going to be okay? The rest of us seem better than her."

"She's improving. The saline is working, and her temperature is up. We'll keep her on the drip the rest of the day. Nurse Harris will disconnect the rest of you from everything after I leave. She'll take more blood samples, and I want urine samples from everyone. Doctor Hill will be in to conduct a simple stick test. I'm not sure if you remember, but he did that before when you arrived. He'll touch you lightly, checking for changes in your nerve endings. The nurses will complete full hearing and vision testing. And, guys, if anything bothers you, anything at all, if you feel sick or even different, call immediately! Any information you give is good, you won't be bothering us. We're trying to understand what happened. Once you're out of quarantine, you'll do an EKG and the other tests. These doctors will perform examines of their own. I'm sure you're tired of these questions, but please answer as honestly as you can. Doctor Knowles and I will start here with Sara."

The other doctors introduced themselves and pulled the curtains around the other beds.

After they left, Liz served lunch, scrambled eggs, and applesauce with tea. "Toast later if this agrees with you. There's water and juice in the cabinet too if you want it. I'll take your blood samples and let you rest. Do you guys need anything else?"

"Television." Oz glanced about the empty room. "Or books?"

"Books I can do, but no television until you're out of quarantine, I'm afraid. TV's aren't worth sterilizing for the short time you'll be in here at this rate of progress. Your parents are waiting to visit. I'll let them in, okay?"

Mrs. Morales and Oz's mother and father showed up together.

"We're told you're doing better." Oz's mother fidgeted by the bed, clenching and unclenching the gloves. "The doctor said you might be out of here as soon as tomorrow and released in a few days. Your father and I agree that he'll stay here. I need to return. Christmas break is a few weeks away. I'll see you then. I love you and am so glad you're better."

Oz dutifully wished her a good trip home and assured her he was happy with the arrangements, which he was.

Charlie gave Oz a rueful smile aware of his mother's drinking problem. While Oz and his dad had little in common, they got along fine. Oz hated going to his mom's house for the holidays. His mother stayed out partying all night and spent the days hungover. Usually, she let him go to Charlie's house instead. Charlie's parents treated him like one of their sons, and he knew Oz preferred it there.

Mrs. Morales sorted the magazines Mary had brought. Camila was a kind woman and meant well but had no idea how Sara felt about being Meredith Barlow's daughter. Charlie winced when she held up the magazine with the picture of Sara's mother on the cover.

"Oh look, pictures of you two on the

cover of Star." She held the magazine out to Stasia with a smile and read it aloud. "Barlow Curse Strikes Again? Two beautiful girls cut down in their prime a fault of the famed Barlow curse?" The picture showed Stasia and Sara hugging after they'd won last year's MMO champs junior division alongside a picture of Sara's mother and grandfather. The article compared the airplane accidents.

The accidents were freaky, Charlie thought as Camila read the story. Sara was the third person to be in a plane crash in her family. The crash hadn't killed her, but still.

Camila waved another paper. "You're all pictured in this one."

This time, the picture was the group shot of last year's MMO champions win; all five wore Team Valor sweatshirts and held the trophy aloft. The caption read, 'The Dragons' Triangle Spares Five, But the Dragon's Flame Won't Be Denied.' Camila read the story of previous unexplained encounters in the same area.

"Didn't your mother crash over the Bermuda Triangle?"

"Sara doesn't like to talk about her mom's

death." Stasia gave Sara an apologetic grimace.

"No, of course, she doesn't. I'm sorry, sweetie." Camila put down the magazine.

Sara shrugged. "It's okay. Yes, both she and my grandfather died on the way to Cuba, at different times."

"That's kind of spooky." Camila shivered.

Sara shrugged again. "Not really. My grandfather flew himself without the proper qualifications. The pilot flying my mother was drunk; at least that's what the reports say. The lightning wasn't anything like that, and we didn't die."

Mrs. Morales nodded, but Charlie saw she wasn't entirely convinced. *Hell, he wasn't either. That was one hell of a coincidence.*

That night, Mary visited and brought keyboard printouts and two computer magazines. "This one has a list of the best models available. Since you have to replace the laptops, I thought you could use it." Aware Oz was their go-to guy for computer problems she handed him the magazines.

"Thanks, Mrs. H, you rock." Oz eagerly took the magazine and flipped through it.

"Darn, we'll need new headsets and everything." Hawk sighed gloomily. "And, I just got that one for my birthday. Do you think Mom will let us use some of the prize money to buy new computer gear?"

Stasia took one of the new magazines. "I'm sure she will, but we had flight insurance on them. Does it count they got destroyed on purpose after we landed? The damage originated on the plane really."

Mary appeared thoughtful. "I'm not sure how that's playing out. Mr. Mitchel has lawyers handling it, and he's representing everyone. I wouldn't worry about that too much. Your mom knows you need a computer to win these tournaments and winning is putting a nice amount of money away for college. I'm sure she'll be fine with replacing them. Speaking of your mother, we had a long talk today and she's catching a flight back tomorrow if that's okay with you guys.

"Mr. Ramos left already and gave me a limited power of attorney for you, Sara, and I have notarized notes for everyone in case you need more medical treatment. Oz, your mom left this afternoon, but your dad's still here. Assure him I'm happy to keep you with me. I think he feels guilty leaving you."

"You sure you don't mind, Mrs. H."

"You know I don't, Oz." Mary smiled and gave him a hug. "When I thought you were dying, that I would lose you too— to lose all my sons—" Mary stopped speaking and cleared her throat. "I'm so grateful you all recovered. Those were the worst days of my life."

Liz brought in cake, and Mary rose to help her.

"Is anyone hungry? I brought cake and good news." Liz handed out cake and milk. "If the three o'clock checks are clear, which I'm sure they will be, they'll officially declare you non-contagious and move you into regular rooms."

"What about them though?" Mary handed a piece of cake to Stasia. "Their blood counts are too low, aren't they? Don't they need a sterile environment?"

"They did but look at this." Liz handed Mary a chart. "This is day one until now. See how the count drops and rapidly the first three days, and then it holds with no change for one. The day they recovered the count is up, and the day after that it's normal. As of the last testing, the blood count was normal. The doctors have no idea how that happened, but it happened to all of them. These tests show they have the same immunities of everyone else, both red and white cells in the exact right mix."

"And you don't know how it happened?" Mary apprehensively examined the graph in her hand. "Has it ever happened before?"

"No, that's why they're doing all these tests. As far as I know, it's a one-time miracle for them. They took an experimental type of Neupogen and Neulasta as well as Potassium iodide and Prussian blue, but nothing they were given should've had this result. The doctors did anything they thought might help, but I'm convinced the prayers did it. But, honestly, we don't know." Liz tapped the last batch of test results.

"So, it's safe for them to leave this room?"

"The doctors think so, and the tests say so. We'll keep a close eye out to make sure it doesn't reverse again but look at them; I'd say they're almost one hundred percent." Liz turned to speak directly to Charlie. "The doctors want you to have follow-up care and more tests over the next year to ensure nothing pops up, but our tests say you're one hundred percent healthy."

Liz wagged a gloved finger at them. "That doesn't mean you should ignore any problems and I mean any! Tell us immediately if you have diarrhea, or headaches, vomiting, dizziness or anything at all. Seriously, even if you get the sniffles, we want to know. Still no sports or strenuous physical activity and some people notice loose teeth, tell us if that happens. The doctors are quite interested in this so no matter how small or insignificant it seems, report it."

Everyone promised to report any new symptoms right away. Charlie almost laughed at how hard they all tried to avoid glancing at Sara.

"Tomorrow you'll be on a regular diet and can eat what you like within reason. Stay on this floor. Don't wander around the hospital."

"Where are we?" Charlie wondered aloud.

Liz laughed. "Okinawa, at Camp Foster, in a U.S. Naval hospital. Technically, I'm Major Harris, but you can call me Liz. When it became apparent you suffered from radiation poisoning, you were medevacked here. There's an alphabet soup of people wanting to talk with you, from the FFA to the EPA. There's even a representative from the Japanese government waiting to meet you."

"We have to see them all?" Hawk exchanged dismayed glances with Charlie and Oz. "That could take months."

"No, you don't have too, but if you would be willing to it would certainly help their investigations. The conference room on this floor can be made available to meet with everyone at once."

"And I thought we'd just have to deal with Tara's paparazzi." Mary patted Sara's hand when she looked alarmed. "I'll talk with the lawyers tonight and see what they say."

"That woman is a three-ring circus," Liz agreed. "Sorry, Sara, you might be used to it, but for the rest of us it's a bit overwhelming."

Sara grinned. "We have a system. I ignore them, and they mostly ignore me."

"Well, not this time!" Mary gave a contemptuous snort. "Tara comes each day, and they film her making dramatic entrances where she gives sound bites about her darling girl. You, I presume?" Sara snickered, and Mary laughed. "Every paper and newspaper is printing stories about her and the poor heiress; it's a backward Cinderella story."

Liz bit back a laugh. "She's definitely milking it for all it's worth. I've never even seen her on this floor."

"Oh God, don't blow her character. I have to live with her. If she's playing the devoted mother, let her. We have a good system. She doesn't bother me, and I don't bother her. Our last gardener gave an unflattering interview and she had him deported. I don't know how she did it when he was here legally."

"Maybe she had nothing to do with it?" Mary suggested.

"No, I'm sure she did. I overheard her bragging to her friend Portia by the pool before it happened; she knew it would. Stay out of her way, it's safer that way."

Mary's brow furrowed in concern. "She hasn't hurt you or threatened you in any way, has she?"

Charlie tensed, suddenly angry, and Liz glanced at him in alarm. He smiled at her with limited success judging by the wan-ness of her return smile. Sara didn't seem to notice the notice the sudden tenseness and Charlie made a conscious effort to relax.

"No, like I said, we leave each other alone. I stay out of her way, and she ignores me. It works for us." Sara smiled at Mary. "Really, Mrs. H, we get along fine. Don't worry about me."

"Sara, I hope you know if you ever need adult help, John and I are here for you. You aren't alone."

Sara hugged her tight, suit and all. "Thank you. I love you too."

Stasia got up and hugged her too. In minutes, all the kids hugged her. "Mrs. H, you've been awesome, your family means the world to us, we love you guys," Stasia said.

"Some more than others," Sara

whispered in Stasia's ear and giggled, then gave Charlie a sad grimace and hugged Stasia hard.

- 14 -

FRIENDS WITH LIZ

The next morning, they moved to new rooms. The girls shared one, the boys another. By nine o'clock, a different nurse hustled them off to tests. By afternoon, they'd been poked, prodded, measured, weighed, and taken every test the doctors wanted. When they returned to their rooms, they showered and gathered in the boy's room.

Tara arrived with a huge bouquet, kissed the air by Sara's face, and then stepped back and surveyed her with pursed lips and a raised eyebrow.

"You look horrible. Couldn't you fix

yourself up some?"

Sara stared at her clasped hands and said nothing.

Charlie was quietly fuming and then inspired. "So, Oz, it was cool of your mother to let you come home with my mother. I know she worried about catching this, but there's such a slim chance of that." He stood and strolled closer, grinning when Tara felt his aura and took a quick step away.

Oz looked startled and then smiled. "Well, she had to return home for work, but it relieved her to be away for the next week until they're sure no one can catch this. Besides, your mom needs us now with Rick still missing. It comforts her to have us near." Oz scratched his arms energetically. "Man, this itches like crazy. I hope my skin still isn't falling off."

Tara took another quick step back. "So glad you're doing better, Sara darling. I hoped we could travel home together, but you might be better off in the company of your friends, for Mrs. Haye's sake. Have a safe trip home, darling."

The sound of her high heels rapidly

retreating made Charlie smile.

When the door swung shut, Sara burst into laughter. "Oh, my God, her face. I bet she runs straight to the hotel shower. That was priceless."

"I hope you wanted to come with us, not her." Charlie grinned at Oz and smiled at the door Tara ran through before turning back to Sara.

"Well, duh, who the heck would want to be with her?" Sara gave Charlie a quick hug. "Oz you're coming too, right? Your dad will let you?"

To Charlie's disappointment, Sara left his side, going to Oz and taking his hands in both of hers.

"Not yet, but he will. No reason for him not too." Oz freed his hands and gave her a quick hug.

"Good, we need to stick together, we're a team." Sara grinned at them. "Besides, I'm dying to see what we can do."

"So am I." Oz grinned back. "Everyone, take a paper keyboard and do passives only. No casts or channels, like a drill. Nothing showy, say if it worked or if your finger memory is off."

The two girls sat on Charlie's bed with his tray table. The boys pulled the table as close as they could.

Oz tapped his fingers on the paper keyboard, scanned the room, and grinned as he moved them again. "Okay, I still remember where Find a Sensor is and Cancel Magic. Hawk, see if you remember where Detect Devices is."

Hawk tapped his fingers on the paper keyboard in front of him.

"Hand me the cards, please." Stasia pointed to the drawer next to her. "In the drawer there, I think."

Without complaint that it was still his turn, or she sat right beside it, Hawk rose and got the cards. Stasia laughed when he handed them to her. She winked and again ran the spell pattern for Sweet-Talk on the paper in front of her.

Hawk slapped himself in the head and laughed. "Har, har! The first one worked; I'll try another."

Stasia shuffled the deck, cast her Precognition spell, flipped a card over, and grinned at the nine of clubs she knew would be there. "Two for two." She dealt herself a hand of solitaire.

Hawk sat with his eyes closed, fingers moving over the paper keyboard. A smile crossed his face. "Two for two," he agreed.

Oz lifted his fingers from his paper keyboard and turned to Charlie as a stranger entered the room.

Obviously not a doctor, the man wore an expensive suit and carried a briefcase. Short, black hair cut in a conservative style framed kind brown eyes and a strong chin.

"Excuse me, I hope I'm not interrupting, I'm Mr. Martin. Sara, your father hired my law firm to straighten this out."

"No, you aren't interrupting. We're practicing our keybindings." Sara got off the bed and shook Mr. Martin's hand. "We can finish later."

"Various agencies want to speak with you. I've arranged to use the conference room here at three today if that's convenient."

Hawk shrugged and ran his finger over the paper in front of him. "Sure, it's not like we're going anywhere."

As Sara said, " Will you be there too, Mr. Martin?"

"Yes, speak to no one about the airplane, or your hospitalization, without me present, excluding your doctors and nurses. Tell the truth but keep it simple. A yes or no answer is best."

"Are we in trouble?" Sara suddenly looked worried. "Did we do something wrong?"

"No, no, not all. This is nothing to be concerned about, on your part anyway, but this will be an official record, and it's easier for us lawyers if we have simple yes and no answers to deal with."

"Okay. Is anything settled as far as insurance for the stuff destroyed? As soon as we can we want to buy new laptops."

"I'm afraid not, and I don't think it'll be settled for some time. Other arrangements need to be made to replace them."

Stasia sighed heavily. "Great, Mom will have a fit if we touch our winnings. She'll let us, but she won't be happy."

"Replacement money shouldn't be a

problem. I've received several lucrative offers for interviews. Some of which should be fine to accept, but please don't speak to anyone unless you check with me first."

Stasia brightened. "Enough for new electronic gear? That stuff isn't cheap."

"Yes, I'm aware it isn't a cheap hobby." Mr. Martin said dryly. "I have a teenage son who games. At your level of play, I'm sure it's even more expensive, but I digress. You'll all probably receive offers from sponsors or advertisers. Again, check with me first before talking to, or god-forbid, signing anything."

Mary arrived with two big suitcases and two smaller bags. "Oh, hello, Mr. Martin, filling them in, I see. I thought I'd beat you here, but finding the right sizes was more challenging than I expected." She handed each of the girls one of the smaller bags, checked the tags on the suitcases, and handed them one. The other she handed to Oz. "Try them on. If they don't fit or you hate them, let me know." She turned back to Mr. Martin. "Anything new since our last talk?"

"No, I was just advising them not to speak to anyone, or sign anything, without me present."

Mary turned to them with a serious expression. "You hear that, guys? No interviews without his approval. Say no comment or nothing at all."

The kids all nodded.

"So, I'll see everyone at three o'clock in the conference room. If you have questions, call me anytime." He handed them each a card.

"With what?" Oz sighed in exasperation as the door closed behind Mr. Martin. "They took our phones."

"I still have one." Mary waved her cell phone." If any of you want to talk with your parents or anyone, you can use mine. We'll see about replacing yours as soon as we can."

"Did Dad call today?" Charlie asked.

"Yes, he hasn't learned anything new and is considering going to Iraq where Rick was stationed but doesn't think he can get a visa to go there."

"Mom, can you bring us a map of the area there? Or, a good atlas? We don't really know where Iraq is or what it's near."

"I'll try." Mary leaned over and felt Sara's

forehead. "Sara, are you still cold? Want me to bring you some thermal underwear?"

"No, I'm fine now, thanks though. With the robe and sweatshirts, I'm all set."

Liz brought them pizza for lunch, which she shared with them. "I'll miss you guys," She said. "Keep in touch; I want to know how you're doing."

Oz smiled as he took another slice of pizza, "You should make a character and play with us sometime. We're online almost every night. You could be a priest like Sara and heal people."

"Or maybe she's tired of taking care of people at the end of the day and would rather slice and dice like me." Stasia grinned at Liz. "I'll help you level up and show you around."

"I'm too old for video games," Liz protested.

"No, you're not," Mary disagreed. "People of all ages play. I have a character myself. I don't raid or play seriously, but it's fun once in a while. The kids take me to castles where we kill monsters and loot gold. My husband plays too sometimes. A word of warning though, gaming can be addicting. Time flies right by while you're playing."

"Well, I will then." Liz wrote her email address and gave it to Mary. "I'm not promising to become a gamer, but I'll try it. Write me when you're home and settled and tell me how to find you online."

Stasia laughed. "Not to brag or anything, but we're kind of famous online. Anyone could tell you how to find us. Once we add you to our friends list, we'll see your chat all the time."

"You know everyone in the game?"

"God no, that would be impossible. Over eight million people play."

"Seriously?" Liz asked.

"Yep, everyone knows us though, well not all, but a lot of them."

"So, you're really famous. I knew you won a tournament but had no idea so many played."

Charlie reached for another slice of pizza. "There's good money to be won from them. Next year we won't play the junior division;

we'll be old enough to try for the big money."

"How much money can you win playing video games?"

"Top prize for juniors was two hundred thousand dollars. The regular division paid four hundred fifty thousand dollars."

Liz halted with the pizza halfway to her mouth. "Wow, I had no idea. And you guys won it, you split the money?"

"Yep, it goes right into our college funds. To get here we won four minors. This was our second win. We won last year and placed second the first time we played."

"You could live off that income." Liz's eyes widened.

"People do, it's pretty serious business. Winning is hard work; it takes lots of practice, but more than that you have to be a team. That's why we win; we're a team both in game and in real life." Charlie grinned as he observed his real-life team.

INVESTIGATION

They were explaining the game to Liz when Mr. Martin arrived. Six men already sat in the conference room when they entered.

"Two more people are expected, but if you'd like to introduce yourselves, please do." Mr. Martin said to the seated men and gestured the kids to take seats at the table.

A man in a blue suit stood and shook their hands, "I'm Mr. Baker from the FAA, that's the Federal Aviation Administration."

"I General Chochin, Japanese Air Force." The general wore a dress uniform, had a small recorder with him, and bowed slightly. "Is good record this?"

"Yes," Mr. Martin said. "Full transcripts can be provided on request. Mr. Leed is from our firm and will record the proceedings."

Mr. Leed had a small video camera set up and a recording device on the table.

A portly man in a brown suit shook their hands. "I'm Doctor Harry Pitt from the CDC; you've met a few of my colleagues already."

"I'm Roger Salmone, and this is my assistant, Fred Kingsley, and we're from the airline."

A man and a woman entered the room together. "Hello, sorry to keep you waiting." The woman offered her hand to them. They shook her hand as the man sat.

"It's fine," Mr. Martin said. "We were getting the introductions."

"Well then, I'm Marie Lopez from NTSB, that's the National Transportation Safety Board." She set a briefcase on the table.

"And I'm with the FBI, Agent Lewis." An attractive, clean cut, dark-haired man in his late twenties, wearing a casual suit, sat at the table, and unlike the rest of them, he carried no briefcase.

"Now that everyone's here, who wants to go first?" Mr. Martin glanced around the table.

"I will," Maria, said cheerfully, "I have a few questions. Were you all touching each other when the lightning hit?" She examined her notes, "Sara, right— it hit you first?"

"Yes, it burst through the window. I'm not sure who was touching who, but I grabbed Charlie's arm right before it hit."

The rest of them agreed they were touching when it hit.

"And you say it entered through the window?" Maria asked still staring at Sara.

"Yes."

"Could you elaborate on that? If you could tell us what happened in your own words, it would be helpful."

Sara glanced at Mr. Martin, who nodded, so she told them what she remembered.

Marie nodded. "That matches the eyewitness accounts. We attributed the entire incident to a freak lightning strike until you became ill with radiation poisoning. Now we're wondering if a weapon was used."

"Excuse me." General Chochin rapped the table with his knuckles. "I hope you no say we attacked the plane? We are unsure exposure happened on plane."

Marie eyed General Chochin skeptically. "Their seats on the plane show radioactivity proving exposure on or before the plane trip. They were on the plane for fifteen hours and showed no signs of illness. After the lightning strike, they sickened within nine hours getting progressively worse within twenty-four hours. I'm convinced exposure happened on the plane."

Agent Lewis turned to face the general. "The FBI had agents test every single spot they were reported to be prior to boarding the plane. There is no trace of radiation anywhere, except the seats they sat in. A trail of radiation followed them in the car they used in Japan, the hotel rooms they used, the game room they used. We're also sure it originated from the plane. The question is— how did it get there? Have you ever seen anything like that before?"

"No never." General Chochin shook his head decisively. "We investigate possibility of weapon. The plane on radar the entire time; we see no missile. We see storm but was normal. If weapon, we no see before."

"Multiple witnesses describe the same thing Sara saw out the window. We even have pictures." Maria opened her briefcase and handed out pictures of the wing of the plane from different angles. In the first picture, a white outline with a blue edge encompassed the wing. In the second, the wing was mostly blue. The third picture they had seen in the newspaper, the wing on fire surrounded by a blue glow.

"The wing is also highly radioactive. What that means, we have no idea. How and why the lightning entered through the window, and only that window, and only affected them, we don't know. Two other people were awake, both reading. Those two saw everything from the put away electronic devices notice to the window blowing out."

Agent Lewis turned to Mr. Martin. "Who removed their belongings? Nothing remained in their hotel rooms."

"At the behest of my government, we took to investigate potential for plots,"

General Chochin said to Charlie's surprise.

Hawk groaned. "Oh, man, I thought you took them because they were radioactive."

"I too was under that impression." Mr. Martin frowned. "You're saying they weren't destroyed, but instead investigated?"

"Yes, we investigate," the general agreed.

"While we have nothing to hide, costs are involved. Are you able to return the equipment?" Mr. Martin asked.

"No, afraid is impossible. I see restitution should be made, will see done." General Chochin bowed slightly.

"The FBI would like access to the devices." Agent Lewis eyed the general thoughtfully.

"Not possible, but reports made," General Chochin said.

Agent Lewis frowned but nodded.

Mr. Martin tapped the table to gather attention. "Does anyone have any more questions for them?"

Agent Lewis turned to the kids, "Do you have any explanation for your recovery?"

"No, sir," Charlie said keeping his voice firm and even.

"You're Charles Hayes correct, the leader of your group? They call you Chief?"

"Chief is my character's name. I'm the guild master of our guild. They're all officers. I answer to Chief, or Charlie, as a nickname."

"It's interesting that you use your game names in everyday life too."

Charlie shrugged. "The game is a big part of our life. We spend half our time there. Besides, it's easier when you're in a hurry, you don't have to think about what you're calling someone."

Agent Lewis leaned back in his chair. "Yes, I can see that you are those characters. You talked about saving the priest in your delirium, and she prays for you all."

"You've been spying on us?" Charlie tensed, trying not to let it show, and kept his gaze away from Sara.

"Spying no, investigating, yes. You feel you need to take care of them?" Agent Lewis swiveled his chair side-to-side as he waited for Charlie to reply.

"We take care of each other."

Sweat beaded on Mr. Salmone's brow. He loosened his tie and moved his chair away from Charlie. Charlie tried to reign in his anger before it empowered his aura and sent the men running from the room. The thought made him smile.

Agent Lewis gaze flicked to Mr. Salmone, then back to Charlie. "I viewed your tournament games, amazing teamwork. Your timing with each other is superb. You must practice a lot. How do you know whose timer you're following?"

"Mine are almost all for Seraphim and hers for me. When they're not, I say the name first."

"So, when you say shield tick, you're telling her when you cast a spell, so she knows when it'll run out?"

"Yes, then she replies tock when she picks it up, it means the timer is continuing, and she has me shielded."

Agent Lewis nodded. "I saw that and wondered what you were doing saying tick-tock, back and forth for four minutes, then a spate of one-word commands that meant nothing to me."

"Timing is everything in this game. We practice every day. Most tourneys don't allow addons, so we use keybindings and macros and do finger memory drills." Charlie mimed typing, being careful not to cast a spell.

"I see, it's like any other profession with its own jargon that you won't understand unless you're in the industry—"

Mr. Martin interrupted, "While I'm sure the mechanics of their game are interesting you might meet with them later to discuss it?"

"Oh sure, but the reason I asked was the nurse reported Sara was praying when the light flashed and I wondered if that was significant. Do you remember what you prayed?"

"You think God answered her prayer?" Marie rose an eyebrow and glanced at Sara.

"I don't know what happened, just checking all the bases," Agent Lewis replied blithely.

"The Hail Mary." Sara stared at her clasped hands. "I thought we were dying. In fact, I believed we had died."

"Could you tell me exactly what you said?"

Sara glanced down and in a soft, nervous

voice recited the Hail Mary.

"Did you sense anything, feel different in any way?"

"The pain stopped, but I was confused. I was scared, my best friend was screaming, dying in agony. Praying was the only thing I could do for her. Afterward, I felt better, but what caused it I have no idea."

"Will you give permission for us to see your medical records?"

"Talk to me after this interview," Mr. Martin said. "A confidentiality contract will need to be signed. We don't want the records spread all over the internet, but we want to help in any way we can."

"Yes, we can agree to that. The records will be sealed," Agent Lewis agreed. "How much longer will you be here? Have they told you yet?"

Charlie answered that question. "One more full day at least until they release us. We're all feeling much better. They're just being cautious because our condition was so strange."

"Would you be willing to take a lie detector test?"

"Yes, but what do you think we're lying about?"

"Nothing, but it would make people happy if you'd answer on the machine if you knew anything about the radioactivity, where it's from, that sort of thing."

Mr. Martin put his hand on Charlie's before he could answer. "I'll agree to let them take the test if I have signed documents saying no charges will be brought based on it. We don't know what systems of theirs the lightning affected. I can't let a false positive potentially harm them."

"That's fine, I can agree to that too. A tech will be here with a machine in the morning. The test shouldn't take over thirty minutes for each of them."

"If their doctors agree, and it doesn't interfere with their medical tests, I see no problem with it."

Agent Lewis shifted in his seat, leaning forward and placing his elbows on the table. "Another reason I ask about the game is because another group of players has gone missing."

Charlie bit his lip and exchanged a quick

worried glance with Sara. "Where?"

"On Monday the plane they were traveling in declared an air emergency and hasn't been located yet. Twenty players from the tournament were on board. It almost seems like someone has it in for video game players."

"Twenty?" Stasia turned a white face to Oz. "Dear God. Who?"

"That's right, you know them all, don't you?" Agent Lewis reached over and patted her hand. "I'm sorry for blurting it out like that. I forgot what a small community that is and you would know them. The names escape me now but I can get copies of the news articles for you."

Tears trailed down Stasia and Sara's cheeks, and they hugged a moment.

Maria cleared her throat. "The disappearance of that plane is still being investigated. We do know it was struck by lightning. The pilot reported both wings on fire with the same blue glow before the tower lost him. Is there anything you can add? Have there been threats or… well, anything?"

"No," Charlie answered before the

others. "Did the plane go down in the area ours was hit?"

"Yes. But no wreckage has been spotted."

General Chochin rapped the tabletop with his knuckles. "My government still searching. Will find. Many small islands; will take time. Large electrical storm. Is unsafe to travel now."

Agent Lewis interrupted. "A Navy rescue boat is in the area and reports a high level of storms with electrical interference. Once the storms pass, the search will resume. While it appears to be a natural phenomenon, the fact that both planes carried video games teams is an awfully big coincidence."

Marie pursed her lips. "So... what— you think someone developed a secret weapon to kill their game competition?" One eyebrow rose as she regarded Agent Lewis.

"No, I guess I don't. That would be crazy, wouldn't it?"

Marie hid a smile behind a hand raised to cover a fake cough.

The meeting broke up shortly afterward, and everyone headed back to the boy's room.

"They're bound to ask if we know what

the light was," Oz whispered on the way to the room.

"Doesn't matter because we don't know what it is. Just tell the truth." Charlie shrugged. "Yeah, they'll think we're kind of loony when we say we think Sara praying healed us, but so what. I think he kind of thinks that anyway."

Liz brought them dinner. Mary arrived with their clothes and an atlas of the Middle East. Oz's father arrived with her.

Oz pulled his father to the corner of the room where they spoke in private. "Dad, I want to go home with them if you don't mind."

"That's fine with me, son. In fact, I can catch a flight home tonight. The sooner I return to work, the better, but you're sure you won't need me?"

"Yeah, we're all better. No one knows how, but we are. I hate to ask, but I could use some money. Whatever you can spare. My ticket is paid for, and Mr. Mitchel bought us some clothes, but all our money was confiscated and destroyed."

"I don't have much." His father took out

his wallet. "I was in a real hurry to get here and emptied my almost empty savings and bought a ticket. The airline said they'll reimburse me, and they gave me an open ticket to return, but I'm real short at the moment."

The worn, brown wallet his dad took from his pocket contained little. After leafing through the bills, he handed Oz two hundred dollars.

"One hundred and twenty dollars left. This leaves me enough to get home on; I have taxis and stuff to pay for. Sorry, son."

"This is more than enough. Are you sure you left yourself enough?"

"Plenty." He hugged Oz who exchanged a surprised glance with Charlie. Oz hugged him back.

"I love you, son. You be safe coming home."

"I love you too, Dad. Thanks for this. As soon as I can, I'll pay you back."

"No need." Mr. Simmons thanked Mary for watching his son. "My boy practically lives with you. You get tired of him, shoo him home."

"That'll never happen." Mary smiled at Oz. "John and I love him like a son."

"Ma'am, I wish he was your son. He could've used a momma like you. I didn't pick him a good one. She's a hell of a woman, and I'm sorry she left us, but she weren't no mother."

"I'll take good care of him for you. We'll call and let you know when we'll return." Mary shook Mr. Simmons hand.

Once his father left, they spent the rest of the night taking turns with the atlas. At eleven, they gathered in the boy's room and watched world news. A short report mentioned the missing soldiers, followed by a longer recap.

ISIS had attacked a convoy of twenty-five Marines and forty-two Army personnel on the road leading from Ramadi. The United States retrieved the bodies of twelve Marines and thirty Army personnel, but the rest were reported MIA. Pictures of the destroyed trucks flashed on the screen. Handheld missile launchers had destroyed both Marine vehicles, one of which contained personnel. Remains were still being positively identified.

"Jeez, what a mess," Oz breathed.

Sara took Charlie's hand, and Stasia hugged him.

The reporter describing the fight finished with, "While this is all conjecture, as there are no eyewitnesses left, it's clearly a big loss for the United States. This attack has the highest causality rating to date for American troops in a bombing of this nature."

Oz turned off the television, and they faced each other grimly. "We can't help him. stuck in here. We need to get out of here and find out what's going on—Oz started to say something else, then glanced around and whispered, "If they don't release us soon, we'll have to release ourselves."

"We give them one more day," Charlie said. "If we break out of here, they're bound to search for us. No one could possibly suspect the truth, but they might think we're involved and have something to hide. As much as I want to go right now, it's better to not raise any suspicions until we have time to figure this out."

Stasia nodded unwilling agreement. The rest of them agreed with no hesitation.

The next morning, they rose and showered early. Wearing their new clothes, they waited for the doctor in the boy's room.

Doctor Allen was pleased with their progress, but still unable to explain it. "All your tests show you're completely recovered. There's no point in keeping you here, you're healthy as horses. After one more battery of tests, we'll discharge you. I've informed your mother already, Charlie. I'll go over the discharge papers with her, but I want to remind everyone, no strenuous exercise, avoid stress, and stay away from large crowds, for a while at least. The test show normal blood counts, but we want you to take precautions. Keep taking the vitamins we prescribed and meet with your doctor at home when you get there. And most importantly, report any changes immediately!"

The morning nurse arrived with their breakfasts, and the doctor left. The nurse took their blood samples and checked their vitals in a professional, distant way. She wasn't friendly like Liz.

Agent Lewis knocked on the open door

and said, "Mr. Martin and the tech are all set. I'll take you one at a time. Who's first?"

"Me, I guess." Charlie accompanied Agent Lewis.

"You take being their leader seriously, don't you?" Agent Lewis said as he led the way to the conference room.

"I don't think of myself as their leader, we're friends."

"The big age differences doesn't bother you?"

"It's not that big, only eighteen months, it's no big deal. Hawk doesn't seem to care either. Sara and Stasia will be fifteen in a few more months."

"How did you meet?"

"Oz and I met in kindergarten, he lives near me, and we met the rest of them online. Hawk was an online friend until we found out he lived close by and met him a few times in real life. My brother had a guild in UBM. We joined and played together almost daily, not raiding, casual play. The five of us made a fully formed team; we never needed to look for a group. Before you knew it, we were inseparable, and we were good, especially together. We started raiding, and here we are now."

"So, the girls aren't serious members, it's just you three guys?"

"Not at all, they're as important and my friends equally, we guys just hung out first. Who hangs out with a girl at eleven? I mean we liked them to play video games with them, but that's all we had in common. Then Hawk was our friend and Stasia visited some. She and Sara were online friends. Sara didn't meet us in person until we became serious raiders and met at my house to plan strategies and stuff. We spend every weekend together and most weeknights. Sara doesn't live as close, but she gets a ride there no problem."

"And your parents don't mind you playing video games so much?"

"No, why would they? We do our homework and stuff, and it isn't just play, we make good money at it."

"I don't know, it seems like you're missing out on other after school things."

"I play football. Hawk used too before he hurt his knee, and Sara takes dance and does track. Stasia is practically a professional shopper she's at the mall so much, and Oz is on the basketball team and in the math club. We seem pretty normal to me."

"How do you find time for all that?"

"We almost never watch television. While the rest of the world is watching, we're gaming."

They had long ago arrived at the conference room. Agent Lewis introduced Charlie to the tech and had him take a seat. "We'll start with some simple questions to calibrate the machine. Try to answer yes or no unless I ask for an explanation. I'll ask all the questions. Ignore the tech as much as you can, ready?"

"Yes."

"Is your name Charles Hayes?"

"Yes."

Agent Lewis asked him his age, grade in school, and if his mother's first name was Mary and if he knew where the radiation originated. Did he think it derived from the lightning or event on the plane? Did he know why it just affected them? Did he know what the light was? When asked to clarify his response on that, he said he thought it was

Sara praying. Did he think a miracle occurred? Agent Lewis asked him to wait next door.

Before long, Stasia joined him. They'd both answered the same questions the same way. When they were together in the room again, Agent Lewis addressed them.

"Well, everyone told the truth. I expected as much, but this will make my supervisors happy. Here's my card in case you think of anything, but I'm finished investigating you. My report will say you were in the wrong place at the wrong time and had no idea what happened or why. It was nice to meet you, and I'm glad you're all doing better." He shook their hands. A thoughtful frown settled on his face and he stared after them as everyone headed off before he turned to the tech. "So, what do you think?"

"Everyone told the truth. Normal amount of nervousness. They seem like nice kids."

"Yeah, they're nice, but something is off here. I can't put my finger on it. Well, pack up and let's head back. I have more reports to read. I wish I could've gotten their cell phones and laptops."

"You think they were involved somehow?" the tech asked, sounding amazed.

"Not at all, but I do think they know more than they're telling."

"Why didn't you ask them?"

"I don't know the right questions to ask, so I asked them the obvious questions."

The tech shrugged. "Maybe there is nothing they can tell you. They seemed pretty straightforward to me. What could they possibly know? Even the doctors don't have an answer."

"Yeah maybe," Agent Lewis agreed, but he continued to frown thoughtfully.

- 16 -

GEARING UP

Mary arrived by noon. "Sorry I'm late; meetings held me up. The Japanese government sent five checks to the hotel that should cover most, if not all, of your replacement gear." She handed them checks written in Japanese.

"How do we cash this? I can't even read it." Hawk frowned at the colorful paper in his hand in consternation.

Sara peered over his shoulder. "It's a check for six-hundred-thousand yen. That's about five thousand American dollars."

Mary looked surprised. "I didn't know you can read Japanese."

"I can't, I recognized the numbers is all." Sara turned away and busied herself packing.

Mary examined Charlie's check as she said, "The Japanese government politely asked me to leave at the earliest opportunity, so I thought we'd go from here to the hotel."

Stasia flicked her fingers, casting Sweet-Talk. "Could we maybe go to a few stores? We'd like to buy some souvenirs and replace some of our electronics."

Mary smiled agreeably, and Charlie hid his grin. Stasia's spell seemed to make his mother completely forget the doctor's warnings on crowds.

Mary said, "You can cash your checks at the hotel, and we can go to a local computer store to see if they have anything. If you want to wait until we're home to spend the money, you can. Then we can go eat and maybe shop some more if we have time before deciding what plane to fly home on using our open tickets. I'm sure they'll make every effort to let us take any flight we want as long as we leave."

"They don't want us here?" Charlie asked in surprise.

"We're quite a disturbance, more than you realize."

"Jeez, is it safe for us to leave here?"

"Everyone agreed it was as long as we don't linger." She gave them all a nervous smile before turning back to Charlie. "Dad called. He can't get a visa to go to Iraq, so he'll meet us at home. He might even beat us there."

"Is there any news at all?"

"None, I'm afraid, but sometimes no news is good news," Mary said in forced optimism. "Let's get you guys packed up and get out of here as soon as possible."

By three Mary had signed the release forms and spoken at length with their doctors. A folded list of instructions and emergency contacts went in her purse. A car with tinted windows waited at the back door of the hospital. People held signs in front of the hospital, and a few news vans and a large group of people with cameras crowded the entrance.

"What's going on there?" Oz asked, craning his neck to peer out the back window.

"You are." Mary's laughing gaze swept them. "Everyone wants interviews. Well, most do anyways; some are UFO nuts who think you're aliens."

Stasia said, "Mrs. H, I need access to a computer before we go shopping. Is there one at the hotel I can use?"

Mary frowned thoughtfully. "I'm not sure."

The driver spoke up, "There's free Wi-Fi there, but no open terminals. A computer cafe is within easy walking distance, or I could drive you there. I'm at your disposal all day. Is there anything I could help you find?"

"No, I want to research different models of phones and stuff before we buy one." Stasia flipped through the computer magazine Mary had brought them.

"Ah, I see. Well, shall I stop?"

Charlie hid his smile as Stasia's finger's twitched casting Sweet-Talk.

"Could he drop Oz and I off please, and pick us up when you're all checked in? I promise we won't leave the cafe."

"I suppose it would be okay." Mary rummaged through her purse and handed them a wad of bills. "This is all the Japanese money I have on me at the moment. Wait there for one of us to retrieve you; don't leave."

Stasia crossed her heart and hugged Mary, winking at Charlie over her shoulder. "Don't worry, we won't be long."

The driver let them out, pointing out the cafe and the hotel.

"What do we want, Stasia?" Oz asked as they entered the quiet café. "This isn't just a craving to shop, I hope."

"No, it isn't. We need gear. Not computers, although we should buy at least one to browse on, but it doesn't need to be gaming quality, any old thing will do. What we need is gear to replace what we normally use. Find us watches with stopwatches built in and compass features and wireless headsets or walkie-talkies. Sara needs a cloak and a staff. We need regular gear, thermoses, protective clothing, good boots, and I need some tools. Hawk needs a bow, and we could all use daggers for the agility buff. The weapons have to wait until we get there, but we can buy the clothes and stuff."

Oz talked to the barista at the counter who spoke fluent English. In a few minutes, they were set up with two computers side-by-side. "Okay, you find us clothes. I'll research the watches and headsets."

Oz tapped keys for a few minutes. "I'll be right back, I need paper and a pen."

Stasia didn't glance up, just nodded. Oz bought a small notepad and pen, returned to the computer, and jotted down model numbers.

"How's your search going?"

"Well, good and bad, I found what I want, but we can't get it. It's mostly military grade. Until we get home, we'll have to settle for regular clothing. There's a shop near here for that and shoes. There's a retro dress shop right next door where we might find a cape for Sara."

Oz nodded. "I've got the watches nailed down, that was easy. The headsets we want are military grade, but we can use walkie-talkies meanwhile. The closest store that has them isn't too close. This lists the best ones. The electronics store near here probably has something suitable. Half this stuff is made in

Japan after all. What are we doing for Sara?"

"Well, it needs to be hollow and at least four feet long. There's a store not too far away we can try." Stasia pointed to an ad on the computer screen advertising weapons of all kinds. "This store's thirty minutes away. They might sell something there she can use, and we might see something we can use too."

"Yeah, but how the heck do we get it on a plane? We can't carry weapons on."

"Can't hurt to check it out. They advertise fancy carved wooden nunchucks. Let's go see. Also, I found a small park within walking distance. Let's go there tonight to see what we can do?"

"Okay, let's check on flights and see where we can go," Oz said.

When Hawk arrived, they were both scanning the available places.

"We're checked in, and we cashed our checks," Hawk said. "You can cash yours later. Are you ready to go?"

"Yep, let's head out." Oz grabbed up his notes and put the computer on Google's home page. Stasia did the same.

Everyone got in the car.

"First stop is this electronics store." Oz handed the driver an address.

"Did you guys find what you need?" the driver asked.

"There's a few stores we want to check out. When we return home, we'll replace our cell phones. For now, we'll use cheap radios." Oz turned to Mary. "Mrs. H, if you don't want to come in, I promise we won't be more than an hour."

"Fine, I know how you guys are. We have time before dinner. Browse away. I'll wait here."

"There are two other stores we want to visit. We won't be long," Oz assured her.

Inside the store, Oz handed Stasia a slip of paper with a model number on it. "Stasia, you and Hawk, go pick out two laptops and five of these. If they don't have those Bluetooth headsets, find us what you can. We want waterproof ones capable of hands-free, small, with no lights. Sara, go find us a mini iPad and see if they sell any good GPS devices with maps in them for the right area, and if you can, get five plastic thermoses, five black or camo backpacks, and five disposable phones. Charlie, come with me."

They split up, each hurrying to find what they came for.

The store was huge and slightly confusing, the signs were in Japanese. Charlie grinned at Oz. He could read them, although he was trying to act like he couldn't. An employee in a red apron helped them. While they couldn't understand him, or he them, they mimed watch accurately enough to get the point across.

"Perfect." Oz spied the watches he wanted in a glass case. "Five of those and five extra batteries please."

Oz pointed at the Suunto Core watch and held up five fingers. The clerk frowned, shrugged, and took one out. Oz gestured for four more, the clerk smiled broadly and took them out. Oz tapped the battery compartment and held up five fingers. With another shrug, the clerk got them out.

Oz smiled. "Great, we need five walkie-talkies too." Oz mimed talking into one. The clerk nodded and led him to the cell phone aisle. Oz shook his head and mimed pulling out an antenna and pushing a button while saying "Roger, over and out."

The clerks face lit up, and he led them to a new aisle. The case displayed what they wanted. Oz checked them against his list, settled on the Midland GXT, and picked out extra batteries and chargers. The clerk helped them to the checkout where Sara waited with Stasia and Hawk. All the items together cost them almost five thousand dollars. The happy clerk walked them to the waiting car.

"Guess you found some stuff." Mary laughed at the big bags they carried.

"Where to now?" the driver asked.

Stasia handed him a slip of paper. He rose his eyebrows at the address but didn't complain.

"A martial arts store?"

"Sara needs a gift for her father; he collects crafted items. We thought we'd chip in and buy him something nice to thank him for all his help."

"Besides, it'll be cool, a real martial arts store," Hawk said enthusiastically.

When they arrived, everyone entered the store, including the driver. Charlie glanced at him from the corner of his eye, wondering if he worked for the FBI or the Japanese government. He grinned to himself and headed to the sword display. No one would ever suspect what had really happened. He still had to pinch himself to believe it despite the continued evidence of his own eyes. Customers made way for him at his approach, some eyeing him nervously and he had to bite back a laugh.

Protective aura made complete strangers bow their heads or sidle away as he passed. Their gazes locked on him as if the rest of the team didn't exist. He wondered what their chaperone thought or if he even noticed.

Oz and Stasia dragged Sara over to a display of handcrafted wooden items. Oz pointed to a wooden staff in the case. "Can you show us that one?"

A small shrug was his only reply.

The driver said something in Japanese and the clerk took it out.

A rapid spate of Japanese followed, which the driver translated. "This staff is handcrafted, but not antique. It has a solid hardwood core, no metal reinforcement, but it's expensive. Are you sure you want that?"

Stasia leaned forward to see. "How does it work?"

The driver said something. The clerk smiled, stepped back, flicked his arm, and the wooden stick instantly became almost five-feet-long. After whirling it around, he showed them how a small wooden button depressed, allowing it to become a one-foot stick again. Closed, it had a three-inch circumference. When turned slowly, intricate carvings of clouds, the moon, and the sun, appeared to rise and set giving way to a full moon.

The staff was a work of art, Charlie thought appreciatively.

"How much? It's perfect," Charlie said.

They paid three thousand American dollars for it.

Charlie and Hawk eyed the weapons on the wall while Stasia examined the packages on a shelf as the clerk rang them up.

"Man, they have everything here." Hawk pointed out the throwing stars. "Stasia, they're just like yours, and they have them in every color imaginable."

"Those are real weapons, not for sale to children. Sorry, guys," the driver said.

"Those would look rad on my wall." Hawk touched one wickedly sharp point with a fingertip.

"Let's get going," Stasia said. "We want to make one more stop at a clothing store." She handed the driver the address.

The clothing store took a while. Everyone tried on boots, and Stasia picked them out clothes to try. Everyone bought new cargo pants in black and long-sleeved black shirts and black combat boots. When everyone was outfitted to Stasia's satisfaction, she asked to stop at the store right next door selling old-fashioned gowns and clothing.

While the rest of them browsed and clowned around with the old-fashioned clothing, she sorted through the racks and bought a floor-length cape of black silk with a light-yellow interior for five hundred U.S. dollars. The clasp was a sun and moon, and heavy embroidery traced the front edges and bottom, again with the sun and moon pattern.

"If we don't get Tara something too,

there'll be no living with her," she explained when Mary asked why she wanted it.

After thanking the driver, they headed into the hotel loaded down with bundles.

"Let's order room service; I'm too tired to go out." Charlie wasn't lying. He was tired. He thought they were all more tired than they let on.

"That's fine. We didn't overdo it, did we?" Mary felt his forehead. "You're not feeling poorly?"

"No, just not in the mood to go out. Besides, we want to open our new gear." He hefted the bags in his hand and smiled; it seemed to reassure her.

"Mrs. H, is there a place nearby I can buy a nail file?" Stasia handed her bag to Charlie.

"There's a small shop here you can check. If they don't have it, we can ask there."

"Okay, I'll run down and check. Sara, wanna come? Order us whatever you're having. Come on, Sara." She pulled Sara's arm, leading her away after handing the packages to the boys who took them with no complaints.

"Shopaholic." Oz grinned at Mary.

"We're used to schlepping their packages."

"I'll order us a nice Japanese meal in the girl's room. You guys can unpack in your room. If you need me, I'm right next door. Any food requests?"

"Nope, you know what we like. Call us when it arrives," Charlie said. "And thanks, Mom, you've been great." He kissed her cheek awkwardly over his packages. Oz and Hawk echoed him and followed Charlie into their room.

"Nice, this beats hospital white." Oz gazed happily around the pleasant room.

Two double beds lay opposite a blue couch and two upholstered green chairs by a small table. A large television hung on the wall over the bureau. Matching nightstands stood on each side of the beds with individual reading lamps. A floor lamp stood at each end of the couch. Flecks of gold paint glittered in the brown walls.

"The girl's room is identical." Charlie put his packages on the bed.

"Let's see what we got." Hawk took a box, tried on a watch, and frowned at the accompanying manual. "Holy cow, this is a paperweight."

"This watch does everything our map did." Oz read the manual as he described the watch. "There's a built-in compass, you can set a direction and it'll tell you if you stray from it. Coordinates and weather display with the touch of a button. There's a built-in stopwatch and a countdown feature. It's waterproof and has a red backlight to not mess up our night vision. If we need precise timing, we have it. We all need to learn to use the features. These walkie-talkies should work like our headsets. Channels can be set individually, and we can use the Bluetooth or the wired headsets; both are hands-free and voice-activated. It has a whisper mic, vibrates and silent mode."

Hawk opened the staff and whirled it around expertly while Charlie plugged in chargers.

"Let's charge the new gear. Put an extra battery in everyone's pack. We should've bought a small screwdriver for each of us. These small screws will be impossible by hand."

Oz didn't glance up from his manual.

"We can pick that up at the airport. I'm sure they have eyeglass repair kits. At one tonight we're supposed to meet the girls and go to a park near here to find out what we can do."

Oz set the manual down to help Charlie open the walkie-talkies and put them on chargers.

"I can't wait." Hawk rubbed his knee and smiled. "My leg is completely better. I want to run and jump and..." he trailed off as the door opened.

His sister and Sara had returned.

"I thought those locked automatically." Charlie twisted the knob to see if it worked.

"They do." Stasia grinned. "I let myself in."

Sara took a manual off the small table and leafed through it, saying, "We're good to go tonight. When your mom falls asleep, we'll come get you."

Hawk peered at the door as someone knocked. "It's your mother. The food must be ready."

Sara let her in.

"Food will be ready in fifteen minutes. Let's see what you got." Mary examined their purchases with interest. "What, no laptops?"

"We got two, but we're waiting until we get home to replace our gaming gear. We'll buy new phones and stuff there. These will work until then." Charlie handed her one of the cheap laptops they'd bought, happy his mother had no idea how much electronics cost.

His mother nodded.

"Once everything is on chargers, we'll be over." Charlie walked his mom to the door.

"We should tell her," Oz said, once Mary left the room.

"Yeah, she needs to know." Sara stared after Mary with a small frown. "We can't disappear on her, she'll freak."

"I agree." Stasia mirrored Sara's worried expression. "She'll keep our secret, and we could use her help to get there. We checked flights. We'll need to go to Turkey and cross the border ourselves. I have ideas, but it depends on what we can do."

Hands on his hips, Charlie scowled at them in exasperation. "If we tell her, she'll tell my father. I guarantee it."

Hawk shrugged. "So, she tells him, big

deal. What's he going to do?"

"I don't know, forbid us maybe. There's no way he'll let us go to Iraq."

"He can forbid it all he likes, I'm still going!" Stasia meet Charlie's eyes; he recognized her stubborn expression. She would go with or without them. The thought of her heading into danger without him tightened his shoulder muscles unpleasantly. His surge of anger was so sharp and sudden he recognized it as a magical impulse. The shock of it stole his breath. He hadn't considered his magic was rage based or that he'd feel compelled to protect his team. The others kept speaking, unaware he was trying to tame his anger.

"Me too, I respect him and all, but we need to go." Oz handed the manual for the walkie-talkie to Sara.

"Besides, he isn't here. It's not like she can say a thing over the phone," Sara said practically. "I'm sure she won't want us to go either, but she'll let us. Or, at the least, she won't tell. With or without permission, we go."

"Let's see what we can do first and think

about it some. I'm thinking plausible deniability for her. We just go. It'll suck for her, but..." Charlie trailed off.

"Don't be a knucklehead! We can't do that to her. Rick is already missing. If we go missing too—well, that's cruel, and I won't do that to her." Oz threw the manual at him and picked up another one.

Sara placed a hand on each of them, getting between them before they fought. "Let's go eat. I'm starving. We'll decide later. First, we need a plan. We need time on the web."

Charlie smiled at her and rubbed Oz's head, happy he felt no compulsion to hit him or any anger at Oz's mild act of aggression. As far as he could tell he'd reacted normally to Oz. His gaze flit to Stasia. Contemplating her heading into danger alone still bothered him. *I'm going with her*, he told himself firmly, and his anger subsided.

Oz took the manuals with him when they went next door to eat.

After dinner, Stasia and Hawk used the computers while Oz, Charlie, and Sara figured out the watches and walkie-talkies.

"We should practice with these as much as we can; we need to be fast at setting them," Charlie said to Sara.

Sara put on a watch and messed with the settings. "It'll be hard to measure our accuracy without target dummies."

"We have this dummy." Charlie put Hawk in a headlock and rubbed his bald head.

"Hey, don't mess with the do. It took me hours to get it just right," Hawk said in mock outrage, pretending to smooth his hair.

"Hawk can time us and let us know if we're slow. The iPad can video us to check that way. Everyone needs to assume we'll be slower though, we can't count on our usual accuracy," Charlie said as he practiced setting the stopwatch feature.

Mary knocked again as they headed to bed for the night.

"She probably wants us to go to bed," Sara said, as she opened the door.

A white-faced Mary stood at the door swaying. "They found him. Oh, my God, they found him!"

- 17 -

DISCLOSURE

Mary burst into tears. Sara grabbed her and led her to a chair.

"Sit down. What happened?" Sara knelt before Mary, clasping her hands, rubbing them between her own.

"It's on the news. I saw him."

Charlie turned on the television, his face white. Team Valor gathered around him. Almost every channel showed the same breaking story. ISIS had sent a tape of a beheading.

Charlie's breath caught, but then he sighed in relief. The soldier they'd killed wasn't Rick. Gathered close together they watched horrified as an angry man shouted in Arabic.

Sara took Charlie's hand in hers and translated. "The infidel dogs must retreat now or pay the penalty. Mohamed demands the heads of the infidels. One infidel will die every day until our demands are met." The camera left the screaming man and panned over a group of tied men. "Rick," Sara breathed, "they have him."

"And his entire squad," Mary said and started to cry again, "Oh, my God, my son."

Sara flexed her fingers and a spark flickered over her fingertips. She flicked it at Mary who sat straighter and spoke more calmly as Sara's Soothe spell hit her. "I don't even know if your father knows. I have to call him." When she rose to go to her room for her cell phone, Oz put a hand on her arm to stop her.

"No, don't call yet. We need to tell you something first."

Charlie frowned.

Sara took both of Charlie's hands in hers. "This is the right thing. We need to go right now, and we need her help. They're going to kill someone else tomorrow, maybe Rick."

"Tell me what? You need help? Oh, my God, are you sick again?" Mary's worried gaze flicked between them.

"No, no, nothing like that. We need to tell you something." Stasia took her arm and led her to a chair. "Just sit please and listen."

Charlie turned to Hawk. "Book us on the quickest route you can, Hawk."

"Okay, I'm booking us on the one o'clock flight to Tokyo. From there we can take another flight at eleven-thirty tomorrow morning to Ankara Turkey where we switch planes and go to Adana. This is the fastest flight available, Chief, and it'll still be almost twenty-four hours. Cheaper flights are available, but it'll take almost three days."

"Do it! Get us there." Charlie grimaced slightly; it would take half his winnings to buy plane tickets.

Mary looked mystified. "Where?"

"Turkey, but don't worry about that," Charlie said, then to Sara, "Show her."

"We don't know how or why, but watch." Sara twitched her fingers and a ball of light formed in her hands. She threw the ball at Hawk. When the yellow ball hit him, it absorbed into his skin causing him to glow for a moment. A flick of her fingers and suddenly Stasia floated. Within seconds everyone floated.

Mary gaped at her. "What? What was that? How are you doing that?"

"That light was my Major Heal spell, and we're floating because I levitated us with Ascension."

"What? That's crazy!"

"I agree, yet here I am, floating."

"But, that's impossible!" Mary stared in amazement, reached out, and touched Sara who floated in front of her.

"Yet, I'm doing it," Sara repeated.

"Why didn't you say anything? This is amazing."

"If I had, I'd still be in the hospital or locked up somewhere else. We want to go get Rick, not whatever the doctors would want."

Mary recoiled and pressed her hands to her face. "Oh, my God! No, you can't! I can't let a little girl go to Iraq, to a war zone with crazy fanatics!"

"I won't go alone, they'll come too."

Mary gasped and crossed her hands on her chest. "Wait— what— you can all do that?"

"No, only Sara can. We do other stuff." Stasia was suddenly foggy as if she'd became a white shadow of her former self. "I've been dying to try that." She laughed and appeared behind Charlie and then was instantly behind Hawk on the other side of the room. "Whoa, that'll take some getting used to."

"What's it feel like?" Oz sat cross-legged and continued to float.

"It's like suddenly waking up in a strange place. Try it, Charlie, waylay me."

Charlie suddenly stood beside Stasia. "Yes, it's odd. We need to practice." He was suddenly beside Sara. "What the heck? I didn't...."

"I did." Sara smiled. "I pulled you."

Oz held up a knife from dinner. "Take it."

The knife appeared in Charlie's hand, and as suddenly disappeared. Hawk laughed as he waggled it in Charlie's direction.

"All of you can do that?" Mary sounded

overwhelmed. Face pale and eyes wide, she searched the room for Stasia, following the other's glances.

"We don't know what we can do. We planned on sneaking out to the park tonight and checking." Sara cast another Soothe on Mary. "We seem to have learned our character's abilities though."

"So, Charlie can do his tank moves and you're still the healer and Stasia can be invisible?"

"So far it appears that way but we need to go make sure and practice."

"How did this happen? When did this happen? How did you realize you could do this?" Mary put a trembling hand to her face.

"Now don't freak out, Mom." Charlie sat beside his mother and took her hand. "Keep in mind I'm okay now, but when a tank dies or receives a blow that would kill him, he gains a second wind, returning half his health to him. I'm pretty sure that's what happened to me."

"One minute I'm in horrible pain, I can't move at all, and I'm completely confused about what's happening. I had the weirdest dreams about the tournament and the game. The next minute, I was stronger but still confused. I thought I was at the tournament and all I could think was we needed to change our strategy. The tank's job is to protect the healer. I cast Waylay and was suddenly right next to her. All the medical equipment ripped off, and it hurt like hell.

"When I saw her lying there, I remembered where we were and I thought I was still dreaming. She cried when she saw me, and I asked her to pray for me, and she did, a real prayer, and I told her to cast a heal on me like we do when we use the paper keyboards and when she did that a ball of light formed on her hands, and she healed me. I still thought I was dreaming it until she healed all of us."

"You died?" Tears sprang to his mother's eyes.

"No, I had what amounts to one hit point left. I was probably taking some of Sara's damage by that point. Like a protection warrior in the game does for healers in their groups, which is a good thing or she would've been too far gone to heal us."

"But, why didn't you say anything?"

"At first, we were afraid they'd take her away, separate us. Then we heard about Rick, and we wanted to go get him. If we'd said something, we'd still be there undergoing God knows what kind of testing."

Mary said, "Even like this I can't let you go to Iraq and search for Rick; the magic could disappear as quickly as it arrived."

"Honestly, you can't stop us so you might as well help us." Stasia gave her a cocky grin. "We're going to the park for thirty minutes, then the airport. If you won't help us, we'll sneak on."

Mary closed her eyes tightly. "God forgive me," she mumbled, "Okay, let's go. I'll pack our bags, order us a car, check us out and meet you at the park in one hour. Don't hurt yourselves doing whatever it is you're going to do."

Sara flicked a small golden light onto Charlie. "No one will be hurt; I'll keep them healed."

Mary nodded and left the room, and they grabbed the walkie-talkies.

"Let's go," Stasia said. "I memorized the

route to the park earlier."

They followed Stasia to a service elevator, which they took to the basement and exited through the laundry area. Twice they stopped. Once Hawk cast a No-See-Um on them when a group of people passed by and once Oz cast Fool Sensors on a wall-mounted security camera. No one seemed to notice them. When they arrived, the park was dark and deserted.

"Cast a No-See-Um on the three of you." Charlie took a few steps away for a better view. "I want to see it from the outside." Three seconds later, he frowned. "Did you try? You all look the same."

"Thirty-minute cooldown, silly." Oz glanced at his watch and set a timer. "He can try again later. The question is, could he tell there was a cooldown, or did he think the cast happened?"

Hawk shook his head and looked embarrassed. "I couldn't tell. I'll pay closer attention next time."

"Okay, stand back. I want to try a fireball." Oz flexed his fingers preparing to cast.

"Wait!" Sara grabbed his hands. "Do those last; they might draw attention, and make sure you're ready to cast freezing rain if you start a fire. I'll go through my spells and Stasia and Hawk can go run around seeing how fast they are, and they can test their fighting moves on a tree or something. Try all your spells that don't cause explosions."

Stasia sprinted off at full speed and leapt into a tree where she disappeared from sight. Hawk grinned and followed, moving inhumanly fast he disappeared into the surrounding trees.

Sara cast her shield spells. "Hey, throw something small at me. I can't see my shield. Is it there?"

A small pink star whirled out of the darkness, hit an invisible wall, and clattered to the ground. "Try again, Stasia," Sara called.

"Where did you get that from?" Charlie eyed the small pink throwing star on the ground with disfavor.

"I stole it from the shop," Stasia said.

"If we try to board a plane with that, it'll set off every alarm on Earth," Charlie complained.

"Nope, it's plastic, no metal at all. It'll be fine, trust me." The star disappeared from the ground and reappeared in her hand. The small pink star flashed through the air, hit Sara's cloak, and fell to the ground.

Sara smiled. "Cloak works." She took out the staff and fumbled with it a bit to open it before setting it into the ground. A ring of light expanded from it and formed a dome over her, which she quickly dispelled.

"So much for subtle." Oz snickered and turned himself and Charlie invisible.

Anything over a whisper broke the spell. Stasia could talk while invisible too, but again loud noises broke the spell. Oz formed a portal, and they stared through it at what appeared to be his bedroom.

Oz said, "No way are we going through that unless we're desperate. We could end up in some crazy alternate dimension or something or fall through the world endlessly like we used to before they fixed this spell."

Charlie agreed with a shiver. Once he'd fallen endlessly through black space after taking a portal and it had taken a game master two days to retrieve his character. The thought of it happening in the real world was scary. Unless his life depended on it, he wouldn't use a portal.

"Let me borrow your staff." Charlie took the staff Sara handed him and did a complicated set of moves. "Okay, guys, concentrate on spell marks. Almost all my spells light my fingertips a small amount before they go off. Do a timing sequence if you can. Sara, let's run a straight cooldown pattern on my mark, tick."

Sara hit her watch.

"Tock," she said and shielded him.

He continued to do his fighting moves, trying not to feel ridiculous while he punched, kicked and stabbed at nothing. When he said, "Tock," she immediately said, "Tick" and recast her shield. They worked the entire sequence.

"I don't know, it seems okay, but I'm sure we're slower," Charlie said when they finished.

Sara frowned at her watch, speaking without looking up. "There's no way my heal-over-time spell is anywhere near accurate. I have to guess on when the HOT will wear off them. There's bound to be chunks of time where they have no HOT on. The only one I'm sure of is you."

"Do the best you can. We'll need to practice and some of our strategies need to be changed. None of us will have the split-second timing we had. We treat this as a new scenario and plan it as a stealth action similar to Castle Dark. On the plane, we'll run through it as if it were an actual game scenario."

Her anxious blue eyes fastened on him. "This isn't a game, Charlie. I won't use harmful spells on anyone. I'm not a killer."

"Me either, we have enough defensive spells, we can use those, but, Sara, if it's them or you— use force."

They practiced until Charlie's mother showed up. Oz cast a fireball and put out the resulting fire with freezing rain. He followed that with a lightning strike, which split a tree with a loud crack.

"People are coming, we better go," Hawk warned, "I warded this place earlier, and someone entered."

Stasia turned herself invisible and outside

Hawk was hard to see. Oz cast Invisible Duo on himself and Sara, and they walked out in a quiet group.

PLANNING

They passed through airport security with no problem, their bald heads and patchy skin caused some gawking, but they ignored it. They bought the eyeglass screwdrivers they needed, and Stasia bought a bunch of candy and granola bars.

"No matter how delicious, I can't live on conjured bread, sorry, Oz."

"I called your father, and he'll meet us there," Mary said to Charlie. "And no, I didn't say anything. This needs to be told in person."

They spread out copies of the keyboards in front of them and opened their notebooks.

"Okay, in this scenario we start with no weapons. The only abilities allowed are defensive. We can disarm and stun. The trick is the conditions are changeable. Let's start with a first condition."

Charlie spoke quietly using the new walkie-talkies. The rest of the plane was still boarding. His mother sat to his left, listening intently.

Charlie, Sara, and his mom sat behind Oz, Stasia, and Hawk in the first-class section. None sat in a window seat. The seats were bigger, letting them turn part way around in their seats, affording Charlie a view of his team's faces.

"First condition- bright lights," Charlie said. "In all conditions, assume armed enemies. Groups of enemies will most likely be on the small side, but we'll run a scenario of forty or more later. Let's assign a code word to not use headsets. If someone says blackout, it means radio silence."

"Okay, and project blackout means turn them off completely, they might be tracking it," Sara elaborated.

Everyone agreed to the call signs.

"Wherever possible we go around lights," Stasia said. "Since we don't want to leave a trace, we can't take out the lights. Walls pose no obstacle for us. Hawk and I leap or climb up, you waylay me. Then Spell-Steal Sara's pull and grab Oz unless he can Wink there, and Sara pulls herself. Everyone jumps down and goes to our next position. That's our standard for crossing walls in enemy territory, no reason to change it."

"Agreed." Charlie nodded and made a note in the notebook. Sara was taking notes too. "When we say normal crossing that's what's meant. Assume the fence has defenses, it senses us and lights up."

"Again, our normal response is adequate. Immediately jump down and I go invisible, and you do No-See-Um."

"Most enemies will stop searching in moments, but let's assume these don't."

Stasia smiled. "I cast Distract, and you Spell-Steal Oz's invisible and use it on Hawk and yourself while he uses it on Sara, and we retreat to the nearest dark, safe area. If there is no safe spot on the ground, I climb to a roof or up a tree, and she pulls herself up, then Oz. Oz can disguise himself if he has to while he waits for her pull cooldown. Hawk is hard to spot if you're outside and if we're inside, he can stay still and cast Imperceptible. If they use dogs, he can charm them away. I come back and distract again, and you cast Waylay on Sara. That leaves Hawk on the ground alone, but unseen and safe. If it remains unsafe for him to jump or sneak out, Sara will summon him, but that's a last resort, we can only use that every three hours."

"Well, technically twice if we use Chiefs Spell-Steal on ally," Oz said. "Let's make that Chief summons him leaving Sara with hers."

"Yeah, that's better," Charlie agreed. "So, that's a normal crossing. Now an emergency cross. We have our standard ones, we use invis and walk right through the gate, and of course, there's sap, trap, and sheep."

"If it goes to hell, you and Sara fear, with freezing rain, cold spot, and a couple shield hits for stuns." Oz paused in thought a moment. "I'm picturing you leap in and shield stun them while I cast Invisible Duo on us and we run away as fast as we can.

Code name, just run, we regroup and see if they stop chasing us."

Stasia grinned at Oz. "We can also use good old distraction. A fireball or lightning strike away from where we are would tend to gather people or at least make them look away."

"Okay, that'll be code named Oz opens the way. Oz picks a spot away from us and casts whatever he chooses." Charlie grinned at Oz too.

"We'll need a mark on that." Sara glanced at her watch.

"I'll use our standard one," Oz agreed. "Inc fire, and the time in seconds, so inc fire fifteen is a fireball in fifteen seconds on my watch. I'm hitting my counter at the word fifteen. Let's practice that timer a few times, and make sure we have that down."

A flight attendant approached them. "We're about to depart. Please, no electronic devices until the captain turns on the light."

"Are the watches okay?" Oz held his out to her. "We're learning to use the features."

"That's fine, but the radios need to be turned off."

The radios went in their bags with their headsets. "Okay, Oz, you call out the time, I want a tock from everyone on his mark. Don't forget to take into account the time needed to make the motions to cast." Charlie watched them hit their timers.

"Inc ning three." Oz used his usual method to warn he would cast lightning and it would go off in three seconds.

It took them a few tries to account for the motion at the end of the cast. They did it until they were all on the mark.

Charlie said, "So far so good, but I want to check it from a distance where we can't see each other. Let's make a note to do it later when we can be separated and walking or something."

He made a note in his notebook and smiled to himself when he noticed Sara write it too. "The timing needs to be accurate. We won't get a second chance at this. If we call out a cast, it has to go off at the right time. Everyone depends on it. If we go and we aren't invisible, or a distraction wasn't set, we might be seriously hurt, and we can screw up if we wait. The key to success will be timing just like always. If you aren't certain, say something immediately. Say three-ish if you aren't positive it'll be exactly three seconds. To acclimate to our new timing, practice any casts you can. Do unnoticeable ones, of course, but practice. It'll take us longer to cast now with both finger and hand movements to consider with no latency to precast."

His team listened seriously, knowing they couldn't afford to screw this up.

Sara was drawing a graph with timers in her notebook as he spoke. Her pencil flew across the paper making computations faster than he could read them. She'd already written out the new timing for her spells, adding the cast to the motions necessary, and had begun to work out Hawk's.

Charlie was awed at her memory as she made the motions of his casts while timing them. He'd played the game for years and was barely certain of his own character's motions.

"Let's talk about our gear for a minute," Stasia said, pulling his attention from Sara. "In this scenario, we go in naked and can only acquire gear from enemy camps. The better our gear is, the better our chances to rescue our captive."

"Not only enemy camps." Charlie tapped his notebook absently. "Unattended ally gear would work. If you got us chest pieces…."

Hawk turned in the seat to gaze thoughtfully at Sara. "Yeah, five, Sara shouldn't count on her cloak exclusively."

"Charlie needs a shield. Even a crappy one will work for a stun," Oz said.

Stasia rolled her eyes. "Not like those are likely to be lying around in either camp."

"You can craft one, right?" Mary said unexpectedly. "That's an acceptable game practice."

Sara laughed. "Okay, one garbage can lid painted black coming up; it'll be a fashion statement. All the first level shields look like crap."

Hawk laughed too. "I'll need a rifle or a bow."

Mary looked alarmed.

"To cast a Knock-Out Shot, I need a weapon. I'd prefer a bow, but unless we craft that I doubt we'll find one of those either."

Oz leaned back in his seat and closed his eyes, deep in thought, and said, "Charlie, Hawk, and Stasia need daggers to activate their passive agility buff. Those should be thick as flies on honey on both sides. Axes for Charlie would be easy to find. Whirling blades are an effective way to block damage, you don't have to use it to attack."

Charlie wrote it down. "I'll want two axes, a dagger, and a shield. All easy to get if we don't care about the looks, which we don't. With two axes, I can cast crossed blades and hold back a rush."

Sara made a face. "You'll need a sheath. You can't run around holding them."

"Sewing was one of my game professions; my character can whip something up," Mary offered. "Belts with tie sheaths are easy enough to make for daggers."

Charlie gave his mother a grateful nod. "Okay, so there we are on the roof. The enemy knows we're near somewhere, assume alarms and more patrols."

Oz opened his eyes and smiled slightly. "I locate our captive, and we roof hop to the right building if we can. That's a standard technique for us. We can cross a twenty-foot gap without touching the ground."

"If we do touch down, do it like always. Charlie, then me, then Oz, then Sara, then Hawk," Stasia said. "We plan our moves in advance, like always, and we use the same target designations as always, T-one, T-two, and so on. Always numbering from front to back and left to right."

Sara nodded agreement to Stasia. "We should make a Leroy plan as well. If every armed man in the area attacks, we'll need a plan to escape. There's no more teleport home."

Charlie nodded. "Stasia should be okay no matter what. She can cast Invisible and run. Hawk to some extent the same. If he can reach trees, he'd be fine too. Sara, you and I and Oz would need to fight our way out if there was nothing to hide behind before Oz's invisible runs out."

Charlie knew he could steal Stasia's invisible and escape, but no way would he abandon Sara and Oz. Being a protection warrior, he didn't think it would be possible to leave them behind even if he wanted to.

"Oz might be able to cast Wink and Invisible Duo and hide, but even assuming you feared them and ran away there would be too many; if you didn't fight, their numbers would overwhelm you. Sara, you could only run if a safe-haven presented itself where you were sure they couldn't follow."

"Yeah, I can see that." Sara thoughtfully tapped her lip with one finger. "If I could reach a bigger group attacking and hide in it, or reach a safe castle, otherwise I'd need to fight and most likely kill them."

"That's a last resort." Charlie took her hand in his. "You don't have to even attempt this scenario."

"We're a team."

"If it's a Leroy, I'm not leaving," Stasia said.

Stasia wore her stubborn expression again, and Charlie grinned.

"I'm staying to fight too," she said. "We treat it like any pug Leroy we ever had. From now on, it's crucial we protect our healer, we can't sacrifice her. Protect Sara at all costs. If she dies, we die too. We group up and fight it out, concentrating on our team and in this case the captive. No matter what other captives are there, it's us first."

Oz laughed, he recognized the look too. "If we can save more captives by blowing cooldowns, we do it, but only if we're ninety percent sure we can escape with our captive alive."

Charlie nodded gratefully. "Yes, I'll call it out if Sara gives the word. She'll call for a total defense or retreat. Targets and sectors, I'll call as usual, but don't hesitate to call for changes. This'll be an entirely new scenario. The hardest part is no more rez."

"Well, we don't know that for sure, but it's a safe assumption," Sara agreed.

Charlie checked his notes. "So, we're on our roof, if they have dogs, Hawk handles it. How do we enter?"

Stasia shrugged. "I can Pick Lock or Sweet-Talk my way in. Oz can blast a door or teleport through a wall. You can rush the door."

"Or, we could just try the knob," Hawk said and laughed.

Sara laughed too. "Yeah, try the knob

first, and there might be windows. And you could always chop a hole, or Oz could blast a hole in the roof. Getting in shouldn't be too hard. Stasia could follow someone else in and open a door for us. It's the getting out."

Oz narrowed his eyes. "Yeah, I don't want to leave any captives behind."

"Sure, but we locate ours first, then the others," Stasia said. "Once we retrieve our captive, we free the others. They wouldn't have problems killing the enemies."

Sara nodded thoughtfully. "True, but they would be unarmed and defenseless."

Hawk shrugged. "So, we arm them. Disable small groups of enemies and take their weapons and give them to the others."

"CC only holds for three minutes, tops," Oz said.

"True, but old-fashioned rope would work; if we can't find rope, we could use conjured bandages."

"Okay, let's assume—"

The flight attendant interrupted. "The radios can be used now and if you could be a tad quieter? People are trying to sleep. Can I get you pillows or blankets?"

Mary accepted the offer. "Okay, guys, just a while longer. You need sleep too. This flight is thirteen hours. You'll have time to work out details."

Charlie nodded and put his headset back on. "Just a while longer, Mom."

The headsets got set to whisper mode, and they turned down the lights over their seats.

Charlie lowered his voice to a whisper. "This is a stealth mission and not just because of the danger. If we're seen using magic spells by the enemy— Well, I think they'll hunt us down." Charlie winced and rubbed his forehead. "You need to be especially careful, Oz. Our spells aren't as, um, flamboyant as yours. Sara's abilities must remain secret. I can't even imagine what they'd do if they got their hands on her. What she can do is priceless. This has to remain secret."

Oz nodded. "If we do attack using showy magic, we can't have survivors. You're right, Sara is at serious risk. Hell, we all are. We need to think about what we're going to do about that—"

Stasia interrupted, "Let's get Rick first, then worry about it. Even if that means we expose ourselves. This isn't a game. He can't start again."

"I agree." Hawk placed his hand on his sister's. "Try to be as subtle as we can, but if it's them or us, we use what we have to, showy or not. There's likely to be injured hostages. If Sara heals them, I'm hoping they'll be grateful to be rescued and keep our secret. As long as we don't go around blowing things up, no one will believe them if they do tell."

Charlie frowned at Sara who sat beside him. "You don't have to come—"

"I'm coming!" Sara leaned over and placed her hand on Stasia's too. "Team Valor sticks together. We're strongest when we're together. Let's get Rick and get out and deal with what happens when he's safe."

"I agree." Stasia nodded gratefully. "If we have to run away to stay safe, so be it. That's a small price to pay for Rick's life."

"Team Valor sticks together no matter what." Charlie took Sara's hand, kissed it, and then ran his hand over her head. "If we do have to run, we stay together." Her amazing blue eyes lit, and he had to clear his throat before speaking.

"Okay, but how do we reach him?" Hawk asked.

"I have an idea to get into the zone." Stasia took out the atlas. "There's an ally base at the border. We, sneak, Sweet-Talk or Hypnosis our way onto transport."

Sara frowned. "With Hypnosis, someone, meaning one of you, would need to drive and I couldn't keep it up long, but maybe we could use it to board transport."

Hawk pursed his lips. "Hmm, I have Mount Mastery. I wonder if that translates to vehicles?"

"Camels maybe," Stasia said. "We can always try to rent some of them or something."

Oz appeared doubtful about that. Charlie was doubtful too. He didn't want to ride a camel through the desert of Iraq searching for his brother either. "I could drive us. I have a learner permit. The concepts are a little familiar."

Sara glanced over at Mary to be sure she

slept before speaking. "Sweet-Talk will get your mom to show us all quick in case we need too. I realize we can't learn to drive in ten minutes but knowing the basics couldn't hurt. The other option is we board transport and use a No-See-Um."

Stasia drummed her pen absently as she spoke. "If we sit quietly and don't move, no one will see us. That option would work better in a supply truck than a troop one."

Oz nodded agreement, seeming much happier with that idea. "That one sounds better. The trick there is finding one going where we want and getting off it at the other end unseen."

Stasia nodded agreement as she spoke. "Oz, your invisible should get them all off. And, we don't actually need to be inside the vehicle, we could ride on top under a No-See-Um. The air base is a good bet to find a ride going where we want. No one will see me spy out our ride. Sara and Oz can go listen to the locals and see if anyone's headed where we want to go. A military transport would be better than a civilian one, I doubt it would be searched or at least not as thoroughly. A No-See-Um won't hold up if we're actually searched for and stared right at."

They made plans for a few more hours. Finally, Charlie said, "Thanks for coming with me. This will be dangerous. If you change your mind about going, I won't be mad or think less of you."

He wasn't surprised when they all whispered they were going.

"Okay, we have a rough plan, a very rough plan. Let's get some sleep. This plane lands in five hours."

They stowed their gear and used each other as pillows. Charlie fell asleep almost instantly and slept soundly, his head resting on Sara. She curled into his side, both of their jackets and her cloak spread over them. No one stirred until the buzzer to fasten seatbelts lit.

- 19 -

SPIES

Charlie felt like he'd been in an airport forever. The plane landed at five in the morning, gaining six hours from the time change. The flight from Okinawa to Tokyo took an hour and a half, but they had a six-hour wait for the flight from there to Ankara Turkey. That flight took thirteen hours and made two stops where they waited almost four hours each time, and then they'd caught a flight to Adana. They'd been traveling for almost twenty-four hours.

Gathered around a television in an airport in Ankara, while waiting for their flight, they watched reruns of the news, praying they weren't already too late. Charlie was relieved his brother wasn't killed but frustrated they were too late to save the other soldiers.

Turkish customs passed them through with no problems. Mary told the custom's official when the captives returned they wanted to be near. She went to rent a car while they picked up her luggage.

Forty-five minutes later, they headed down the road. After a quick stop at a McDonalds, where they got food to go, they got on a two-lane highway bordered on both sides by high-rise buildings. In twenty minutes, the buildings disappeared replaced by brown grasses, low bushes, and the occasional pine. The empty landscape changed to industrial concrete buildings and then two-story wooden and stone houses, most surrounded by fences. It didn't appear that much different from home to Charlie.

Sara had the iPad mini out, and the maps app opened. "Siri, where's the closest department store?"

Siri directed them to a small shopping center. The plane had arrived at five-thirty in the morning local time. An hour remained before the store opened. Stasia talked Mary into showing them how to drive the car. Hawk excelled at it. Charlie, Oz and Stasia were passable and Sara was nervous.

"Don't buy axes, Mrs. H, I'll get them," Stasia said when the store opened. "Buy black spray paint and whatever you need to make Chief's ax holder. What should we use for knife sheaths?"

"More material. I'll make them, but you might be able to get the sheaths where you get the knives," Mary said.

They left the store with those items and a box of Slim-Jims.

"This is the ass end of nowhere, and they have McDonalds and Slim-Jims, that's amazing," Hawk said as he happily ate his Slim-Jim.

Stasia asked Mary to stop by any hotel or motel they passed.

"Nice, this ought to do it. Pull over I'll be right back." Stasia said when Sara pointed to a rundown building with one old wreck of a car out front and a broken sign advertising room for rents.

The invisible spell made her appear foggy to her teammates, but Mary couldn't see her. In ten minutes, Stasia returned with two axes. "Let's go down the street and spray paint these bad boys black."

Mary pulled the car over onto a side street and quickly sprayed them, pretending to read a map while they waited for them to dry. People passed them infrequently, but no one stopped or seemed interested.

"Can you heal my mother?" Charlie asked Sara. "I'm wondering if you can only heal group members."

Sara cast a shield, which showed as a faint outline in the ground and a heal that traveled to her as a ball of light. The light ball made Mary glow for a moment.

"Yep, but she's my friend. I should try it on a stranger. Most of my spells are party or ally only. I probably couldn't cast on a stranger."

Mary sprayed the axes again and frowned. "Will you be able to heal Rick?"

"Probably, he's my friend too. If it works for you, it should on him."

"Maybe it only works on me because I

was on the plane," Mary said.

"Try it on my dad. If it works on him, it should work on Rick." Charlie gave his mom a quick hug. "Hawk, cast a No-See-Um on my mother."

"Can't," Hawk said after a minute. "That's a party only spell. Make it a raid."

"Mom, I invite you to join our raid." Charlie crossed his fingers.

"I accept," Mary said.

"Try now." Charlie glanced anxiously at Hawk as he cast.

Mary faded to a foggy image.

"Sweet, it worked!" he exclaimed in relief.

"Nothing changed," Mary protested.

"It worked," Stasia said and grinned at Mary. "From inside the spell everything appears the same, but you appear faded to us. This doesn't prove it'll work with a stranger, she's raided with us before."

"Doesn't matter." Charlie shrugged. "All I care about is us right now anyway."

"True that." Hawk gingerly touched the axes, testing the drying paint. "One more quick spray ought to do it."

They were back on the road headed to

the hotel when Charlie's father called.

"Where are you? I'm at the hotel," John said.

"Hi, dear, you're on speaker phone. The kids and I are on the way to the hotel. The rooms are reserved under our name. You should be able to check in."

"What the hell is going on?"

"We'll be there in... when, Sara?"

"Thirty-two minutes, according to our GPS."

"Thirty minutes or so," Mary repeated.

"I heard her. Do their parents know where they are?" John said, sounding pissed.

Mary exchanged a rueful glance with Charlie before saying, "Not really, no. They know they're with me. Look, we'll talk about this when we get there. Sara needs orange juice. Can you see if you can find any small cans of premade orange juice, not the fake stuff, the real stuff?" Mary turned to Charlie. "Does he need a car too?"

Charlie shrugged. "I don't know, but it couldn't hurt."

"Hun, do you have a rental car there?" Mary asked her husband.

"No, I took a taxi. Why didn't you fly into this airport?"

"Couldn't," Hawk said loudly so his voice would carry from the backseat to the phone. "This was the only flight available; we would've had to wait until tomorrow."

"What's the hurry? What's going on?"

"Rent a car. We'll be there soon and talk in person. Love you." Mary hung up without waiting for a reply.

"Oh boy, he's going to have a fit," Charlie said, his voice a mix of laughter and dread.

"Did you guys have time to run a cave scenario?" Mary clutched the steering wheel, tapping her fingers in a nervous rhythm.

"We spent a lot of time on that," Charlie reassured her. "We figured it's actually the most likely one. We have a plan, but first we need to get there. Stasia, Hawk, and I'll see about finding us gear and our ride. Drop us off anywhere by Incirlik base. There's bound to be supplies there."

"Couldn't I drive you to the border?"

"Yes, but it's a big area. We aren't sure if Rick's in Syria or Iraq. We might need to check both places. First, we'll check the Sinjar Mountains as it's the most likely spot. The border there is heavily patrolled. If we can hop on a transport heading there, it'll be easier for us."

Stasia leaned forward from the back seat and placed a hand on Mary's shoulder. "Sara and Oz will go to the Turkish base. She can check there for transport. Mrs. H, when we find one, we're leaving. There won't be time for long goodbyes. We'll be as careful as we can be."

Oz put his arm around Stasia. "We'll be as fast as we can be too. The next beheading is nine hours away."

The reminder silenced them. No one spoke except Sara giving directions. "Those fields are part of the base, we're almost there," she said.

Mary slowed, and everyone eagerly stared out the windows.

Oz pointed to a sign written in English. "Yep, look, there's a sign. This is the right spot. Drive by the main gate. Let's see what it looks like."

Mary drove by, going as slow as possible

without attracting attention. A four-lane entrance with open electronic gates led into the base. Armed men stopped the cars, questioning the drivers. A soldier with a dog walked around each car while the dog sniffed diligently. One strand of razor wire topped the eight-foot-high fence that surrounded the base as far as they could see.

Charlie gestured for his mother to keep driving. "This place is huge. Go around the base and stay as close to the fence as you can. We're searching for somewhere to cross."

They cruised slowly down the road, keeping the fence in sight.

"Stop!" Stasia said as she grabbed her backpack from the floor of the car. "This'll work. Let's go."

A sprawling group of bushes grew against the fence. An untended lawn with overgrown, dead grass and an abandoned building stood in front of them. Scrubby bushes filled an empty field bordering a few low concrete buildings on the other side of the fence.

Sara leaned over and hugged Stasia. "Be careful. We'll be listening. If you need a port out, call me."

Stasia exited the car and Hawk climbed over the seat and followed her. Sara hugged him too. Charlie got out of the front seat and fist bumped them through the door.

"Go, Team Valor. See ya soon." Charlie slung his almost empty backpack over his shoulder and the three casually headed to the building. Stasia was already invisible. The boys formed a cradle with their hands and threw her over the fence.

"Whoops, didn't mean to throw you that far. I'm not used to being stronger. You okay?" Charlie grimaced apologetically at Stasia, relieved when she gave him a thumbs up.

He boosted Hawk over the fence, cast his Waylay spell on Stasia, and stole her invisible with his Spell-Steal when he appeared beside her.

"Let's split up. This place is huge." Stasia's voice broadcasted clearly over their headset.

The three of them ran off in different directions.

"Okay, Mrs. H, let's go," Oz said. "The

Turkish base isn't far. Drop us off and go check in. When we need a ride, we'll call. Can you set up the chargers, please, if you have time?"

"I'll get everything ready; you be careful," Mary said.

The Turkish base was twenty minutes away, and it too was guarded and fenced. Mary passed the main gate slowly.

"How will you enter? Want me to drive around it?" she asked.

"No, we'll use the front entrance," Oz said. "Drive up to the gate but stop on the side of the road and go ask for directions to the hotel. Leave your door open. We'll be gone when you return."

Oz and Sara ducked down in their seats as Mary drove up. She didn't get in line with the other cars; she pulled over and got out. A whistle blew, and a man yelled in Turkish.

Mary held her hands up and walked towards the gate. "English, please. I'm sorry, I don't understand you. I just need directions."

Oz whispered, "Invis three."

Sara counted it off, climbed over the seat, and ran through the gate, ignoring the commotion behind her. As the soldiers surrounded Mrs. H, she and Oz headed into the base at a run.

- 20 -

MARY TELLS JOHN

Mary headed to the hotel as soon as the gate guards let her go. When she pulled into the parking lot of the hotel, she parked the car and took a deep breath before opening the door. John would be angry. Her palms were sweating when she called him on the cell phone.

"What room are we in?" she asked.

"Room fifty-one on the second floor. The kids are in the rooms on either side," John said. "Do you need help with the bags?"

"No, I got them. I'll be right up."

Mary hung up the phone before he said anything else. If he came to help and realized the kids weren't with her, he might cause a scene right there and this disclosure required privacy.

She tucked the bag of sewing supplies under one arm, threw her coat over the ax handles sticking out, and frowned at the garbage can lid; she'd come back for that, she decided. Awkwardly grabbing the two handles to pull the suitcases, she slammed the trunk and hurried inside, passed the desk, to the elevator.

The sign right outside the elevator pointed to the room, and she knocked on door fifty-one in moments. John answered with a frown on his face and let her into the small room. The bags hit the floor, and the axes tumbled out as she hugged her husband. To her relief, he hugged her back just as tightly.

Finally, he pulled away. "Where are the kids?"

She took a second to pick up the axes and gather her thoughts as she set them on the bed. "I dropped them off. They had things to do. Have a seat. I have things to tell you that you won't like much."

"What sort of things?" he asked suspiciously. The frown on his face deepened, and he stood with his feet apart and his hands on his hips. "And what are they doing?"

Mary shrugged lightly and turned to the suitcases. The chargers were in a tangled ball, and she started sorting them. "I need to plug these in. I have things to do too, and our time might be limited. Can you give me a hand?"

John took the bag, placed it on the floor, and took her hands. "Mary, what's going on? This secrecy isn't like you. Is this about the kid's condition?" he asked, his brow creased in sudden worry. "Is something wrong with them?"

Mary gripped his hands, hers trembled. "There's nothing wrong with them *per-se*, but they do have a condition, and I don't know if it's permanent or not. This'll sound incredible, but they've become their UBM characters."

"What?" John dropped her hands, laughed, and rubbed his eyes with both hands. "Jesus, Mary, that's it? I was really worried. Is it the plane crash, or hair loss, or what? And, how do you know? They always call each other by their game names, and it never worried you before."

"I know because they showed me. Right now they're out getting what they call epic gear. Well, some of them are anyways. Oz and Sara are scouting the Turkish air base."

"What the hell are you talking about? Why would they do that and how did they even enter it? That base is totally restricted."

"Why— they're looking for a ride into Iraq. How—they snuck in using their new abilities."

"Mary, sit down; you're not making any sense." John pushed her down on the bed and sat beside her. "Iraq? Why would they want to go there? Are you sure you're okay?" he asked in sudden alarm. "Jesus, are you sick too?" More frown lines formed as he felt her forehead.

She brushed him away and grabbed his searching hands. "I'm fine. Listen to me! The kids are going to Iraq and maybe Syria to search for Rick. Oz's has a locate spell they think they can use to find him. With their new abilities, they think they can rescue him. Right now, they're at different bases looking for gear and a way over the border."

John pulled his hands from his wife's grip.

Tears rose to her eyes as she grabbed his hands again and held tightly. "I know that sounds crazy, and I didn't want them to go either. New power or not, they're just kids, but as they pointed out, I can't stop them. They're going with or without my permission, and John they could do it; they could bring Rick back safely. Rick could come home." Mary held his hands beseechingly.

"Mary, honey—" John stopped and bit his lip. An expression of deep sadness on his face, he cleared his throat before he spoke. "I love Rick too. If I could magically save him, of course I would. But, honey, it's just a game. I realize you're all desperate. Hell, I'm desperate too! But they absolutely can't go, and we can stop them. Tell me where they are and I'll go get them and talk with them. Somehow they convinced you—"

He grabbed her shoulders as she turned

away from him. "I'm not blaming you. I know how much we want Rick back, but the kids can't find him or rescue him. We have to leave that to the professionals, and they're looking, honey. Have faith they'll find him. I'll get the kids, and we can lock them in their rooms if we have to. Once we're home, we'll find them professional help to get over this delusion." He pulled his wife into a hug. "We'll get you help. Where are they? I'll go pick them up."

Mary pulled away from him. "They'll call me when they're ready to come back here. I'm sorry, honey, you'll have to trust me. I'm not deluded or crazy. They really can do the things their characters could. No locked door on Earth will stop them now." Mary started plugging chargers in.

John stood in the center of the room and watched her unpack the kids' bags, his lips pressed tight together, his face sad and worried. When she'd plugged everything in, she started sewing. In a few minutes, she'd made a pouch for Sara's staff, and she started on Charlie's ax holder. John squatted in front of her.

"What are the axes for?" he asked.

"Charlie needs them to deflect an attack." Mary kept sewing.

"Please, honey, think about what you just said. Charlie can't use axes to deflect an attack— no one can. It's a make-believe skill in a make-believe world. Here, in this world, we use them to open doors in a fire. Where did you get them?"

"Stasia stole them from a motel on the way here. I plan on paying for them, I don't want her to steal, but we needed them, and I didn't think I could go in a store and buy axes."

"Listen to yourself, sweetheart; we can't let the kids do any of these things. They could get hurt. You say they're out there right now stealing things and sneaking around. That's not how we raised them! That is in no way how you want our kids to behave! Can't you see something is wrong?" His voice rose as he pleaded with her.

"It's wrong, but Rick needs them. John, ISIS, could behead our son tonight. We can't stop it, but they can. Sara could save him with her spells. She really could. They just have to find him. I need my suitcases. I'll be right back." Mary hung the backpack with the axes in the small closet and left the room.

John stayed and sat on the bed with a thump. "Holy mother of God, what am I going to do," he said aloud, his voice soft and full of worry. His head was in his hand when Mary returned with her cases and a black trashcan lid.

His eyes were sad as she made a Velcro loop and attach it to the backpack. Ten minutes later, her phone rang. After a minute of quiet conversation, she asked him what color car he'd rented.

"A dark-blue, four-door sedan."

After she repeated that, she said, "I'll send your father."

"Give me the phone!" John command, but she'd hung up.

"Sara and Oz need a ride. The guards at the gate might recognize my car. You better pick them up in yours. Go down the street to the left of the main entrance of the Turkish base. They'll be on the street there. When Charles is ready, I'll get him."

John put both hands on her shoulders

and shook her slightly. "Don't go anywhere else without telling me! Get the kids and come straight back here! Promise me."

"I promise."

He searched her face a moment before kissing her quickly and leaving to pick up Sara and Oz.

SARA AND OZ

Oz pointed to a big building. "That one. Seventy-two seconds left, let's go."

They ran through the doorway, slowing as they passed people. No one noticed them. Oz grinned at Sara and pointed to an open office door and they ran inside. A man spoke on a phone in the outer office, but the inner office was empty. Another small door stood to the left of the one they entered that when cautiously opened proved to be a closet. Oz tapped his watch and entered the closet, waiting for Sara to enter before closing the door.

She held up one finger. With her back

against the wall hidden from sight, she listened to the man on the phone.

Oz tapped his watch again.

Sara nodded but remained.

Oz kept an eye on the timer and held up two fingers, warning it would be two minutes before he could cast Invisible Duo again as the fog surrounding Sara disappeared. The man on the phone finished his conversation. File drawers opened and closed and the phone rang again. Once the spell cooldown passed, Sara tapped her chest indicating she would lead.

Stasia's voice came on the line. "I've located a storage room and retrieved some gear."

"Until we know what will break my invisible, I better scout while you get the gear," Charlie replied. "The far hanger has lots of activity. I'll head down there and see if I can find out where they're going."

"Meet me back at the fence, sis, and I'll carry the gear. There aren't enough plants to hide me close enough to do any good," Hawk said, sounding annoyed.

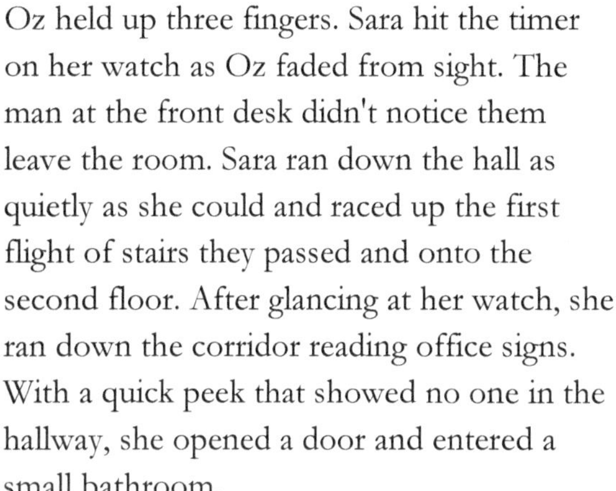

Oz held up three fingers. Sara hit the timer on her watch as Oz faded from sight. The man at the front desk didn't notice them leave the room. Sara ran down the hall as quietly as she could and raced up the first flight of stairs they passed and onto the second floor. After glancing at her watch, she ran down the corridor reading office signs. With a quick peek that showed no one in the hallway, she opened a door and entered a small bathroom.

Oz peered under the stalls and ran into the last one.

Sara followed.

Sara whispered, "That man on the phone said he'd send the schedule right up to dispatch. That's on this floor but I didn't see it yet. Let's wait until the next timer and run down the hall to see if we can find it."

"Okay, Stasia, I've got this stuff," Hawk said over the headset. "See if you can find us a ride."

"One minute until invis," Oz whispered.

The door to the bathroom opened and

someone entered and used the second stall. Oz stood on the toilet while Sara stood in front of it. He tapped her shoulder, held up three fingers, and turned foggy as the person next to them flushed. Sara didn't wait; she ran out the door and into the hall and raced down the hallway reading the door signs.

With a quick glance at her watch, she stopped by one and hurried inside. Four desks in the front room were all occupied by men in uniform busily working on their computers. Three opened doors lined the left wall. Sara tiptoed to the first and glanced in. Four more men sat at desks in that room as well. A man stood in front of a filing cabinet behind a large desk in the last room.

She crept inside and peered in the cabinets the man had open. After glancing at her watch, she returned to the door. Tacked to the wall by the door hung a large map and she paused to examine it. Another glance at her watch and she hurried out the door. They ran back to the bathroom and entered it as the spell wore off. They both peeked hurriedly under the stalls.

Oz tapped his watch. "You cut it close."

"There's a map on the wall," Sara said as they entered the last stall again. "It shows where their bases are and there are pins showing the locations of enemy forces."

"No word on a ride though?"

"No, not yet. I'll check the third room on the timer."

"There's a plane going to Baghdad at eight tonight we can board easily," Charlie said. "I'm going to keep looking, see if I can find ground transport going earlier."

"Ready?" Oz glanced at his timer.

Sara nodded. Oz held up three fingers, and they ran straight to the third room. The filing cabinets were closed now. She paused at each desk and observed what the men were working on and then headed into the big office where the map hung until Oz pulled her out. They ran back to the bathroom and returned to the last stall.

"Okay, there's a supply truck scheduled to leave here in one hour going to Ocalan. That's on the border of Syria. A list of planned stops was on the desk in the third room but I only had time to find one stop. Charlie, call for our pickup. We're going to steal that list and map and get out of here. Oz, we need a distraction, maybe a fire alarm. When they leave the room, we take the stuff."

"Okay, I'll pull it in" –Oz glanced at his watch— "Eighteen seconds. Once that room is empty, if it empties, take it and come back here. We wait out the timer and run out."

Oz held up three fingers, putting them down one at a time as the seconds ticked by and they were invisible again. Sara ran into the office where she'd seen the list. The alarm sounded, and the employees stopped work.

The man in the big office stomped into the hallway. "This is the third goddamn drill in a week— let's go!" he said in Turkish and motioned the people in the office to pass him, making sure everyone left before leaving himself.

Sara kept an eye on the time, counting the seconds remaining until she had to run. Oz entered the room as the last man left and Sara darted into the now empty office and scanned the desk where the list was before.

The list was gone. Oz returned to the hallway to watch for returning men. Papers scattered as she searched frantically. The invisibility spell wore off, and she still hadn't found it.

"Two minutes, Sara, hurry the heck up!" Oz shouted in a whisper from where he stood at the stairs watching for returning men.

"Got it!" Sara sighed in relief, waved the paper at Oz, and got the map. She took it down, ran to the copier, and copied one part at a time. The whir of the machine sounded loud in the quiet office as it made the copies.

"Sara, I hear people coming, hurry."

"One second, I'm almost done. Let's go right out on this cast." Sara returned the map to the wall, folded the wad of papers, and hastily stuck them under her shirt as she ran to Oz. "Let's go."

"Invis three." Oz grabbed her hand, and they ran out the door and down the hallway. They tiptoed down the stairs past men returning to their offices.

Sara peered at her watch, tugged on his hand, and pointed to a door they passed. 'Bathroom,' she mouthed.

Oz nodded and returned to the door,

glanced up and down the hall, shrugged, pushed the door open, and pulled her inside.

The bathroom appeared empty.

They both ducked down and checked the stalls. Oz climbed up on the seat of the last stall while Sara again remained on the floor. "Two minutes, thirty-two seconds to recast. Any ETA on our ride?"

"My father is coming for you," Charlie said. "He's driving a dark-blue four-door. Run down the road to the left as you exit. If you can't find a safe spot to hide, walk down the road and try to look casual."

Oz counted down the seconds until he could cast Invisible Duo again. People passed in the hallway talking, and it sounded busy.

"Let's wait until it quiets before we go," he said.

Sara nodded agreement.

Someone entered and used the first stall. Oz put his hand over his mouth to stop the laugh as the person entered talking to himself. In a moment, he wasn't laughing, his eyes watered from the smell. The bathroom door opened again, someone exclaimed, and the door slammed shut. Oz switched his hand from over his mouth to holding his nose. Sara pulled the neck of her shirt over her nose and mouth, her eyes dancing with mirth. Oz rolled his eyes and held up three fingers, he was getting the heck out of there.

On three, they ran out the door. Oz glanced at his watch and tugged her faster as they headed through the gate. Nothing on the road could hide them. Invisible would wear off in three seconds. Oz put his arm around Sara's shoulder and slowed to a walk.

"Just keep walking. Nothing to look at here— we were here all the time," he mumbled when a car slowed as it passed.

Stasia snuck down a long hallway carrying a bulging pack. She exited the building right behind a soldier carrying a briefcase and sprinted across the empty square headed towards a big building with trucks parked in front. Empty cargo trucks with rolled canvas sides were backed into the loading docks. Men gathered on the loading docks with forklifts holding large cardboard boxes. She eavesdropped shamelessly.

"A bunch of trucks here are going to Silopi at noon. Where is that?" Stasia asked.

"That's on the border of Syria and Iraq," Sara said. "Head back. We'll group up and pick a ride."

"On my way." Stasia sprinted back to the main entrance.

The dog sniffing the cars glanced at her but didn't bark or otherwise acknowledge her. Charlie and Hawk waited outside the gate where they'd jumped the fence with the gear she'd already borrowed.

Stasia hefted her pack triumphantly. "I got us everything on our list, and I picked up a radio. Maybe he can use it to call for help or a ride."

"Good idea," Charlie said. *It wasn't stealing,* he told himself. *I'll give it all back when we're done with it.* "Mom is on her way to get us. Oh, here she is now. Let's go." Carrying the stolen gear, they ran to the car and got in. "Back to the hotel, Mom. How did Dad take it?"

"Not good!" His father's angry voice said on his headset. "You're all certifiable. Don't you dare leave that hotel until I return!"

"Yeah, I would definitely say not good." A small, ironic smile crossed Mary's face as she turned the car back to the hotel. "He didn't believe me, but he will. Don't worry about that. How'd it go?"

Stasia met her eyes in the rearview mirror and smiled. "Good, we got the gear. We need a few minutes to check the maps and dress."

- 22 -

JOHN RELUCTANTLY AGREES

They headed straight to their room when they arrived at the hotel. "We have three rooms. I didn't want to rouse suspicion if anyone checked up on us." Mary handed Charlie a room key as they entered the building. "We're on the second floor."

She opened a door and gestured them inside. The small room held one double bed, one nightstand, and one rickety chair. A small table with a lamp sat before drape-covered windows. A quick peek in the door beside the open closet revealed a small bathroom with no tub, only a shower boasting cracked linoleum.

"Plug in and charge up while we settle

this," Charlie said as he dumped his bulging pack and rummaged through the stuff until he found the charger for his headset.

Hawk took the walkie-talkies into the next room where the chargers waited. After hooking them up, he headed into the bathroom.

Sara and Oz arrived a few minutes later followed by his irate father. Without speaking, they put their electronic devices on chargers. Sara took out the copied map and laid it on the table, and they gathered around.

"The truck I found leaves in eighteen minutes to go here." She pointed on the map. "The truck Stasia saw leaves in an hour and a half to go here." Sliding her finger further north, she pointed to a different spot. "Stasia's truck brings us closer, but mine leaves sooner. Or, we can get on the plane headed to Baghdad. The flight from here to Iraq is three hours, but the plane doesn't leave for eight, and we'd need to travel about six more hours to reach the area we know ISIS controls. It'll take us seven hours to reach Silopi, the ride Stasia found, and five to reach mine, but Stasia's is closer to where we want to be. It's also an English-speaking base so she could scout out our next ride there."

John slapped his hand on the makeshift map emphatically. "Wait one damn minute! No one's going haring off to God knows where into a war zone for crying-out-loud. None of you are going anywhere, except home."

"Mr. H, you can't stop us." Oz laid his hand on John's arm. "I'm sorry, sir, you know I respect you, but we're talking about Rick's life here. We're going."

"I understand you think you're the game characters now, a delusion my wife somehow shares, but, son, you're not. And sneaking around army bases, especially enemy army bases can get you shot. Please, everyone, sit down, and we'll talk calmly about this. I love Rick too. I'll do everything I can to get him home safe, but I won't let my teenage son and his friends sneak onto army transport in a war zone where they have no business being. You won't be able to find him. I'm sorry, guys, but you're not living in a video game. This is—"

"Mr. H." Stasia tugged his shirtsleeve and

when he faced her, turned herself invisible.

Oz cast Invisible Duo on himself and Sara. Hawk made himself invisible. Charlie stood in front of his gaping father.

"Dad, we're going. We aren't crazy. We can find him. Oz has a locate spell we think he can use to find Rick if we're in the same zone."

John sat weakly on the bed. "Oh, dear Lord." He rubbed his face with his hands. "You're just children. I can't let you go, even with this…"

"Magic," Stasia said helpfully, popping into sight sitting in the room's only chair. "The word you're looking for is magic. We can do magic. Why we can, I have no idea, but we can."

"Dad, you're not letting us, we're telling you we're going. You can't stop us. The most you could do would be report us and who would believe it? I'm so sorry, Dad, but we can't obey you in this. We know it's a war zone, we'll be very, very careful."

"The window to take my truck is closing." Sara tapped the map on the word Silopi. "Let's take Stasia's truck. The hour we lose now we can make up once we reach the next stop."

"I agree." Oz nodded, peering over Sara's shoulder at the map. "While Sara and I can sneak around, it's less likely that Stasia will be caught. We'll lose one hour though, and I can't bear to think of arriving too late."

"Either way we'll be too late today." Stasia moved away while speaking, opened her suitcase, and grabbed her black clothing. "Someone will die today, even if we left right this minute and drove as fast as we could, we couldn't reach him in nine hours."

"I don't know what to pray for. If I pray my son isn't picked, I'm praying for someone else's son to be." Mary put her head in her hands and cried.

Charlie's father got up, hugged her, and met his son's eyes over his wife's bowed head. "Okay, take Stasia's truck. What do you need from us?"

"Mom, did you make me the ax holder?"

She nodded against her husband's shoulder. "Hanging in the closet."

"I got us all knives and one handgun for you, Hawk." Stasia took the gun from her pack and handed it to Hawk.

"Jesus Christ, I'm sitting here listening to my kids talk about arming themselves." John turned a stricken face to Stasia.

"Then you'll hate hearing this. I have grenades in this bag. The black ones are live; the green are flash bangs. Or was it the other way around?" she said, sounding confused.

John stared in horror at the bag she held.

"I'm kidding, I know which-is-which." Stasia snickered.

Charlie bit back a laugh at his dad's expression and turned his attention back to Stasia. "Everyone put on a vest and take a knife and sheath. Long-sleeve camo shirts are in one of these bags. We should wear the black shirts and black pants. The camo shirt is good for the day, but we're more likely to be sneaking around in the dark."

"I picked up four flashlights and food I thought you could use." Mary rummaged in her bag as she spoke and pulled out the flashlights. "John got a bunch of orange juices too."

"Okay, pack up." Charlie headed to his room to change. "Make sure you have your extra batteries and the small screwdriver in your pocket."

"Bring an extra pair of socks; keep your feet dry, you don't know how far you'll have to walk. I can't believe I'm doing this," John mumbled as he helped Sara tighten her bulletproof vest over her black shirt.

Mary handed Sara a small black cylindrical pouch. "For your staff if you're not carrying it."

After threading the belt through the belt loops, she turned and hugged Mary. The sheath tied to one leg, the pouch for her staff on the other.

"I feel like Lara Croft." Sara grinned, grabbed her backpack, put orange juice into the outside pouches, and added her plastic thermos with water and the granola and food Mary had bought.

Hawk handed her a shirt with desert camo on it. The sleeves were long on her. Heaving an annoyed sigh, she rolled them up. Finally, she donned the cape Stasia bought in Japan.

"I'm ready, I guess."

"What are we going to tell their parents?"

John asked as he watched them dress, his lips in a tight line.

Mary shrugged. "Nothing, we lied to them. The kids called and told them we'd be in Japan for two more days. If they call me asking for them, we make excuses. They made recordings on the laptop to leave fake messages, but I figure we have three to four days before any of them even begin to think something's up and I hope to God the kids are back by then."

Stasia held her belt in her hands and made small slits in the top. The nail file she'd bought days ago slid into the small slit. She tied two sheaths with daggers to her legs and put on her vest and the camo shirt. The sleeves were too long, and the front was tight on top and loose on the bottom.

"Boys clothes never fit me right." She tried to pull the shirt together more over her breasts to make the gap in the buttons disappear.

After checking to make sure she could reach the file and replace it easily, she added her throwing stars to her side pants pocket and put a grenade in the other one.

She dumped the contents of her backpack onto the bed and handed everyone a set of handcuffs and a flash bang grenade.

"I thought maybe we could use these, and I found myself this."

She held up a weighted blackjack with a wrist strap, put it in her back pocket, placed a small case in her top-front pocket, and then added an extra pair of socks, food and water to her bag. "I'm ready too."

Oz and Hawk did the same, putting on the vests and tying down the sheaths. They packed their backpacks, adding food, water, socks, and the flashlights. Oz added the iPad mini to his bag.

"One second for a bathroom break and I'm good to go too," Oz said as he headed to the bathroom.

"Good idea." Sara went next door to use that bathroom, and they heard sudden laughter.

Charlie entered, his face bright-red.

"Don't you dare," he said warningly as he arrived.

He'd gotten ready in the other room and wore his headset again with his black cap over it. He wore his black cargo pants and black shirt with a desert colored camouflage shirt over it like the others. A black backpack hung on his back, and black ax blades peeked over his shoulders. In his left hand, he held a metal trashcan lid painted black.

Hawk snickered and Stasia bit back a laugh.

"I didn't say a word!" she said as she passed him to retrieve the charging walkie-talkies.

Both girls laughed in the other room and his blush deepened. He hugged both his parents.

"Don't be worried if you don't hear from us. I don't expect there'll be cell service where we're going. There's notes saying we ran away in my suitcase. If we don't come back, maybe you can use them to stay out of trouble. There's also a video message saying the same thing as the notes in my email box addressed to Dear Mother. You know my password. Do what you think best with it."

Sara and Stasia returned, now wearing their headsets and black caps and both hugged John and Mary.

"We'll be back, have faith." Sara kissed Mary's cheek.

Stasia kissed Mary, then John. "And, we'll have Rick with us. One week tops, you'll see."

Oz hugged them both quickly too. "Our plan is simple— we cross the border of Iraq, and I'll try to locate him. ISIS territory could be considered a different zone, so we'll try there too. Then we'll try Syria. If we still haven't found him, we'll go to each ISIS stronghold, they have three different towns we know of. I hope that by then either my Magical Locate spell or Stasia snooping, or even the military, they must be searching too, will have found him. If we have no leads in one week, we'll come back here."

"I feel like a selfish bastard sending you into harm's way to save my boy. God knows we all love him, but he'd be the first to say don't risk yourselves on his account." John put his hand on Hawk's shoulder. "That gun isn't a toy. If you shoot someone, they *will* die. You're much too young to make that kind of decision. You can't go unarmed into a war, but guns and children—" John paced.

"You're all armed with knives. On one hand, I wish they were Uzis, on the other, well, I wish—" he stopped talking and closed his eyes, hugging Hawk.

"We don't want to harm anyone at all," Oz said as he squeezed John's shoulder a moment. "But, if it's them or us, we'll use what we must to survive. Hawk has a gun because he has a silenced stun shot. The weapons aren't for damage, they're for defense, same as Chief's axes. The plan is to sneak in, not attack."

"Oh, I almost forgot." Mary reached into her purse, pulled out a small bag, and handed each of them a mini travel toothbrush and toothpaste kit. Then she pulled out a wad of cash. "Divvy it up." Next, she handed Sara a credit card. "This is the card your dad gave me. I don't know if it'll be usable there or not."

"Let's go. We have an hour and thirty minutes to get in place," Oz tapped his watch face and gestured to the door.

A final flurry of hugs followed. John took the toilet paper from the bathroom, which he handed to Charlie. "The toothbrushes made me think of it, you might be hiking awhile and watch out for bugs. In fact, let's stop and buy bug spray. There's a small store not too far from here."

"We'll meet you in Mom's car. We can't go through the lobby like this," Charlie said.

A shrill squeal sounded as Charlie forced the window in the room up. No one was in sight, so he jumped to the ground. Stasia and Hawk followed. Sara and Oz jumped, she casted Ascension, and they fell slowly to the ground.

John observed from the window and shook his head in wonder. The kids headed to the car and got in quickly.

A few minutes down the road they found a grocery store. John entered the store.

"Drop us by the same bushes, Mom, and don't worry, we'll be fine." Charlie glanced at his watch. "What's taking him so long?"

Five minutes later, Charlie's father appeared carrying two big bags. "Bug spray, one for each of you, and food. Eat one sandwich now and take one with you. There's chips and soda in there too." He passed the bags into the back seat.

"Mom knows where we want to go, she'll direct you." Charlie took a sandwich from the bag. "Nice… pickles, here." He handed a pickle and a sandwich to Sara and one to Stasia before handing the bag back to Hawk and Oz. Sara glanced in the other bag, took out a soda, and passed them out.

Hawk grinned as he grabbed a Twinkie. "There's Twinkies in this bag, Twinkies! This country is amazing, first Slim-Jims, now Twinkies."

"Yeah, just don't look at the expiration dates," Stasia said.

"Twinkies don't expire, do they?" Hawk examined the package with a worried gaze.

"I was teasing, dolt. Give me one." Stasia held her hand out for one.

"YOLO," Sara said and held her hand out for one too.

"Dad, when we arrive, pretend to have car trouble or something. We only need a minute to jump over the fence."

"Charles, invite your father to the raid, he'll be able to see you then."

"Dad, I invite you to join our raid," Charlie said while making the key clicks on an imaginary keyboard to invite him he'd have made in the game.

"Um," John said doubtfully.

"Say you accept, dear. It worked for me, and you've raided with them before, it should work for you."

"I accept the invitation to join your raid, Charles, err, Chief," his father said.

Sara took the bag of leftover sandwiches and put them in Charlie's pack. "Radios on and time check. It's ten fifty-eight on my mark." She waited a few seconds and said, "Tick."

They agreed they had the correct time.

Sara said, "Mr. H, if you can buy one of these walkie-talkies somewhere we're using channel thirteen-b. It should be just us in there. The backup channel is twenty-two. We'll be long gone by the time you can find one, but that's where we are."

Charlie handed his mother a slip of paper. "These are all our email addresses and passwords. If you find out anything we should know, email it. If we get a chance, we'll check our mail. Leave messages on Sara's home phone number, *her* number, not her dad's; she can check messages from any phone. Be discreet, and there's no guarantee we'll receive it."

Cars passed them on the road, but no people walked the street.

"Everyone, out of the car. No hugging!" Charlie said and pulled Sara to his side as she reached to hug his mother. "People will wonder if they see that. Let's go. We want no attention. Love you, guys!" Charlie said to his parents.

"Be safe. We love you guys too." John opened the hood, and Mary stood beside him. The kids ran to the fence without a backward glance.

STOWAWAYS

Charlie and Hawk boosted an invisible Stasia to the top of the fence. Hawk leaped to the top and jumped down. He sat and faded into fog.

Sara used her pull and was suddenly by Stasia, she jumped down to Hawk, levitating to break her fall. It took them less than three seconds to cross the fence.

Oz cast Wink and teleported through the fence.

Charlie cast Waylay on Stasia and jumped down. Hawk cast a No-See-Um, and they faded out of sight.

"Head to that building over there, while I

line up our ride." Stasia pointed to a building across the base.

No one was near them. They hid in the brush of a big empty field. Big concrete buildings stood six hundred yards away. A road ran in front of them. More buildings and a row of wooden houses lined the opposite side of the street. In the distance, people walked on the street and cars passed, but no one seemed to notice them.

Stasia said, "I'm pretty sure those buildings in front of you are empty barracks, at least they were empty earlier. Kids our age are on the base and people are wearing civilian clothes. Chief needs a disguise though. No one is carrying around a black garbage can lid." Stasia snickered and sprinted away. She jumped over a small fence by the road, darted around a corner and disappeared from sight.

"I'm ready to cast my disguise, but where are we going first? It'll break stealth when I do," Oz asked.

"Head to the back of the building, use invis on you and Sara. They won't notice Hawk, and I'll be what?" Charlie asked.

"A soldier like one at the gate," Oz said.

"Okay, you guys go along the backs of these buildings here until we reach a good spot. What's your time on No-See-Um?" Charlie turned to Hawk.

"Twenty-six minutes," Hawk said.

"I'm going to casually walk over that way, I'll meet you there. Hawk, if you stay in the grass, you won't be seen." Charlie took a deep breath. "Okay, let's go. If you're spotted, don't run, walk, and if they hail you, answer. We're here touring the base. We entered through the front gate. Tell the same story my mom told the customs agent."

Charlie stole Oz's disguise spell and made himself resemble a soldier.

Oz cast Invisible Duo on himself and Sara. They ran along the backs of the buildings until invisible ran out and hunkered down to wait the two minutes until he could cast it again. "We came here to make out if anyone comes along in the next two minutes."

Sara nodded and grabbed his hand. They waited out the timer.

"Invis three." Oz pulled Sara up and they

ran again.

"I could probably walk down the street," Sara said as they ran. "Lots of people are dressed like us with packs and everything. If you disguised yourself no one should wonder about me."

"We'll check at our next stop." Oz pulled her along by the hand and peered at his watch. "Here, stop here. Stand here like we're having a nice, cozy chat."

"I see you guys," Stasia said. "Cut straight across on the next invis. See that big truck headed north? Run down that road and take the first left. Run as far as you can. You can stop anywhere there against one of those buildings just like you are there. I'll find you. I have our ride picked out and I'm clearing a spot for us on it. Hawk, where are you?"

"I'm behind the buildings in the field still. Sara and Oz are ahead of me."

"Chief, where are you?"

"I'm almost at the building you indicated earlier." Charlie wished he'd rolled a mage now. Sara was always with Oz, and it worried him. The two of them were holding hands, and he couldn't decide if she sounded happy or not about being 'cozy' with Oz.

As far as he knew Oz wasn't interested in Sara, but maybe he was, he dated everyone, and he was staying glued to her side when he could easily disguise himself. Giving himself a mental smack for worrying about that right now, he glanced around to make sure he was still headed in the right direction.

Stasia said, "When you reach that building, go behind it. A big warehouse with seven trucks loading up is on the right. We want the third truck with a Hawaiian hula dancer hanging from the mirror. Let us know if you can get into it. If you don't think you can, go steal Oz's invis. Hawk, if you reach the dog kennels, you're too far, go back, I'll come and get you after I get Sara and Oz."

"Twelve seconds," Oz said. Twelve seconds later, he took Sara's hand, and they ran across the base and down the road that Stasia sent them too.

Sara glanced at her watch. Twenty-two seconds left. Stasia beckoned them, and they caught up to her as invisible wore off.

"We can keep walking down this street and cut through this yard here. Go to the green trucks getting loaded now." Stasia pointed to a group of trucks backed into a loading dock. "Our ride is there. On the next invis, Sara should enter the back. Oz, wait here for Hawk. I'm going for him now." She sprinted off still talking. "That house you're at is empty, Oz. Sit there on the steps like you're reading or something."

"The people loading the trucks will see me get on, I'll head to Oz," Charlie said.

Sara and Oz sat together on the back steps of a house holding hands with their heads close together, and he couldn't decide if they were acting or not. Sara turned foggy when Oz cast Invisible Duo on her, and she ran to the truck Stasia had picked out where he lost sight of her.

"Hawk, I see you. Turn around I'm behind you." Stasia waved at him; he waved back. "Come between these houses here." She ran back to the houses and stopped. "Oz, will invis you, and I'll lead you to the right truck."

"I'm in, and rearranging the boxes back here, I'll be careful," Sara whispered. "There's still loading going on here; watch out for them."

Four minutes later, Charlie whispered, "I'm in. We're hidden."

Five minutes later, Oz, Hawk, and Stasia, were in the truck. Stasia had cleared a space earlier in the center of the stack. By putting their backs against the cartons and their feet against others, they braced themselves. Charlie put some bigger cartons over them.

"These might have to be held in place," he said. "Be ready to give us a No-See-Um and be prepared to brace the cartons from falling in on you."

Stasia kept watch out the back of the truck. "We have twenty-six minutes before they leave. Try to nap on the way."

The cargo area was dark and stuffy as they waited silently for the truck to move. Eventually, they heard doors shutting and motors starting. Loud music issued from the cab. The truck lurched forward, but the cartons didn't budge. After two minutes, the truck stopped and started again with another lurch and sharp turn to the left. The hum of the tires on asphalt built steadily as it picked up speed and settled into a steady rhythm.

Stasia stood and slid the box over them to the side. She climbed up to peek out the back. The ties holding the canvas top down loosened easily to peer out.

"Three trucks are behind this one," she said. "The one directly behind us has three people in the cab. This highway is going through empty countryside. There's nothing to either side of us except fields and scrub brush. Hawk, there's room above where you are. If you climb up, you can lie down up there. Three of us can fit up top here. Two of you stretch out down there. Let's try to rest. I'm sure we'll hear the truck when it stops and have time to jump back down. Don't No-See-Um unless you have to. Night all."

"I'll go up." Oz winked at Charlie. "You two stay here; we're less likely to be spotted than you are if we don't wake soon enough." Oz climbed up and settled in.

"Lay down here, Sara, use this as a pillow." Charlie put their backpacks on one end and patted the floor beside him. Sara knelt, removed her cape, and lay next to him, spreading the cape over them.

"Night, Team Valor," she whispered and

snuggled beside Charlie, closing her eyes.

Charlie sighed heavily, he wanted to kiss her and pull her even closer. Instead, he laid his arm across her and closed his eyes.

Six hours and twelve minutes later the truck slowed enough to wake him. "Time to wake up," he whispered and gently shook Sara. Again, he wanted to kiss her, to run a finger over her perfect brow line, to put his face in the crook of her neck and kiss it, but he didn't.

She opened her eyes, smiled at him sleepily, and leaned forward. For one glorious second Charlie thought she would kiss him, but she hugged him quickly and stood. "Are we there?"

"Don't know, but soon. It's almost six-thirty." He put his pack back on.

Sara put her cape on and took out her water bottle. Both took sips before she put it away.

"We're somewhere; the trucks are going much slower," Stasia whispered. "Better hide." The truck turned and sped up. A few minutes later it slowed and turned again. "Yeah, we're here. I think it's a base anyways

There's lots of armed men and a ten-foot fence with two strands of razor wire." The truck slowed and stopped. It started, then stopped again. "We're at the gate."

The music coming from the cab stopped, and they overheard people talking, but couldn't make out what they said.

"This is our stop." Stasia peered at them from the top of the boxes. "Hawk goes first and heads to the first patch of grass that can hide us. Go now. I loosened one corner."

Oz and Hawk climbed up the boxes as the truck stopped again. "Three invis." Oz held up three fingers and put them down one by one as the seconds ticked by.

Hawk eased through the loose flap and said, "They're waiting to park at the loading dock. I'm to the right of the building. There's a bunch of scraggly bushes there. Head there. I'll find out what's behind this building." A minute passed. "Oh, nice, we can hide right here. There's nothing behind this building except an empty field surrounded by more fence. When you come out, go right. You'll see the bushes. Go to the back of the building, there are more bushes there. I'll be there. I'll cast a No-See-Um if anyone comes, but it should be clear. I've warded the area. I'll know if someone is coming," Hawk whispered.

Charlie stole Stasia's invisible and waited beside her.

"The truck is pulling into the loading dock," Stasia said three minutes later. "I'm hoping off. Okay, I'm clear. Be ready, they're opening the back. I have a distract ready, but we only need two minutes. They're moving the first row of boxes." Stasia described the unloading process, letting Oz know when the loading dock cleared. "Oz, your cooldown should be up. They're moving boxes out, there isn't much room, be quick. When I say go, you can hop down and out. Invis now. Okay, go it's clear, still clear— okay, I see you. They're headed back, but you have time— okay, run." Everyone ran to the back of the building.

Charlie squatted beside Oz. "Oz, see if you can locate Rick, then Hawk can No-See-Um us. Stasia, go find our next ride."

"Nothing." Oz shook his head as Stasia sprinted off.

"If anyone has to pee, now would be good before I cast," Hawk said.

"Now that you mention it— everyone face that way!" Sara said, pointing back the way they came. "No one turns around until I say."

She dropped her pack, took off the cape, and did what she had to do. The boys took the opportunity to go too.

"I'm good, you guys all set?" she said a minute later.

"We're good too," Charlie said.

Sara said, "Hand me some of the toilet paper for later. That was my only tissue."

Charlie took off his pack and handed her the roll. She took some off and gave it back. They moved further down the wall and sat with their backs against it. Sara took out her water bottle, poured water over her hands, and took a sip. She offered the water around. Charlie took a sip, the others declined.

"No-See-Um in five." Hawk sat cross-legged on the ground and closed his eyes. "We're out of sight here. Stasia, any luck?"

"Jeez, give me a minute." A toilet flushed in the background.

"Make sure you wash your hands," Sara said so enviously that Charlie laughed.

"Oh, I will, and my face. I would fix my hair too if I still had any. The border is twenty miles away. I don't know if that's the road or as the crow flies. One minute, a big group is standing around chatting by the trucks, I'm going to listen."

They sat and waited. She returned in ten minutes and squatted in front of them. "This is a small depot, not a real base at all. The trucks are heading back to Incirlik. They do cross the border frequently, but in jeeps. We can't hide there. They also use helicopter patrols. We need to get out of here and borrow a car or— I overheard a guy saying a specialist was coming, a survey thing. Maybe Oz could impersonate him. The guy coming is surveying by helicopter."

"How could we pull that off?" Charlie frowned doubtfully. "He's bound to need documents and whatnot."

"I'll need time to look around and find out how they do the helicopter patrols, what the procedure is. This might take me more than a few minutes. Do we want to try it or, um, borrow a car?"

"Try it," Sara said immediately. "If we got on a helicopter, especially one where Oz told the driver where to go, that would save us a ton of time. If we can get near Rick, we jump out and levitate down."

"Yeah, try it. Go find out what the procedure is." Charlie's frown deepened, "We're too late tonight anyway. We couldn't reach him in under an hour. And, Stasia, if you can find out who it is, would you?"

"Of course. I'll be silent a while. Don't worry about me." She laid her hand on Charlie's shoulder and squeezed lightly. "I'll let you know as soon as I hear anything. Stay here until dark at least and try calling your parents to let them know what's up." With a final gentle pat on his shoulder, she stood and sprinted around the corner.

"I wish I'd rolled a rogue," Charlie said, staring after Stasia.

"If you'd rolled a rogue, we wouldn't be here." Sara squeezed his shoulder lightly too and he was suddenly fiercely glad he was a protection warrior. She would need protection.

- 24 -

ON BASE

The sun set as they sat quietly, waiting for Stasia to return. Their phones and internet weren't working. Oz scrolled through the maps on the iPad while Sara scrolled through the small map on the GPS they bought in Japan.

"There's like no roads here. How the heck do these people travel?"

Charlie shrugged. "There aren't many people there either, especially now. They've all been evacuated. Only bad guys are left there."

"This place is extremely ugly." Hawk eyed the waist-high dead grass with disfavor.

Clumps of small prickly bushes interspersed with the dead grass surrounded them. No effort had been made to beautify the concrete buildings that squatted in the barren landscape.

"Iraq is uglier." Oz gestured to the iPad. "Where we're going is even drier than this, but at least the temperature is nice."

"No wonder they hate us; we live in heaven compared to this," Hawk said.

Stasia came on the line. "Can you guys move to the building where the helicopters are? I have an idea, and we won't have much time to pull it off. The building is pretty active, but there's a supply closet on the second floor. The two of you can hide there, and I'll take Oz with me. There's a computer he can use in a locked building. They're expecting the major tomorrow morning, but I got the day codes for today and stole some letterhead. We need to print up our orders and present them before shift change at eleven. Hawk, go around back, as close as you can to the helicopters. Find us a good spot. They need to be able to board a copter in less than three minutes."

"As much as I'd like to be in a dark closet alone with Sara, I think we can safely stay here while Hawk looks," Charlie said and grinned at Sara.

Sara giggled. "We'll be fine here. If we don't move, No-See-Um should hold even if Hawk goes. Hawk can No-See-Um us again when you go meet Stasia. Where should he meet you?"

"Stay there, I'll come for you. Shift change is in three and a half hours, but I'll be happier if we can do it one and a half." Stasia appeared in front of them, hunkered down, and drew a rough map in the dirt. "This is us and over here, are office buildings, and that's the hanger. The helicopters are right outside, lined up in a long row. Guards patrol along this road here and here," she said, pointing out the spots on the map. "The fence is electrified with motion sensors. Oz, we're going to this closed and locked building. We'll go in there and use a computer. I have a log on code from the guy in the front office." She giggled. "I turned his computer off four times in a row, and he had to keep logging on. The code for the day was harder to find. I got lucky on that. It could take me all day tomorrow to get another one, and I don't know when they change it."

"What's this guy look like?" Oz asked.

She shrugged. "Like a regular guy. I only glimpsed his picture for a minute. He has a crew cut growing out and dark brown hair and eyes. His ID said five feet eleven inches, one hundred seventy pounds."

"Sure, I can do that." Oz nodded. "But, once I cast a locate I'll lose my disguise."

"Tell him you need to be in the back. I'll scrounge us some random stuff, and you whip up a device and pretend to use it. If you sit right behind him, he won't be able to see you."

Oz sighed. "Okay, it's worth a shot, but first I'll need to test to make sure locate works from the air."

"That's no problem." Charlie tapped Hawk's sidearm. "Hawk can leave his gun on the ground, if you can find it, we know it works. If you can't, tell him you need to land to test the device quick occasionally."

"We'll be flying over hostile territory, what if they shoot at us?" Hawk asked.

"I'll shield us, and we fly out of there as quick as we can," Sara said.

"Okay, we'll need a tarp and a device we can pass off as the secret Major Warley is testing." Stasia stood and dusted off her pants. "Let's get going."

Charlie glanced from Stasia to Sara and bit his lip. "If I steal your invis, I can help, but I'm not sure what breaks it. When we get the time, we need to test that."

Stasia shrugged. "Oz and I got this."

Charlie nodded, he didn't like the idea of leaving Sara alone here more than he disliked the idea of Stasia and Oz darting off alone.

Oz and Stasia ran off.

When Charlie and Sara sat back down, he kept her hand in his. Hawk cast a No-See-Um and glided away.

Hawk didn't have a true invisible while moving, but outdoors he was almost impossible to spot. If he stood still or sat, he could be truly invisible both indoors and out. Charlie and Sara sat so close their shoulders touched.

"We missed the dance." Charlie's heart pounded. This wasn't great timing, but his uncertainty about Oz was killing him. "I hoped you'd go to the next one with me?" He held his breath waiting for her answer.

"She says yes," Stasia said. "We can hear you guys."

Sara laughed, turned to Charlie and leaned back to see his face. "I do say yes."

Charlie removed his headset, reached out, removed hers, and leaned in, moving slow trying to read her. *She appeared serious, but not unhappy.* The moment was oddly clear as if every sense he possessed was hyper-alert. A light breeze caressed his face and the dead grasses surrounding them were a rich perfume as he gently kissed her lips while an insect symphony played.

When she sighed and leaned into him, the kiss deepened, and he held her hand tighter. The scent of her skin made his head spin and his pulse race. When the kiss ended, he pulled back and ran a finger over the curve of where her eyebrow would be if she still had hair.

"For two years I've wanted to do that," his voice was deep and husky.

For answer, she leaned in and kissed him

again.

Placing her face by his neck, she breathed deeply. "And I've wanted you to."

The urge to pull her even closer, to feel her entire body pressed against him was almost irresistible, but he didn't want to break the No-See-Um. He wanted to tell her he loved her but didn't want to freak her out. Still holding one of her hands, he used the other to hold her to his chest, her face still on his shoulder, her breath warm on his neck, her arm around him. Minutes passed in silence as they held each other.

Charlie had never felt like this before in his life. Words couldn't express what he felt; he couldn't think of a strong enough one. He pondered words as he held her, good, amazing, happy, none did what he felt justice. Complete was the closest he came. Sara belonged next to him. He tightened his arm around her waist and kissed her again. Heat from the kiss filled him, spreading outward from his center until every part of him heated and his skin felt flushed.

When she leaned back, her eyes shone a brilliant blue. "We should put the headsets back on. They might need us," she said.

He picked up the headsets, handed her one, and hesitated. He wanted to make this official somehow. To make her his so she would know that he didn't think this was just a kiss. *God*, he thought in sudden panic, *suppose she kissed him because of the danger they faced. What if she meant nothing by it?*

Sara squeezed his hand, leaned in, and kissed him again. Her hands cradled his face. "I love you," she whispered her blue eyes sparkled, and her cheeks flushed dark red. "Don't let this freak you out or scare you away; I want you to know just in case—"

Relief made him lightheaded, and his voice tremble. "You're braver than I am. I've loved you for years but was afraid to tell you. Afraid I'd make our friendship awkward and you'd go away and I'd never see you again."

Without waiting for a reply, he kissed her again, pressing her tight against his chest, wishing they weren't wearing the bulletproof vests so he could feel her pressed against him. Her hands clutched his sides, and she moaned a soft breath of a sigh, leaning hard into his kiss.

Reluctantly, he pulled back from her, his breath coming hard. "I love you, Sara Mitchel. I'll love you until the day I die."

"She loves you too, stud. Now put the freaking headsets back on. You gave me a heart attack," Stasia said as she appeared behind them. "Why you two pick now to declare your undying love when everyone on Earth knew already, I don't know. Your timing sucks. Head in the game guys." Stasia grinned and hugged them quickly. "I'm happy for you, but you scared me. No more mic silence unless you tell us in advance."

"Jeez, Stasia, relax. We were off mic for like five minutes."

"Try twenty, Romeo."

Sara sheepishly put her headset on. "Sorry, guys. We lost track of time."

Oz snickered. "Yeah, it happens, but keep the headsets on. There's a mute button, use it."

Sara turned red. Charlie felt so euphoric there was no room left for embarrassment. The words I love you echoed in his soul until his heart felt like it would burst.

Stasia patted her hand and said, "One

more hurdle left. The paper work's finished. We just need our device. Hawk, is there a spot to hide near the copters?"

"Yeah, you can reach here in one invis if you run fast."

"Okay, Oz, head back and give Sara an invis and make sure they reach Hawk. Then meet me back at the other building. I'll scrounge us up a tarp and device."

Charlie stole Stasia's invisible and Stasia ran off.

Charlie hit the mute button. "Sorry about that. I didn't mean to embarrass you," he whispered.

Sara shrugged and fumbled for her mute button. "It's fine." Another light blush filled her cheeks. "I want everyone to know you're my boyfriend. I wish I'd been braver sooner."

"Me too." Charlie's eyes darkened, and his voice lowered as he leaned in to kiss her again.

Oz cleared his throat noisily, and Charlie straightened up.

"This is weird; it's like seeing my parents kissing." Oz winked at him.

"It's more like seeing the Easter bunny."

Charlie heard the laughter in Stasia's voice clearly. "You wish one existed, but you don't think you'll ever really see one."

Hawk snickered quietly.

"Back to work guys, invis three." Oz was laughing too and not bothering to hide it. Charlie rolled his eyes, then grinned. Oz was his best friend and knew what this meant to him.

"Okay, invis three." Oz cast his spell, and they ran to Hawk.

- 25 -

BORROWING A HELICOPTER

Charlie and Sara reached Hawk with five seconds left on invisible. Blood raced through his veins, not from the run, but from her hand in his. Heat still filled him.

When she met his eyes, the heat intensified. Hawk cast No-See-Um on them when he sat down. Sara handed him his pack and leaned into his side. He wanted to kiss her again badly, but Hawk's presence inhibited him. The No-See-Um would break if they moved and people walked too close to talk safely, so he sat still, running his thumb over their clasped hands.

Stasia ran up with a tarp, which she laid

on the ground near them. "I'll bring it when we get on the helicopter. A stack of metal poles was outside the hanger door. I borrowed a few for the fake device." Metal poles stuck out of the duffle bag in her hand with a few pieces of red and black wire.

"Wish us luck." She threw the bag over her shoulder and hurried away.

Men came and went to the hanger in front of them. The place was quiet, the helicopters unattended.

Stasia's spoke in a whisper, "He's approaching the door as Major Warley. He's in, I'm following."

Oz strode to the door and walked in. In the first office, a corporal was busy typing at a computer. Oz tapped on the door. "I'm Major Warley; bring me to the duty officer. The guard at the gate said I could find him here."

"Yes, sir, follow me," the man rose from his desk, led him down a hallway, up a flight of stairs and knocked on a closed office door.

"Come in," a gruff voice answered.

His guide opened the door and said, "Captain Marshal, Major Warley is here to see you, sir."

Captain Marshal rose and saluted.

"At ease," Oz said, hoping it was the correct response, glad he carried items, so he didn't have to mimic the salute.

Captain Marshal returned to his seat, leaned back, and frowned. "I thought you were arriving tomorrow, major?"

"HQ thought it would be best to test my, um, device at night, so sent me earlier. This isn't too much of an inconvenience, I hope?"

"No, not at all, but I'm afraid I'm unclear on what you'll need."

Oz nervously shifted the bag on his shoulder. "I'm afraid my work is top-secret. I'll need a pilot and a helicopter at my disposal for a few hours."

Captain Marshal leaned forward and tapped his fingers on the desk. "I see," he said after a moment. "Do you have a flight plan?"

"Yes, in my orders, but it's classified. Once we're in the air, I'll inform the pilot.

This device is a prototype. My tests will be quick and unobtrusive." Oz's gaze darted to Stasia and away quickly.

Stasia crossed her fingers.

The captain nodded and picked up the phone. "Hank; send me your most discrete pilot. Have him ready to roll in ten minutes. Yes, tell him four hours, tops. This is need-to-know. No, I don't. Yes, right to the hanger. Thank you." Hanging up the phone, he held out his hand.

Oz handed him the forged orders.

Captain Marshal gave them a cursory glance and placed them on his desk. "Will you need help with your gear?"

"No, thank you." Oz lifted the bag with the metal poles sticking from it. "I'll need a moment to set up in back. The maps are all set. I'll direct the pilot from there." He turned to the door with his hands full, so he wouldn't have to return the captain's salute.

"Sergeant Yellis will escort you there. She'll meet you at the front door here. If there's anything else we can do for you, don't hesitate to ask." Captain Marshal saluted.

"Actually, there is one more thing. Who

did they execute tonight?" Oz asked and cleared his throat.

The captain's face grew grim. "Apparently, they're going down the chain of command. Staff Sergeant Hanley was murdered tonight."

"I'm sorry to hear it," Oz said. The poles clinked together as he shifted the bag, acting as if it was heavy. He held the door open with his foot to give Stasia a chance to leave. "That went well," he murmured to Stasia as they left.

"Too well. I'm tempted to go listen to see if he's calling security."

"Gee, that's encouraging." Oz glared at her. "Like this isn't nerve wracking enough."

Stasia smiled and winked. "We'll know once you leave the building."

Neither security nor Sergeant Yellis were there when they walked out. Oz fidgeted with the poles while he waited.

"A man got in a helicopter and is starting it up," Hawk reported.

"That's our ride," Stasia said. "Be ready to go. Chief, I'll bring the packs. Damn, I should've given Oz the tarp. I'll try to get it."

Stasia sprinted off at high speed.

"Hello, you must be Private Yellis." Oz greeted the private who arrived. "Captain Marshal said you'd escort me to the helicopter. There's a tarp by the hanger door he said I can use if we can stop there first please?"

Private Yellis nodded agreement and gestured for him to follow. "This way, sir."

She led him to the hanger where Stasia stood grinning by the tarp. Private Yellis carried it for him and led him to the helicopter. After introducing him to the pilot, she left.

Oz got on the helicopter, arranged the tarp, and messed with the device. "This device needs frequent calibration, so I need to stay back here. We might need to land, I'm not sure yet. I'll give you the first destination when we're in the air."

The pilot handed him a headset. "I'll be able to hear you, sir. Can you strap down?"

"Yes, I believe so. But first, I need to, um… I'll just walk over to the grass there. I'll be right back."

The pilot chuckled. "By all means, there's

no bathroom in here."

"Is he looking, Stasia?" Oz whispered.

"Nope, he's reading a map, go." Stasia stood in the doorway of the helicopter observing the pilot. "If he looks up, I'll cast distract."

Oz walked into the grass, waited for Charlie to Spell-Steal his invisible, cast Invisible Duo on Hawk, and disguise on himself again.

Charlie headed to the helicopter and carefully climbed on, trying not to jostle it. He eased under the tarp beside Hawk and Sara. Oz got on straightening his pants. Stasia climbed in carrying the packs and snuck them under the tarp. Oz put on the headset the pilot handed him, putting his in his pocket.

"Okay, could you rise and hover a moment at your normal cruising height? I want to calibrate my device," he said.

"Is everything strapped in back there?" the pilot asked.

"Good to go."

The helicopter lifted into the night sky. After a moment, the pilot said, "Ready sir, this is my usual height here. How are you carrying that device alone? It must weigh a ton. I'm lifting like I have five hundred pounds back there."

Oz cast the locate spell and found Hawk's gun on the ground while he said, "No, it's about a hundred pounds, maybe I need to diet. Okay, the calibration was successful. Can you proceed to the coordinates please?" He gave Stasia a thumbs up. Stasia nodded and told Hawk to recall his gun.

"Um, that's ISIS territories. Are you sure that's right?" the pilot asked nervously.

"Yes, we have special clearance."

The pilot said nothing. The helicopter picked up speed, and they headed off.

"How many times have you flown over here?" Oz asked.

"Almost a hundred, I guess," the pilot said, "but never alone like this, always in a convoy. The Iraqi's are funny about their airspace. Everything takes days to receive clearance. Frankly, I'm surprised at this last-minute jaunt. It must have been uber secret. I hadn't heard we were going, and I usually know days in advance."

Oz winced. "Yeah, well this is a super-secret cut your own throat before disclosing it kind of mission. They told me my pilot could sneak in. Iraq didn't give us clearance. If they see us, the mission is scrapped. No one told you?"

"Holy shit! you're kidding me? No, sir!"

"Our side knows what's going on. Can you keep under their radar? I assumed you were fully briefed."

"No guarantee, but I can try, sir." The pilot sounded aggravated. "If they hail me, I have to answer."

"By all means. I was told I had the best pilot and if anyone could do it, you were the man. I'm just a computer geek here to press buttons. This can't be tested without you."

"I'll do my best, sir. Can I ask what you're testing or is that classified too?"

"It is. I'm sorry I can't tell you about the device, but if you can keep a secret—" He waited until the pilot agreed he could. "It'll help us locate the hostages."

The pilot was silent a few minutes. "Approaching the Iraq border now, sir." A minute later he said, "We're officially in Iraq airspace."

Oz cast a locate spell. "Head south please." He grinned and gave a thumbs-up to Stasia.

Not bothering to cast a new disguise, he jotted notes in his notebook. The pilot left him in peace concentrating on staying low, doing his best to stay under the radar.

"Could we go west now, please?" Oz gave directions, having the pilot circle, then cross above Rick. With an excited grin, he gave the pilot precise coordinates, "Could you head back to these coordinates? Then it's back to base."

"Yes, it's on the way and not far." The pilot turned the helicopter around.

Oz scribbled a note asking if they should jump out or tell the pilot he was leaving and handed it to Stasia. After reading it, she shrugged, leaving the decision to him. Oz took a deep breath and said, "Hover there a few seconds. I'm disembarking with my gear."

"Sir, are you sure? This is enemy territory; this wasn't in my orders."

"Your orders are to assist me in any way

necessary. The device works, but I need to stay and run some tests. Drop me off, and your part is done, and thanks, you've helped save lives here."

Charlie crawled from beneath the tarp with Sara and Hawk. Oz cast Invisible Duo, pointed to the open helicopter door, and nodded.

Charlie Spell-Stole invisible for himself and Sara and grimaced, hoping the pilot wouldn't get in trouble for this.

"Thanks, this is my stop," Oz said as he threw the device out. They jumped after it before the pilot could protest. The helicopter paused a second before continuing away.

- 26 -

FINDING RICK

"Rick isn't far away. We passed directly over him earlier. I must've cast locate a million times in the last two hours," Oz said.
He led the way while Charlie, Sara and Hawk shrugged their packs back on. The exercise felt good. They'd been sitting still for hours.

"I didn't want to land right on top of him, better if we sneak in."

Charlie knew both Oz and Hawk were casting as they walked by their finger movements.

Fifteen minutes later Hawk warned of humans, "Two hundred yards away are humans." He pointed in the direction he sensed them.

"How's that work, Hawk?" Charlie gazed in the direction Hawk pointed and saw nothing except dark, rolling hills.

"No idea." Hawk closed his eyes and spread his arms out, turning in a slow circle. "I can sense them by thinking about the surrounding area. A yellowish glow appears in my mind's eye that I somehow recognize as a person. You guys show up to me as brighter distinct lights mostly white with a greenish tinge, and I can tell which one of you I'm sensing. It works with animals too. The snakes in front of us are tinged with pulsing red. They're dangerous to me, I know it.

"The animals here are mostly soft white specks. Only a few are tinged red. When I concentrate on them, I can tell what kind of animal they are."

A small delighted laugh burst from him, quickly stifled as Hawk moved his fingers slightly, opened his eyes and dropped his arms.

"Three Macrovipera lebetina, blunt-nosed vipers, are coiled together six feet from us.

They're extremely dangerous. I'm scaring them off now. They're agitated, pulsating brilliant red. My magic is showing me everything about them. What they eat, where they prefer to nest, all I need to do is think the question. This is so cool…I never even heard of these kinds of snakes and I know everything about them.

"Yeah, cool." Charlie made a face and rolled his eyes.

Stasia laughed.

"I'm glad you played a ranger. This would totally suck without you, Hawk." Sara gave Hawk a quick hug. "Snakes are gross."

Hawk kept an arm around Sara's shoulder and closed his eyes again. "They're moving away; besides, it's not like we couldn't kill them or cure their bite."

"Keep moving them away. I don't want to see them, whether they can hurt us or not," Sara said.

Charlie laughed as Sara stood on tiptoe, leaning into Hawk's side. "The snakes won't bother us." With another chuckle at her expression, he pulled her away from Hawk and brushed her lips with a quick kiss. "Want me to go kill them?"

Eagerness filled him, and with a small shock, he realized he wanted to kill something for her. A frown crossed his face, he'd never wanted to kill something before, but there was no denying he wanted to now. The thought of slaying those snakes felt good. The snakes scared her and should be dead, destroying them felt right.

"No, as long as Hawk keeps them away, I'm good."

Her hand touching his face broke his concentration. Warm breath feathered his neck as she pressed against him, still on tiptoe. The desire to go kill the snakes faded. He debated mentioning his sudden urge to kill them, then decided it didn't matter now. All that mattered now was finding Rick.

"Okay, five-minute bathroom break." Charlie rummaged in his pack, pulling out an energy bar and bottled water.

Everyone did the same, settling onto the rocky ground in the dark, they ate the bars and spread out to take a bathroom break.

Charlie waited until they'd taken a short break before gathering them up. "Stasia and

Hawk go check it out. Keep an eye out for minefields and traps. If you spot any, let us know. We'll be following."

Stasia and Hawk ran off at full speed and disappeared in the dark. Charlie, Oz, and Sara followed at a walking pace.

Hawk returned a few minutes later. "A minefield is ahead of us, but we can easily avoid it. Stasia and I can both sense them. This place is the creeps, there's like a million snakes around here." The dismayed sound Sara made caused him to laugh. "The surrounding area is clear right now. I've scared them away, besides most aren't dangerous."

Hawk was quiet a moment as he cast, using the animal's eyes to see around them. "Guards are posted, and they have dogs. Three small buildings are in front of us, one built right into a hill. Eight men are patrolling the area, and two men are on top of each building with six sentries farther out. None are in the actual buildings except the one built into the hillside. Six men are spread out in that one. The mine field ends right in front of me."

"How close is he, Oz?" Stasia asked.

"Not sure. He's still in front of us. If I can get in sight of the building with people, he might be in it."

"How can he be there? There should be more of them than six." Stasia peered worriedly at Oz now.

"Jeez, I hope you found our Rick and not some random dude named Rick," Hawk said.

"Yeah, that would suck," Oz agreed.

Stasia led them past the landmines and turned to Oz. "Well?"

"As far as I can tell, Rick is in front of us. Maybe more houses are over the hill?" Oz appeared worried now too.

Stasia led them through the minefield and around the houses.

The minefield ended, and Hawk ran ahead, leaving Stasia with the others. "No houses or buildings are in sight," Hawk reported.

"Rick's under us," Oz said after a few more minutes of walking.

"There must be a cave entrance somewhere," Oz said, sharing a relieved glance with Charlie. "Yep, it's behind us. This spell was the best gold we ever spent." Oz grinned at Charlie, and they bumped fists.

"Maybe that house built into the hill." Stasia turned and ran back the way they'd come. "Let's go back there, and I'll check it out."

Hawk caught up with them on the way back. With a grin at Sara, he warded a spot for them to wait in while Stasia tried to find a way into the building.

Stasia reported, "No openings. The windows are boarded up. I can open the door, but they'll see that. One of them needs to open the door so I can sneak inside."

"If I pushed one over the roof you don't think it would kill him, do you?" Sara asked as she eyed the man on the roof in front of her.

Charlie stifled a laugh.

"I doubt it, there only like ten feet high. Be careful though, they're red tinged too," Hawk said and shrugged.

Hawk obviously didn't care if the man broke his neck or not, and Charlie stifled another laugh.

"Okay, Hawk and I'll go closer, and I'll

use hypnosis to push one off. When they open the door to see what's going on, try to enter, but for the love of God, don't become trapped in there!" Sara said.

Sara and Hawk headed to the west side and crept within twenty yards of the building and the man visible on the roof. The hypnosis spell let her use his eyes, and she spent a few seconds examining his gear.

"Stay out of sight, guys. They have night vision goggles and the rifles. Night vision might show an invisible person. Get ready, Stasia, I'm throwing him now."

The man tumbled off the roof, his black robe fluttering, and landed with a thud and a scream. Charlie hoped he'd think he was sleepwalking.

Other men yelled and raced to the scene and more outdoor lights lit. Sara wiggled backward down a small hill and crouched behind a rock. "Stay there, Hawk, they shouldn't spot you unless they look through the night vision. Don't No-See-Um us unless you have to."

The door opened in the building Stasia wanted to enter, and she slipped inside, easing past the armed men in the front entrance. The first open door led to an empty room with a rough pallet on the floor and weapons lined up on the wall by a boarded-up window.

A cloth hung over another doorway. The cloth slid aside with barely a sound, and she found another hallway lit with lanterns. Men spoke in the next room, but she couldn't understand them. Lantern light cast wavering shadows on the walls. Two armed men stood guard in front of a wooden door at the end of the hall. Distract wouldn't be enough to sneak by, they would see the door open.

A quick search of the rest of the house turned up a small kitchen with a camp stove, a few boxes of food and jugs of water. Another room held a black and white flag with the ISIS symbol hanging on the wall and a video camera set up on a tripod near a small generator. In the next room, a table stood in the corner with a bottle of water and a small pill container. Six empty chairs sat before it, and a stack of folded blankets lay beneath it.

Men returned and stood talking outside

the open front door. One man had his hand on the doorknob and stood staring out the open door. A quick distract spell, and she sprinted past into the darkness.

Stasia squatted in front of Charlie and drew a crude map in the dirt. "Only the wooden door was guarded, the prisoners are likely behind it. If Hawk can get underground, his track humans will work, and he can tell us how many are under there."

"Okay, we need them all out or at least the doorway clear for us to pass." Charlie gave directions in his usual way. "Then we distract, sap, hypnotize the two at the door. Sara targets right, Stasia is left. Stasia opens the door. If bad guys are there, I'll shield stun them and Oz and Hawk tie them. We grab Sara's target, gag him, tie him, and then yours. We take them with us and close the door. Any guards tied up we drag to a convenient spot. Then we search the place.

"If Rick is there, we release him and any others we find, being as quiet as we can. If he isn't there, and there are no hostages, we retreat, open the door, and I stun the two men there, and we tie them and throw them behind the door. We invis and run out, and Hawk No-See-Um's us until it settles down.

"If Rick is there, which is most likely, we'll have to fight our way out. We can stun the guards at the door, but there is no way we're getting over twenty people out stealthed. It becomes a Leroy, and we do what we have to, to protect them." Charlie's gaze flitted from one to the other. Everyone appeared serious.

"There'll likely be more guards beyond the door and as we search. We sap and tie them if we can, but if Rick is down there, we use force if we have too."

"I'm good with that." Sara squeezed his hand. "But, how do we distract them again? Another roof jumper might make them suspicious."

"I'm thinking the dogs could attack," Charlie said. Hawk, make the dogs run and attack something with a lot of growling and barking. How long until No-See-Um?"

"It's up," Hawk said.

"Is everyone ready?" Charlie waited until they nodded, then stood. "Let's go."

"I've got the dog going now." Hawk kept his eyes closed, concentrating on the dog under his control. Dogs barked and snarled as men yelled and the dogs barked louder.

"The doors opening, get ready, Oz." Stasia was stealthed, peeking over the hillside at the small house. "Okay, let's go."

Oz cast his invisibility spell right after Charlie stole it, and they ran down the small hill to the door. A man dressed completely in black stood in the center of the open doorway. Two men dressed the same way stood behind him, and three stood outside. They spoke in loud, angry voices none of them understood except Sara.

She poked Hawk, mimed closer, opened her hand, and made the talking motion. He nodded, and the sound of barking approached. A snarling dog ran up to the door and barked at the man standing there. The man took a step back and rose his gun.

The dog backed up, ran off a few feet, and glanced back at the man. It barked again and ran further away and then stared out into the night and snarled. A spate of talking and yelling erupted and the man in the doorway stepped into the yard.

Charlie peeked at his watch; thirty-seven seconds remained on invisible. The other two men retreated into the house and Charlie seized his chance. He passed the man in the doorway so close he almost brushed his arm and headed straight to the room where Stasia had seen the guns.

Behind the curtained doorway, two men talked to the guards still blocking the wooden door. Charlie glanced at his watch, fifteen seconds left. They retreated into the room with the guns. The two men entered the room and headed to the guns.

Charlie followed Stasia through the curtain and into the hallway. Distract made both men peer behind them and she sapped the guy on the left as Sara hypnotized the one on the right and made him go lean on the wall and close his eyes.

Stasia already had the door open and used her knockout punch on Sara's target, gagging him as fast as she could.

Oz and Stasia each took one of his arms, preparing to drag him behind the door.

Charlie grabbed the person Stasia had

sapped and clamped his hand over his mouth while Sara tied and gagged him with Oz's bandages. Once he was tied, Charlie picked him up. Improvised shield in one hand, and tied man under the other arm, they went through the door right as invisibility wore off.

No guards stood opposite the door, but a man walked down the hallway. Hawk lifted his gun, and the man fell to the floor mid-yell. The gun hadn't made a sound.

Stasia rushed forward and grabbed the man while Oz created bandages. She pulled him to the side of the hall. A quick check found a pulse.

Charlie pointed at a doorway leading from the short hall and Stasia ran forward to check it.

A minute later, she returned. "One sapped man in there needs tying. Is Rick here?"

"Ahead of us." Oz busily conjured bandages.

"Still not sensing more people. I'll let you know when I do," Hawk said.

They dragged the men into the room and

left them gagged and blindfolded in a corner. "Those ties wear off in three hours," Oz warned as they left the room and the unconscious men behind them.

"Yep, let's move it, timed scenario here. Those men could be missed or found at any time," Charlie said as he led the way.

Stasia rushed ahead around a small corner. "The floor turns to dirt here, and it's a sharp ramp downward." After a few seconds, she whispered, "Two more guards here in front of a door."

"On three, I got right," Hawk whispered and leaned around the corner and shot one as she cast distract and then sapped one. Oz and Charlie used their handcuffs on them, gagged them with Oz's bandages, and dragged them along as Sara followed Stasia and Hawk.

"Thirty or more people ahead of us," Hawk warned. "All green except for five. The five red are at the end of the hall. Rick is here in the middle of the biggest group of green."

Hawk and Oz traded high-fives

A locked door blocked them until Stasia unlocked it.

"He's here," Oz said excitedly. "Sara, you go in. We'll go take care of the last five."

- 27 -

RESCUING RICK

Sara eased into the pitch-black room. A slice of light from the corridor illuminated a group of men clad in Army fatigues shackled with chains to the rock floor, their mouths gagged. Light formed on her hands as she cast her Hands-of-Sun and walked the row of men until spotting Rick.

All the people chained were dirty, bruised, and blood smeared. The light showed Rick's amazed expression. Everyone around him wore the same amazed, hopeful look. The gag in his mouth released, but she couldn't budge the chain on his ankle.

"Hey, Rick, long time no see." A

delighted grin lit her face.

"Sara?" In a combination of disbelief and dismay, his voice cracked with disuse.

Sara didn't answer, busy removing the gags of the surrounding men. "Stasia, when you get a second, come unlock these guys, the chains won't budge."

"Stasia is here too? are you kidding me? Jesus, Sara, what happened to you?" Rick asked in alarm, taking in the bald head and patchy skin.

"Who is this, Rick?" the man next to him asked.

"Sara Mitchel, my brother's friend." Rick sounded completely confused.

"Rick, I'm giving you my headset to talk with Chief a minute. When he invites you to the raid and passes you lead, you need to invite everyone else, okay? I know this sounds nuts, just do it. Say I accept, mean it, and invite them." Sara took off her headset, placed it on Rick's head, and continued removing gags, trying to be as gentle as she could to the injured men and women.

"Chief, how the hell did you guys get here? What the hell is going on? What? Yes, I accept, What? Why? Yes, I accept lead to your crazy raid. Jesus Christ, fine!" Rick turned to the man next to him and cleared his throat, then asked him to join his raid. Six people had joined the raid by the time Stasia arrived.

Tears filled her eyes as she dropped stealth and cast Waylay and appeared before him instantly. Before he could say anything, she leaned down and kissed him.

"Another one. Jesus, Rick, girls follow you everywhere," the man next to him said laughingly.

"Stasia, good God! How the hell did you get here?" Stunned amazement filled Rick's eyes at her sudden appearance.

Stasia hugged him again, then laid her fingertips against the chain locked on his ankle. The chain unlocked and fell away from his leg. "It's a long story, Rick, and Sara needs her headset back. We'll tell you later. They're going to notice the missing guards any minute. There's food and water in my pack, be careful though, there's grenades in there too."

Rick handed her the headset and

snatched her pack. "I'm so hungry I could eat this pack."

"Oz, can you come make some food here?" Stasia stared as Rick wolfed down a granola bar.

"Oh, Jesus, of course Oz is here and Hawk? Don't tell me he's here too?"

"He is, he's busy now, but he'll be along." Stasia grinned at him. "Don't stop inviting. We need everyone on our team. This is a Valor raid."

"This is retarded, but sure, okay, whatever you say." Rick turned to the woman beside him and asked her to join his raid. Most agreed instantly, but everyone agreed when Stasia asked them to join.

"Okay, Sara, they're all yours." Stasia stood back.

Sara strode to the center of the room and thumped her staff on the ground. A ring of golden light expanded from it and covered the room. The force of it fluttered her cloak.

"Jesus Christ, what was that?" someone yelled, and a loud babble broke out.

Sara ignored it and twitched her fingers. The light brightened and shrunk to a glowing ball over her staff. The ball bounced around and randomly hit people.

"Jesus, Sara, how the hell are you doing that?" Rick asked as the small cuts and bruises on the man next to him disappeared. "I know what that is, but how the hell?" he trailed off into silence.

Oz entered and created a food tray beside Rick who watched with dawning comprehension.

"Good to see ya, man," Oz said, hugging Rick with one arm around his shoulders, rubbing his crew cut with his other hand.

The air between Oz's hands shimmered and turned into another tray of food. "Go with Stasia, Rick. We need to get into the other room and invite the people there. Sara will help. Move everyone into one room and, Rick, I'm glad you're okay, man." Oz gave him a quick hug and hurried from the room.

Stasia handed her pack to the dark-haired woman in Army fatigues beside Rick. "We'll return as soon as we can," she said. "There's a flashlight in here and food but be careful of the grenades. Keep everyone in here while we retrieve the others, please. The guards are disabled, but we need to be quiet. Once we're all together, we'll go over our options." Stasia didn't wait for an answer, hurrying from the room, she went to unlock the rest of the captives.

Sara followed Stasia and Rick followed Sara. In the hallway, Rick put his hand on Sara's shoulder.

"This feels like a dream. I can't believe you guys are here and what you're doing. Thank you for coming for me." The hand on her shoulder slid to her back as he pulled her into a hug. Cradling her face with one hand, he leaned down and kissed her.

Charlie entered the hallway as his brother pulled Sara into a tight embrace and his heart constricted. Maybe when she'd said she loved him, she meant as a friend. No, he couldn't be wrong. Those weren't friendly kisses she'd given him. But, here she stood with his brother. Sweat sprang up on his brow and his pulse raced. An innocent hug shouldn't provoke this reaction. *I need to get a grip. Sara came here, risking her life for Rick. Of course, she'd hug him.*

Rick leaned down and kissed her.

The pain he felt was unlike any other he'd ever felt.

"Don't let me interrupt." He'd sounded cold and angry. He'd meant to sound disinterested.

Rick released Sara and hugged him. "God, Charlie, I thought I'd never see any of you again."

"I'm glad to see you too," Charlie said stiffly.

Rick's eyes flicked to Sara, then his brother's furious face, and he hugged him again. "Hell, I'd kiss you too if I saw you first."

Charlie stood there undecided on what to do. He loved them both and wanted them to be happy, but he couldn't bear the thought that Sara preferred Rick.

Sara leaned into his side and laid her cheek against his a moment while she held his hand, running her thumb over his clenched fist.

"We should've brought more headsets." She kissed him. "I gotta run, play nice."

The relief was so great he almost sagged to the floor. *Jeez, get a grip,* he told himself and straightened.

Sara went through the door Stasia had opened, and he turned back to his brother and embraced him again, this time much more sincerely.

Stasia was already busy unlocking people in the dark room.

Sara entered and lit the room with her glowing hands. "Go next door; there's food there. If you're hurt, stay here."

The men gawked at her. Two stood rubbing their wrists indecisively.

"The rest of your platoon is next door." Sara did a quick head count. "Stasia, there's only six people in here."

"Go next door please," Stasia said, and the men filed out unable to resist her Sweet-Talk.

Charlie returned to the hallway.

Rick stood in the doorway. "What can I do to help?"

Stasia hugged Rick again. "Are we missing any people— was everyone in these two rooms? Hawk says there's no more."

"Hawk would know better than us. My squad is accounted for. The attack was confusing. I'm not sure how many they took." Rick knelt by one of the injured men.

"Rick needs to invite them." Sara indicated the four left in the room. Two lay unmoving on the floor. The other two sat staring at them in astonishment. Ripped clothing formed crude bandages. The smell of rot was pervasive.

"Sam, open your eyes. It's me— Rick; I invite you to my raid, say you accept."

Sam groaned and forced his eyes open. "I accept," he gasped out.

Three seconds later, a large ball of yellow light sank into him and lit him from within. Sam sat up straight and felt his side in amazement.

"What the hell was that?" he asked, his wide-eyed gaze glued to Sara.

Sara didn't answer, she knelt by the other injured people. "Invite the others." When they'd accepted the invitation Rick issued, she formed more balls of light between her hands and threw them, healing them as they stared in amazement.

"Hawk doesn't see more people underground, but they could've been brought elsewhere," Stasia reported. "Everyone reported MIA on the news is accounted for though, so it's likely just this bunch here.

Rick nodded and went to confer with the others.

"How did you do that?" a woman asked after Rick left.

"It's a long story, and I'm not sure what I'm at liberty to tell, but honestly the answer is, I don't know."

Everyone gathered in the first room.

"So far, no one seems to have noticed we're in here," Stasia said to the gathered group jammed into the small room. "Some choices need to be made. We have this radio," she held up the radio she'd stolen, "and these grenades. The bad guys have sidearms, rifles, and night vision. Twenty or so men are on the roofs and patrolling, and mines surround the houses. It isn't a problem if you follow one of us and we could defuse the minefield with a little time. The men here pose no problem for us to disarm, but I assume they have help nearby somewhere. What do you want us to do?"

A big burly man pushed to the front of

the group. His Army fatigues were ripped and stained; his partially bald head covered in dirt and dried blood. "I'm Staff Sergeant Guthrie, the highest-ranking officer left," he said. "Your friend Chief told us what happened to the other three officers, which puts me in charge of this group unless you outrank me." Guthrie eyed their ill-fitting gear doubtfully.

"No, we have no rank in the armed service," Sara agreed. "None of us do. I'm second in command of Valor though, and we have skills and abilities you'll want to consider when making plans."

"Valor?"

"Yes, it's what we call ourselves. We're Team Valor."

"How old are you kid?"

"Almost fifteen, how old are you?"

"It doesn't matter," he said after a minute of meeting her eyes.

"No, it doesn't," she agreed, grinning at him, then examining the group in front of her. "Is anyone hurt?"

A young, red-haired man in a Marine uniform, sitting with his back to the wall, held up his hand. "My leg is busted. I'll need a crutch or something, but I can still hold a gun."

Sara formed a heal in her hands and cast right at him. The yellow ball of light hit the injured man and sank into him, causing him to glow translucently for a moment. A mass intake of breath sounded when he stood up and stamped his foot.

"Better?" she asked.

He ran a disbelieving hand over his leg and stamped his foot on the floor a few more times. "Yes, how the hell are you doing that?"

"Um...."

Charlie walked in. "That's classified. It's a long story we don't have time to tell right now. Take our word if we say we can do something, we can. Speaking of which, we need a plan ASAP. Sooner or later they'll notice those missing guards."

"You say we can take the house and the weapons?" Guthrie glanced at Charlie's garbage can lid and rose an eyebrow but didn't ask.

"Yes, easily."

Guthrie nodded decisively and said,

"Okay, let's do that. Get the weapons, and we can reassess the situation. The radio isn't reaching anyone. It might be because we're underground. We can try again up top. What do you want us to do?"

"Follow us but give us room to work. Pick some men to guard our prisoners." Charlie turned to his brother and said, "Rick, come with us. You know what we're doing."

Stasia removed her bulletproof vest and handed it to Rick. "Put this on, they'll never see me."

He took it from her and smiled slightly, appearing bemused.

She stood on tiptoe, kissed him and turned foggy, appearing instantly in the hallway behind Hawk, but they couldn't see her. A mass exhalation followed by exclamations sounded.

"That's some tricky girl you got yourself," Guthrie said to Rick. "You'll have to tell me how she does that later."

SHOWING MAGIC

Rick equipped the bulletproof vest and followed Sara from the room. The rest of the group trailed them.

"Same drill." Charlie held an ax in one hand with his garbage can lid held in front of him. "I'll stun as we go through the door. Rick, you tie them. Use force only when necessary. Stasia always targets left, Hawk right, Sara gets center. Let's go."

"Two on the other side of the door," Hawk whispered. "Two by the front door and three in the room we entered by, one in the room we didn't go in."

Stasia stood with her hand on the knob

ready to fling the door open. "Doors unlocked," she said.

"Open it on three," Charlie said and prepared to charge.

Stasia swung the door opened. Charlie charged through and hit the men standing there with his garbage can lid. The guards stood swaying slightly.

Rick grabbed one in a headlock and pushed him to the floor while Stasia sapped one. They used ties and gags made from Oz's bandages to truss the men. Rick retreated through the door, dragging the men, returned with two Marines from his squad, and nodded to show he was ready.

At the next doorway, Sara held up three fingers, and her cast and Hawk's shot went off simultaneously.

Stasia sapped her target as his comrades fell.

Sara walked her hypnotized victim over to Rick and stood him there while they tied his hands and feet and gagged and blindfolded him.

Rick and his friends took the captives back down the hallway into the tunnel.

Stasia snuck up on the third person and sapped him.

Charlie and Oz had him tied by the time Rick reappeared with his friends.

"Take them down and use the chains on them. These bandages disappear in two hours." Stasia glanced at her watch. "Send everyone up. Hawk, where are they?"

Guthrie handed out the guns as Team Valor made plans. "You're going right through the front door?" he asked doubtfully.

Although night, the exterior lighting was bright enough to light most of the surrounding area.

Charlie nodded. "They won't see us, just the open door. First, we'll take out the sentries and work our way in from there. If we alert them, they won't expect you to be free in the house." Charlie took out a pad and paper from his pack and drew a quick sketch of the area with little stick figures of where Hawk said the men were. "These six guys we take out first, then these eight. Six more are spread out on the roofs of these three buildings. When we take the men out front, they might see it. Either way, we'll take them out too. I hope no one has time to call in anything. Oz, Sara, and Hawk will be trying to silence anyone on a radio. Speaking of that, is the radio working?"

Guthrie shook his head.

"Okay, stand away from the door out of the line of sight. Let's go, Valor."

"Invis three." Oz cast, and they ran out the door as Stasia opened it. She followed them out.

Stasia had already sapped the first man by the time they crested the small hill. Charlie held him with one hand over his mouth and one arm around his waist while Oz and Hawk tied him. In eleven minutes, all six sentries were tied and gagged.

Charlie said, "Okay, Sara, you take T-six if he comes up otherwise let him be. The other two men are too far to notice anything. Oz, disguise me like one of them."

Oz cast disguise, making Charlie appear as one of the sentries to the enemy. To Team Valor he appeared to stand inside a ghostly image of the sentry.

"Hawk, takes right T-one, Stasia, left T-three. I'll get the middle guy. Oz, invis and follow me. Tie my guy first, then Hawk's, then Stasia's."

Charlie walked up to the man in the middle. The man said something to him, but he ignored it, beckoned him over to the wall, and grabbed him as soon as he got in range. The other man who watched this in mystification dropped to the ground when Hawk shot him.

Stasia sapped her target, and he stood swaying. He would continue to sway, unable to move, both blind and deaf for three minutes.

Oz used the bandages he'd conjured and tied Charlie's victim, both blindfolding and gagging him, and then did the same to the others' targets. They pulled them up against the building and dropped them in a pile.

"Okay, same plan. Disguise me like this guy here." Charlie poked the man with his foot and again approached a man patrolling in the yard on the other side of the house.

The house the hostages were in faced him and he wondered if any of them watched. Placing himself in what he hoped was a strategic spot, out of sight of the watchers on the roofs, he beckoned his quarry. The man he was after came near. Charlie grabbed him and held his hand over the man's mouth while he struggled in his grip.

Oz tied him in moments.

"Give me this guy's face." Charlie pointed to the tied man.

Oz obliged, and Charlie walked around the building to where the other two sentries stood. He turned his back so they couldn't see him talking and said, "The guy on the roof of the second building might notice this. Stasia, take him out. There's two up there and two across from you on the roof of the building I'm at. I'll grab one of the men on the ground by me. Hawk, shoot yours and climb on the roof to cover Stasia. I'll intercept-stun the guys on this roof. Leave the person Hawk shoots to tie last, tie my guy's first, Oz. Sara, hypno the second guy by Stasia. We'll tie my two up and head over to you. If it goes bad, fear and run."

Charlie turned and headed to his target.

Guthrie and Rick observed from a crack in the boarded window.

Stasia ran across the yard, leapt, and swung herself onto the building opposite them in one fluid move. The men there continued scanning the mountain in front of them. Every few minutes they used the night vision goggles but preferred their eyes.

"How come they don't spot her?" Guthrie asked in bewilderment. "They must be blind to miss her."

"Notice how she appears foggy to you?" Rick waited for the answering nod. "Well, she's invisible to them. Only people in her raid can see her."

Guthrie stared at him opened mouthed. "You're kidding, right?" he finally said.

Rick shook his head, his eyes glued to the scene in front of him.

Stasia crouched behind one of the unsuspecting men, her sap held ready. She nodded and held out three fingers. Sara used her pull and appeared on the roof behind Stasia, floating into position so quickly it appeared as if she flickered.

Stasia sapped the man by her. The other man turned and froze as Sara hypnotized him. A commotion sounded on their roof, it quieted after a minute, and Charlie was suddenly on the other roof in front of Sara.

"I bet he has that macroed," Rick said under his breath and watched while Charlie grabbed the man standing frozen and a second later Oz appeared on the roof.

Stasia took off running, leaping from the building onto the ground. She landed gracefully and passed from sight.

Charlie and Oz tied the remaining man and Charlie jumped down.

Oz and Sara fell slowly to the ground. Ten minutes later, everyone appeared in the doorway.

"It's clear. Send three or four men to round them up. Stasia and Hawk can show you. Take them into the cellar and chain them. Our ropes won't hold long," Charlie explained. "I'm almost sure they didn't get a peep out. What do you want us to do now?"

Guthrie rubbed his chin in thought. "What was your plan?"

Charlie grinned sheepishly and said, "Honestly, we didn't have one for getting away, just for getting here. The plan was to grab Rick and go. We can still do that.

Everyone can go. Stasia and Hawk can lead us out safely."

"And you have no communications?"

"We have an iPad mini, and five prepaid cell phones that don't work here and a small GPS, and Stasia has her iPod. We have unlimited bread and water and four flashlights. Sara can make light too. That's all we have. Oh, and we have bug spray, a lot of it, and one roll of toilet paper," Charlie finished.

"Yes, I see you're well prepared." Rick smirked and chuckled. He took the sting from his words by putting his arm around his brother's shoulder. "What's with the bald look and patchy skin?"

Charlie laughed and left his brother's side, pulling Sara in for a quick kiss. "All the cool kids are doing it. You should try it."

"Seriously," Rick said, his expression concerned. "Is that from the plane crash? Mom thought you were dying. She was really upset. If our convoy hadn't been hijacked, I would've been there, I got leave to go."

"Yes, we'll tell you about it later." Charlie turned to Guthrie. "The man on the recording in the news isn't here, and they have limited supplies. That means more men are coming back. While we could fight them and win, they would know we're here and might air strike us. Sara could heal us through a lot but blown to bits I don't think she could fix, and I don't want to find out."

"Could you find us a safe spot to hide until we can get back-up?" Guthrie asked.

"Oz can find anything at all, but he needs to know what to look for. What should he search for?"

"When you say anything, what exactly does that mean?"

"You know, anything, my shoe, the closest bus, a specific bus, a lost earring, my brother, that kind of anything. A safe place is too vague, but an empty house, or abandon mine, or a small cave, those we could do."

"If I asked you to find their leader, you could?" Guthrie asked in sudden excitement.

"Yes, but I won't. We came to rescue Rick, not fight a war. I won't put Sara in danger like that." Charlie pulled Sara closer to him and narrowed his eyes at the sergeant.

Guthrie eyed Sara and nodded. "Okay,

we get out of here and leave these Ali-babas tied up. Head southwest to the border. Our radio will hopefully pick up something, and we can catch a ride out of here."

Rick threw his hands in the air in aggravation and glared at his brother. "Oh, man— we can't leave them tied here! Anyone could find them and free them. There's no way they get away with murder like that. They beheaded those guys in cold blood, not to mention the hundreds and thousands of innocent people they killed and drove out of their homes."

Charlie frowned at his glaring brother and said, "You want us to what? Take them with us?"

"No, but— God, I don't know. There must be something we can do," Rick said.

Oz laid a hand on Rick's arm, and Rick stopped pacing. "I'll fireball the entrance and see if I can bring it down," Oz said. "When we get help, we send the Iraq police or whatever here. I'll fireball the hell out of it. They'll be trapped there for a while."

"Okay!" Guthrie shouted. "Gather what gear you can, we're moving out now.

Everyone, we're moving through a minefield. I want you all single file. Follow the person ahead of you as close as you can. There is no danger if you follow correctly."

Two lines formed, and Stasia and Hawk led them through the minefield. When Stasia reached the end of the field, she motioned for people to pass her.

"Follow Hawk, we'll catch up," she said.

She ran inhumanly fast back through the mines, going straight across, jumping the mines in her way. "Hawk is leading them away, let's go."

Oz grinned and rubbed his hands together, and Stasia laughed.

"Oh, man, I've been dying to do this. Back up," he said.

An orange glow filled the space between Oz's hands and he hurled a fireball. It struck with a sizzling crash. Fireballs and lightning bolts slammed into the house until all that remained was a giant heap of rubble. "That ought to do it." He dusted his hands off, then blew on and pretended to holster them.

Sara rolled her eyes and laughed. "Let's go."

Stasia led them through the minefield, and they jogged after the group.

Before long, they caught up with Hawk and slowed to a walk.

"They got further than I thought they would," Guthrie said through panting breaths.

"Hawk has a speed buff. Any group he's in travels faster," Sara explained.

"I don't think we should tell him anything, Sara." Charlie pulled Sara closer to him.

"Sorry, bro, but your secret is well and truly out. I don't think you're going back to your old life." Rick put an arm around his brother's shoulders.

"True that." Oz slung an arm around Stasia. "Our ride on the normal train has come to a complete stop and we're now firmly buckled into the crazy train."

"Yeah, I guess we are." Charlie held Sara's hand tighter.

"Do Mom and Dad know?" Rick asked.

"Yes, they know we came for you. We couldn't let some crazy man cut off your fool head." Charlie punched his brother's arm lightly and laughed when he winced.

"And I thank you for that," Rick said and smiled at them as he rubbed his arm.

"Me too," Guthrie said. "I would've been next. We didn't know what happened to the men they removed, but we knew they didn't come back. You've saved my life, and I won't forget it. Trouble might be headed your way though." He lowered his voice to barely above a whisper. "Don't go all the way back with us. You don't want to disappear in a government lab somewhere. Get yourself representation or something to make it impossible for them to take you. I never said that." He winked at them as he straightened.

- 29 -

PARENTAL DOUBT

John and Mary Hayes returned to the hotel room. Mary sat in the only chair in the room and her husband squatted in front of her.

"Did we do the right thing here?" he asked.

Mary nodded and took his hands. "What else could we do? No matter what we said or did they were going."

John pulled her into an embrace and held her without speaking for a few minutes. "How do we help them?"

"Information— we find out anything we can. Let's go to the base and see if we can meet with someone who knows something."

"Yeah, we can do that. Let's buy the same walkie-talkies they're using first though."

Mary kissed him quickly, went to the girl's suitcase, and got the manual for the walkie-talkie, then looked up the model on the laptop. John read over her shoulder.

"No stores close by stock this," Mary said. "We can buy it in Mus. Maybe I can call the store and get them overnighted to us?"

"Yeah, try that. If they'll deliver, we'll have more time to go to the base today."

Mary called the store. To her relief, someone there spoke English. Two walkie-talkies overnighted directly to the hotel cost one hundred dollars extra on top of the regular fee, and she happily paid it. A glance at her watch showed the time was twenty minutes past noon, plenty of time to visit the base during regular working hours.

John browsed the internet, looking at the different phone models available. "I wish we'd thought to purchase a satellite phone."

"I wish we had more time to outfit them better too, but we didn't. If we're wishing things, let's wish Richard was home safe, and the kids never got struck by that lightning."

John nodded and closed the laptop. "We did our best in the time available. I'm sorry I didn't believe you."

Mary laughed and kissed his cheek. "If you'd told me that story, I wouldn't have believed you either. The kids were right when they said no one would believe us if we tried to stop them. Can you imagine that phone call? Hello, police, my child is going to use his superpowers and run away. I want you to stop him."

John smiled grimly. "They were right; we couldn't have stopped them even if we tried. I feel bad I didn't try though."

Mary sobered, her expression serious and a bit sad. "Me too. I'm taking advantage of them, and I don't like the feeling at all. I keep telling myself they would've gone anyway."

John headed to the door. "That's what I tell myself too, it's cold comfort. Let's see if we can find out something for them."

The guard at the gate of Incirlik Air Base made them wait while he made a call. Finally, an officer arrived and spoke to them. Kind brown eyes filled with sympathy as Captain Sanders apologized that General Flores wouldn't be able to speak with them personally. The captain told them they had no news, but several teams of men stood ready to go at a moment's notice. John thanked him and told him they'd be at the hotel for a few days waiting for news.

Mary took the captain's hand. "Please, would you tell us who they kill tonight? The news is too horrible to watch. Any information you have would be such a comfort."

Captain Sanders patted her hand. "I assure you, I'll send word when information becomes available."

"Is there a number I can call?" Mary asked.

The captain thought a moment, running a hand through his sandy-blonde hair. "I'll give you the general information number for the base here, but that one won't do you much good. Our chaplain's number is better; he knows all our procedures for MIA and service funerals and putting families in touch with injured soldiers. This third number is mine. I don't know what else I can do for you, but I realize how hard this situation is.

There's no need to stay here. We can contact you at home as easily."

"We needed to be close." John took his wife's cold hand in his. "Any word on where they're being held?"

"No, I'm afraid not. The search is ongoing, and we won't stop looking until we find them. Everything possible is being done to bring them back safely."

John shook his hand, and they left. Mary called the chaplain from the car and spoke with him for twenty minutes, but he knew nothing either.

"What do we do now?" Mary asked her husband when they once again stood alone in their hotel room.

"We wait."

- 30 -

THE ESCAPE

Silvery moonlight gave off enough light to travel by. They didn't bother with the flashlights or Sara's Hand-of-Sun, instead, hiking in moonlit darkness. The hills they traveled through were rocky with small patches of low-growing scrub brush.

Only the occasional tree loomed up out of the dark to break up the monotony of austere rolling hills. A thick mat of dense green vegetation grew on the bottom slopes, making walking difficult.

The weather was comfortably cool now, but once the sun rose so would the temperature. No one had stepped on a snake yet, Hawk kept an eye out for them, and Sara had fixed two sprained ankles so far.

At dawn, they rested and viewed the sunrise as Oz made food trays and passed them around. Sara cast heal-over-times on everyone to heal sore, tired feet and legs. The phones and iPad still got no reception.

"I can't understand a word they're saying," Guthrie complained as he fiddled with the radio dials.

The radios reception remained spotty, and no one replied to their repeated hails. When Sara did eventually receive a reply, after casting Ascension and being held in the air, the man on the other end called her a fascist whore.

"Okay, on your feet, scrubs, let's move out!" Guthrie bellowed. "The Hajji on the radio was rude to the little lady and could be on his way, drive on. We'll look for a safe place to hole up and sleep awhile. I want everyone's ears wide open. Anyone hears a plane, we all hit the dirt. You copy me?"

"Okay, let's move!" Charlie said and took Sara's hand. She glided smoothly over the rough ground. "I have an idea," he said.

"Everyone, line up again in two lines. Stasia, you take the lead on one and, Hawk, the other. Sara, levitate us. I'll carry Sara so she can recast. Stasia and Hawk can run for a while. Holler out if you fall behind." A minute later Charlie eyed the lines of floating people. "Okay, guys, run."

Stasia and Hawk ran, pulling the group with them, picking up speed and jumping forward in thirty-foot leaps. Sara kept recasting Ascension, refreshing the spell on everyone. Twice they stopped because someone let go and fell behind. Both times, the groups slid to a stop, crashing into each other. After an hour and a half, they stopped. A deep gully with a steep overhang loomed before them. Stasia and Hawk circled around, bringing their groups to a slow stop.

"Want to jump down and rest there a while or jump over and keep going?" Stasia asked Guthrie.

He glanced over the tired group. "Yep, this is the spot. We rest here six hours. Everyone gets some shuteye. I want two volunteers to keep watch." He picked two men at random. "Two-hour shifts, wake us if anything comes along."

Oz made them bread and water and Hawk cleared the area of snakes. Stasia sat on the hard ground and heaved a tired sigh. Rick sat beside her and spoke quietly before settling her against his shoulder. Hawk sat with them, using his pack as a pillow. Oz lay by him.

Sara spread her cloak over them; putting her head on Charlie's shoulder. She was asleep in moments.

Charlie held Sara in his arms while she slept. Despite the danger they faced, and the uncomfortable surroundings and uncertainties, he'd never been happier in his life.

Her murmured 'I love you,' after she kissed him goodnight gave him a sense of peace. The soft, warm weight of her body felt exactly right against him.

Returning home and being separated from her held no appeal; he would almost rather stay here. He laughed at himself, leaned down and kissed her temple.

This wasn't good for her no matter how much he enjoyed it. Safe, comfortable surroundings were better for her. He'd ensure she had them. A few more days of hiking, carrying her occasionally, and holding her while she slept would have to do until they were older. The memory of this would have to suffice him. Day dreaming of their future, he drifted to sleep holding her.

Charlie woke to low talking. Early afternoon light revealed the gully where they'd taken refuge blocked on three sides by steep, shale-covered ledges peppered with loose rock and dotted with low bushes. Oz pointed east.

"The easiest way out is that way. Hawk scouted already this morning. Let him and Stasia pull everyone for a while and we can make good time."

"Sounds good," Charlie agreed. Sound asleep, Sara relaxed against him, while he and Oz conferred quietly. When she stirred, yawning and rubbing her eyes, his attention turned to her. "Are you okay?"

"Tired." She pushed herself higher on his chest and kissed his neck before resting her face on his.

Oz cleared his throat. "I'll go wake everyone." The air between his hands shimmered as he started to conjure the food and water they needed while moving away.

Charlie barely noticed him leave. All his attention was focused on the girl in his arms. The warm caress of her breath on his neck made him shiver. When her lips touched his, time stopped. He could kiss her forever. The blood rushed from his head, and she moaned softly when he deepened the kiss.

The uncomfortable surroundings ceased to exist. Escape was suddenly not a priority. Instead, he wanted to stay here all day kissing her, hearing her sigh, learning how she liked to be touched. The sounds of guns racking and people talking brought him back to reality.

With a groan, he released her. He wasn't thinking with his brain. After tracing a finger over her brow line, he reluctantly rose. All the things he wanted to say to her stuck in his throat.

Sara's luminous gaze met his as he lifted her to her feet, and she took a deep trembling breath.

"Me too," she said.

A smile flitted across her face as she went to find Stasia, giving him one last poignant glance over her shoulder.

Charlie grinned.

Two hours later, they crossed a dirt road. Guthrie called a halt while he studied the GPS for a few minutes. "Okay, we know where we are now. If we keep going on this road, we'll reach Mosul, but we don't want to do that. ISIS controls Mosul. We need to head straight west. Sara, try the radio again. Maybe we can reach Americans."

Sara fiddled with the dials and held the radio to her ear. "Uh oh, there's a group talking back and forth searching for us. Let me see the maps." Everyone crowded closer to see as Sara marked two spots with pebbles. "From what I can make out there's two groups of people searching for us, here and here." She pointed at the pebbles. "Both groups originate from Mosul. This road is a death trap for us. Stasia, Hawk, you guys need to run us out of here, go in thirty."

Everyone linked hands. Charlie picked

Sara up in his arms, resisting the urge to kiss her, letting her concentrate on Ascension timers.

Thirty minutes later Hawk called a halt. A hand held shading his eyes, he peered straight west into the setting sun. "Hostiles at the edge of my range coming closer fast."

"Group up!" Charlie yelled and beckoned Guthrie. "Thirty yards is Sara's healing range. You need to make sure everyone stays within thirty yards of her." Raising his voice to be sure everyone heard him, he shouted, "The healer is in charge of positioning. If Sara tells you to go somewhere, do it right away."

Everyone stopped what they were doing, and all eyes turned to Charlie.

"Trust her to know where it's safe even if it goes against traditional defense. Let's see what we can find for cover and line-of-sight. Oz is calling out DPS targets, and your Sergeant Guthrie will be doing the same."

"DPS target means target to fire on," Rick explained hurriedly.

Meanwhile, Hawk closed his eyes and jumped from one animal mind to another, using their eyes to search for a better spot to fight while Rick explained their targeting system.

"Follow me!" Hawk said and led them south over a small rise, and up a steep hill. The hill formed a small, protected semi-circle on the backside where water run off had cut a deep channel. Grooves led off in multiple directions, some shallow, and some deep. The hill at their back would protect from attacks in that direction, and the grooves made good foxholes.

Charlie slapped Hawk on the back. "Good job." Turning to the raid, he rose his voice again. "Everyone, group up as tight as you can. If you're not touching someone you're too far away."

Charlie loosened his axes, pulled one out, kissed Sara, and lifted his garbage can lid, trying not to feel ridiculous as he took his usual position at the front. Team Valor grouped up in front of their raid taking the positions their characters used when entering tournaments. Oz stood on Sara's left, Hawk on her right with Stasia behind her.

Mirrored shields formed around them and dissipated, the magic stored in Sara's staff as she gathered her magic preparing to cast a major shield. The deep thwapping sound of an approaching helicopter had them shading their eyes and peering into the sky.

Hawk cast a No-See-Um, but Charlie knew it wouldn't work. No-See-Um could only hide five people. Two helicopters flew over them, banked, and flew back, spraying bullets as it passed. A mirror-bright dome of light formed over them as Sara slammed her staff into the ground.

"T-two," Charlie called.

A fireball whizzed by his ear and hit the lead helicopter dead on. Oz cast twice more in quick succession, and the two helicopters spiraled down, landing hard, out of commission. Armed men ran from them using the wrecks as cover as they fired their guns.

The raid returned fire from the protection of Sara's shield.

Charlie knew her shield wouldn't hold much longer, he yelled his attack cry and cast Waylay, appearing instantly behind a man firing on them. One swing of his ax cut the gun in half. The men near Charlie dropped their weapons as he cast his drop weapon spell.

Stasia jumped into their midst, still invisible, and sapped one, dropped a flash-bang grenade, and sprinted away.

Panicked men fled from the grenade into the fire of the men standing behind Sara.

The ax in Charlie's hand spun in a circle deflecting shots fired at him. Oz cast a blinding light followed by a lightning strike on one of the downed helicopters and men screamed and ran from it into the fire from the men behind Sara.

Sara was busy throwing glowing yellow balls of light at her teammates and keeping shields up on the people crouched behind her.

Hawk shot a man taking aim at Charlie. The gun barked in his hand, and his target sailed back twenty feet and stayed down. Knock-Back shot wasn't a damaging attack in the game, but it damaged people here, and Hawk's shrug showed he didn't care.

Rick moved up, lying in front of Sara, and picked men off with his stolen rifle as they showed themselves, being careful with his limited ammunition.

Hawk shot another man with his Stun-Shot, this time the gun was silent, and the man slumped to the ground.

Hawk winced, sighed, shrugged, and straightened his shoulders as more shots sounded behind him, killing the man he'd stunned.

Charlie rushed around, swinging his ax to great effect, knocking people back and out. Red spots bloomed on him as shots got through. Sara kept a HOT on him, and a Major Heal caused him to glow yellow every so often. Blood appeared on Charlie's face and neck in sudden red rivulets, and he staggered as a group of men converged on him, firing on full automatic. A brilliant flash of white light surrounded him as Sara screamed shrilly and used a cooldown, casting an emergency heal on him.

The attacking men were stunned when Charlie charged forward and slammed them with his garbage can lid. More shots sounded behind Sara, and the raid moved forward led by Rick. Oz winked to Charlie's side and cast Polymorph, turning a man into a fluffy black sheep.

Hawk snorted a laugh and grinned at Oz. "Holy crap, that actually worked!"

The sheep turned into a dead man lying in a pool of blood as shots fired from the raid hit him.

A wave of darkness spread from Sara's staff, sending the men it touched fleeing in terror.

The raid followed, firing as they ran.

Charlie wiped the drying blood off his face with the tail of his shirt as they caught up and a small firefight broke out, leaving all their attackers dead. Light flew from Sara's fingers as she healed the wounds her raid took.

"No one except us is alive in my range," Hawk reported.

A stricken Stasia appeared by Sara and grabbed her hand.

Charlie kissed them both on the forehead, putting his arms around them. The raid returned and stood silently, watching them.

Rick hugged them all. "They probably got word out. Here's hoping our side heard it too. More could arrive anytime. Should we move on or stay here?"

Guthrie hesitantly approached them and laid a gentle hand on Sara's back. "Stay, this is a nice defendable position. The girls don't need to fight or protect us. This is our job. We'll give them a fight they won't forget."

Sara heaved a deep sigh and moved away from Charlie. "No, it's our job now too." Tears filled her eyes as she faced her team. "Don't fight unless you mean it. We can't afford to hold back like this."

"You were holding back?" Guthrie said in amazement, staring at the wrecked helicopters and the dead men littering the ground.

Charlie nodded as he too examined the dead men and helicopters. "We weren't using any of our offensive spells, but we can't afford to do that here."

Sara gripped his shirt. "If you go out to fight again, go for the quick kill. They're just as dead if Rick shoots them. Don't go near them if you won't really fight."

Charlie nodded, kissed her, and ran a thumb along the purple crescent under her eyes that showed her exhaustion.

Stasia gripped her hand tighter. "I don't think I can, Sara."

"Then don't, stay with me. The boys can handle it and the men here."

"Yeah, we can handle this. You two stay in back." Guthrie awkwardly patted Stasia on the back.

"Incoming," Hawk warned.

"Hawk, you and Oz too." Sara turned to them. "Please, don't put yourself in harm's way unless you're willing to use deadly force to stop them. No one here will think less of you. I couldn't stand to see either of you hurt."

"Okay, spread out this time! Use these God-given foxholes, people!" Guthrie bellowed and put his large hand on Sara's shoulder. "Honey, we can do this, you don't need—"

Sara cut him off, "I can do it too. I have offensive spells."

The sound of approaching helicopters interrupted them and Sara ran to get into position. Three smaller helicopters approached.

"T-three, two, one," Oz said and cast when the helicopters appeared in his line-of-sight, but this time he didn't stop.

When they crashed, he continued to hit them until smoldering wreckage was all that remained. No one emerged from them.

"Yes, I see. You were holding back," Guthrie, said his voice dry, his hands on his hips, as he surveyed the smoking helicopters half submerged in the rocky ground.

Hawk nodded toward his sister. "Yeah, you don't want to make Stasia mad, she's our top DPS."

Sergeant Guthrie gawked at him. "More damage than that?"

Hawk nodded. "Oz is super strong on grouped targets, she's strong on spread ones."

"Good to know, I'll be careful to keep on her good side."

Charlie approached. "Think they'll send more?"

Guthrie scratched his stubbled cheek as he said, "Not in helicopters, planes maybe, or infantry. Let's make a break now though while they rethink their strategy in case it's missiles next."

They headed west again, cutting straight across country. Rick fiddled with the radio. With a shrug, he handed it to Sara. "I heard something but can't understand them."

The lines between her eyes deepened as she listened, appearing to try to force words from the static. "Calling for our surrender. He says we're going to start a war. Now he's saying he'll burn our women and children. Jeez, this guy is rabid." Arabic voices broken by static sounded as Sara flipped channels. In sudden excitement, she perked up. "He's speaking English." She put her ear closer to it. "Can you connect me to the American Embassy?" The man speaking broke up badly. "Boost me up." Sara levitated herself and held the radio in the air as Guthrie lifted her. She listened hard. For a moment, it came in clear. "This is Baghdad base... Hear... reports... tell... can," then broke up again.

"I can't make it out." Sara gazed over the tired group and shrugged. Giving Guthrie an apologetic grimace she said, "This is Staff Sergeant Guthrie's group. We've escaped from our captives and are fleeing under attack." Static was her only reply.

The hike continued. They took turns trying to use the radio. At four thirty-nine, two jets flew over them.

"Too high. I can't tell," Hawk said as he shaded his eyes trying to see them.

"They're ours," Rick said in excitement. "Try different channels, Sara."

She was already flipping the dials. The jets returned going much slower and a lot lower. One peeled off, and the other circled them, waggling its wings before following the other.

"They know where we are." Rick grinned at Charlie. "We'll get home yet."

"Drive on people. It's a long walk!" Guthrie bellowed.

Walking resumed with only minor complaints. The sight of the jets had invigorated them. Sara mixed in with the crowd and sparks flitted from her fingertips as she cast a heal on everyone, easing sore muscles.

Stasia and Hawk resumed pulling them.

Guthrie spoke to Stasia, whose hand he held, as she ran. "At dark, we walk. There's too much chance we lose someone at night if they fall asleep and let go. Let's say three more hours or until we find a nice spot. Then we rest until dawn. Sara, pass the radio to Todd. Lance Corporal Todd Jones is now our radioman. Keep checking all channels for an American."

After three more hours of walking, they settled into a rocky hillside. Oz again made food trays. Hawk checked for snakes, scaring the ones he found away and warded the area before they slept. Guthrie assigned sentries, but Hawk woke first when his ward went off. He glanced at his watch and grimaced. It was almost five in the morning.

"We have multiple incomings!" he yelled, as people got to their feet staggering and groggy. "Both ally and enemies are coming in. If you aren't sure who-is-who, don't shoot until I call the target. Right now, the enemy is approaching from the south, and our friendlies are from the west."

Guthrie stood and cupped his hands around his mouth to yell, "Okay, people, spread out, but try to stay within thirty feet of Sara. Make sure you have a clear field of fire.

Haji is on his way. Let's give him a warm welcome."

A jet flew over them at a high altitude. Guns sounded in the distance, and bright flashes lit the sky. A helicopter hove into view and cheers broke out when Hawk said it was friendly. The helicopter hovered over them and men in armor, carrying machine guns, slid down lines.

Another helicopter flew up from the south followed by four more.

"Enemy's," Hawk informed them.

Oz prepared to cast fireballs not waiting for Charlie to call targets.

The helicopter over them turned and opened fire at the approaching helicopters. A missile screamed toward the helicopter overhead. Hawk blasted it away using Deflect-Shot. One after another, he shot down missiles using his sidearm. In less than thirty seconds, the enemy helicopters were all down, and Oz kept on fireballing them.

"A large group of men is approaching from the south, so many, so close together, I can't differentiate them," Hawk warned.

Pale-gray dawn light broke over the

landscape. Headlights appeared in the distance, and the sound of engines rumbled through the still air. Hawk holstered his gun and grabbed a rifle from a surprised soldier.

Charlie followed Hawk as he ran up a small incline, lay down, and fired. The sharp crack of his gun caused return fire. Still almost a mile away and barely visible through the early morning gloom, the enemy was too far to hit them, and the gunfire stopped.

Hawk wasn't too far, he fired again and headlights went out one-by-one.

One of the new arrivals lay next to Hawk using binoculars. The enemy marched half a mile away now, and the rate of Hawk's fire increased as more targets presented themselves. Hawk was using an old beat up Ak-47 and hadn't missed once. For every shot he took, a man fell, or a light extinguished. The enemy soldiers fell back behind the tanks, using them as cover, and stopped advancing.

"Our air support better get a move on, we won't be able to hold back those tanks." Two of the new arrivals talked quietly together over Hawk's prone body.

Another of the men in armor climbed the small hill to survey the approaching enemy. The nametag on his chest identified him as Major Nelson, and he carried a machine gun that required two hands to hold. The other four men spread out on the hilltop, picking vantage points to shoot from.

Sara stood behind Hawk with her staff planted on the ground, holding Stasia's hand.

Stasia glanced behind her at the men taking cover and preparing to fight. Her eyes met Rick's. A sad smile crossed his face, and his grip tightened on his stolen rifle.

Charlie stood with his hand on Stasia's shoulder and met her eyes, and they both glanced back at his brother. Rick was filthy and tired and determined to do his best with only a stolen rifle and a bulletproof vest against the overwhelming odds facing them.

"You girls go take cover now." Major Nelson placed his large hand on Sara's shoulder and tried to pull her away. "There's nothing to be afraid of. We can hold them off until help arrives. Helicopters should arrive shortly to take us out of here, and reinforcements are on the way."

Stasis turned to him, her suddenly blue eyes cold. "I'm not afraid of them, they better be afraid of me," she said and disappeared.

LEROY

"Oh jeez, Stasia's gone Leroy!" Sara charged up the small hill. "Hawk, you see her?"
"Where the hell did she go?" Major Nelson hollered and stared in consternation as the kids ran over the hill.

Over a thousand armed men approached them half a mile away accompanied by tanks and jeeps. Stasia ran towards the enemy in front of them, her invisible form barely making a ripple in the knee-high dead grass covering the hill. Before they knew she was coming, she would be upon them.

Hawk and Oz ran by Sara who stood on the top of the hill with her eyes shaded, watching Stasia. After one backward glance at the group of outnumbered, outgunned men behind her, she followed.

Charlie grabbed her arm.

"Sara, you don't have—"

A soft kiss stopped his words. "And let you be killed or hurt? This is my fight too. We came to save Rick, so let's save him."

Charlie grabbed her hand, and they raced forward together. Team Valor grouped up into their usual position six hundred yards away from the advancing enemy.

"Tick," Charlie yelled his battle-cry, a loud arghhh oorah, and charged.

Crossed Axes blocked the first volley of shots heading to him as he leapt into range.

Light shimmered on Sara's hands as she cast shields on Team Valor.

"Tock," she said.

A large yellow ball of light flew through the air and hit Charlie, making him glow for a moment. He wondered what the attacking men thought as he swung his ax and their bullets bounced off him.

"Tick," Charlie said as his defensive spell ran out.

The silver sheen of a magical shield

formed around him. The staff in her hand flared with black light as a wave of blackness spread from it. Those it touched shrieked and ran, clutching their heads.

Oz took position by Sara's side, and fireballs hurtled through the air, colliding with the approaching tanks. The tanks aimed at Oz and Sara and opened fire.

Charlie laughed as the missiles passed him, knowing Sara would reflect them.

Sara slammed her staff into the ground and a mirror-bright shield formed around her. The shots from the tanks arced around the shield and headed back to the tanks, impacting with a tremendous explosion. Fire and smoke filled the air and debris rained down in a wide arc. Their own warheads had destroyed them.

Lightning forked from the clear sky and men ran screaming as it branched out in multiple tendrils seeking them. Charlie charged in, yelling his taunt, forcing the enemy to attack him. The garbage can lid in his hands stunned the men in range of him and Stasia appeared, a whirlwind of death, her daggers flashing in the dawn light.

The attacking men in the front ranks dropped back under the ferocity and unexpectedness of the attack. Fireballs continued to fly into the vehicles, hitting violently, pushing the smaller jeeps over. Every vehicle in sight burned, sending up thick, billowing clouds of black smoke.

Armed men tried to hide behind the wrecks, using them as cover, but Oz kept the fireballs landing, forcing them to retreat and spread out while using his lightning on groups of enemies in line-of-sight.

Shots buzzed around Sara like angry bees.

Hawk's shots hit what he aimed at with magical accuracy, forcing the attacking men to seek cover and keep their heads down. The enemy grouped up in small bunches, using the landscape, hiding behind rocks, taking desperate shots at the death approaching them.

The staff in Sara's hand glowed with a white light while balls of bright-yellow light flew to her teammates, healing them.

Oz teleported forward, changing direction randomly between casts, making himself hard to target.

When Charlie yelled, "Tock," Sara used her pull and yanked him out of the group of attacking men.

Blood covered his clothing and face. He absently used his sleeve to clear his eyes and glanced around. Gunshots felt like paintballs, short, sharp stings and he laughed as they empowered him, making him stronger. The ax in his right hand dripped gore, and his dented shield was clutched in his left. The rocky ground and cactus didn't slow his charge as he yelled and rushed forward into the heaviest fire. Sara followed.

Using her pull to go to Charlie, she fought side-by-side with him. The staff in her hand wasn't just a receptacle for magic, it was also a weapon. Swinging it in a skilled arc; she used it on the attacking men. More light balls formed in her hands as she threw heals at her teammates.

The dull thud of Charlie's ax hitting flesh was swallowed by the screams of the men near them. Although the men fought desperately, their weapons couldn't stop Team Valor's advance.

One group, either braver, or more

desperate, attacked Charlie in force. Using their bodies to hold him down, trying to stop him by brute strength, they converged on him. It took twenty to do it and cost twenty more their lives in the attempt. A bolt of lightning arced down, slamming into the men pushing Charlie into the ground. Another bolt followed the first, and a black cloud flowed from Sara's staff covering them, they screamed and tried to run as Sara cast Smite.

Hawk ran to a vantage point where he could keep the attackers pinned down and stop the advance. Charlie struggled free of the men covering him, climbing over the corpses, violently throwing them from him. A major heal from Sara hit him followed by a mirrored shield. Blood covered him, some from his already healed wounds, but most was from his enemies. He clenched the garbage can lid in his hand and summoned his ax into his other one as he screamed his battle cry and charged.

Oz attacked every large gathering of men. The attackers realized the folly of forming big groups and spread out farther. Men in leapt from concealment in an organized assault and fired at Charlie. Automatic gunfire ripped through the air, hammering the invisible shield surrounding him. They'd forgotten about Hawk.

Hawk vigorously reminded them of his presence. Casting his Rapid-Fire, he killed every man standing, forcing the rest to fall back and seek shelter.

Terrified shrieks followed Oz's casts. Fire and lightning flickered over the countryside. The attacking horde stayed away from the wrecked vehicles, approaching one brought a rain of fire on it.

Charlie leapt from one cowering group of men to another. Stasia appeared, and together they killed them while Sara followed, healing her teammate's wounds.

Hawk called his sister as he ran to change position again, "There's a group to your left twenty feet up, Stasia, hiding behind that big rock. I have no line-of-sight."

Stasia waited for a new shield from Sara before disappearing and leaping forward.

Charlie waylaid Stasia, and they both attacked, leaving bodies scattered on the ground. Sara kept within thirty yards of them, sometimes using her pull to go to them, sometimes using it to remove one or the other from a dangerous spot.

Hawk shot as fast as he found targets. The ground where they fought was rocky, with dips, and scrubby brush, but he always knew where the enemy hid and informed his team. Enemies that appeared in his line-of-sight he killed, but he remained untargeted. Hawk pointed out another small group and Charlie leapt into their midst's, casting taunt, followed by Stasia.

Oz teleported forward and cast lightning.

The incoming fire dwindled away until only silence remained, broken by the whir of insect wings as they arrived to feast. Hawk reported no enemies in range. No one alive was within half a mile of them.

Charlie ordered them to regroup. A single leap brought him to the top of a still smoking tank tipped on its side. Oz had cast so furiously on the tank it had tilted and partially sunk into a large crater. Dead men surrounded it and already bugs covered them. The scene should've horrified him, but it didn't.

Team Valor joined him there, and they surveyed the battlefield together. The boys bumped fists and Charlie put his arms around the girls.

Slashed, burned, and gunshot-riddled corpses littered the ground in clumps and singly. Some lay face up, sightless eyes staring into the dawn sky and some could barely be seen, their bodies hidden in tall weeds or bushes revealed by an out-flung arm or boot tip. None moved. No one had survived Team Valor's attack.

Charlie knew he should be sickened, or remorseful, or feel bad, but he didn't. He felt powerful. This was what he was meant to do. The Charlie from before the lightning would've felt bad. That Charlie couldn't have brought himself to kill so many people so coldly, but that Charlie had died. Chief had replaced him, and Chief was a warrior who lived for the kill. Even now, with no enemies in sight, he wanted to kill, to hunt them down to the ends of the Earth and ensure his team's safety.

Magic covered him as he stood atop the tank until a blue cloud engulfed his entire body. The blue haze spread, coating all of Team Valor.

The blue glow of Stasia's eyes brightened further as she examined the carnage.

Emotions played across her face. Pride, triumph, disappointment, Stasia had died as well. Stasis stood by his side now. The entire team had fiercely glowing blue eyes and stood like Stasia, both eager and disappointed. Except for Sara, her glowing blue eyes appeared troubled.

Charlie placed a hand on Stasia's shoulder. "Stasis?"

Stasia's blue eyes met his, and she nodded and touched his hand.

Sara bit back a sob.

Charlie knew they were eager to fight and disappointed no more enemies existed, he knew because he felt their eagerness. Adrenaline coursed through him. The ax in his hand felt good, but he wished it were his gladius. A gladius and more enemies to kill— the thought excited him.

Stasis ran a thumb over the edge of her dagger.

Hawk crouched, eagerly scanning for

movement.

Oz lifted his glowing blue eyes to his and smiled as lightning flickered from his fingertips.

Yes, they were all eager.

"Seraphim?"

"No, I'm still Sara, well, mostly Sara. Charlie— come back to me. Don't let the magic take you."

Sara's glowing gaze flitted over her team, and she pleaded with them as tears of shining white trail unheeded down her cheek. "The magic has us, I feel it too, but we aren't them. This thrill of the fight isn't us, not really. Killing these men was necessary, but if we go looking for a fight— if we give into this, I don't think we can come back. The people we were will truly be dead. Don't let it take you. I need my best friends back, please…."

Another small sob sounded as she grabbed his blood-coated hand in hers and squeezed.

Chief surveyed the battlefield again, enjoying the sight, being Chief. Team Valor would follow him, he could lead them in a battle and destroy ISIS, destroy every man, woman, and child who stood against them. He could embrace his rage, encourage it, become an unstoppable force of destruction.

Then he turned to the girl by his side. That girl didn't love Chief, she loved Charlie. After taking one long last glance at the bodies littering the ground, he jumped down from his vantage point. The desire to fight, to kill, he pushed away. He released the pride he felt at the destruction they'd wrought. The blue mist of magic dissipated, absorbed into their skin. His eyes were brown when he held out his hands to her.

A brilliant smile lit her face as she jumped into his arms.

A matching smile crossed his face as he leaned down and kissed her.

For the girl at his side, he would be Charlie.

The entire raid stood on the ridge, watching them return. Major Nelson was on a radio when they reached the waiting raid.

"No, we don't need air support we need transport," he was saying. When his call ended, he put the radio away and approached slowly. "That was— um—"

"Impressively scary," Rick said. "Are you guys okay?"

"Yeah." Sara grabbed an orange juice from her bag on the ground and offered one to Oz who accepted.

No one spoke as they sat and drank their juice.

"So, um, what was that?" Major Nelson asked finally.

"That was Team Valor not holding back," Guthrie said and smiled at them as proud as if he'd invented them himself.

Oz examined the silent group observing them and smiled slightly. "Harmful magic can't be used on teammates," he said. "We couldn't hurt you even if we wanted to." The orange ball of fire Oz formed fizzled out before it left his hand. "See, I can't cast on teammates. Sara can, but only beneficial spells. There's no reason to fear us."

"That was impressive. Where did you learn to fight like that?" one of the armored men asked.

"The internet," Stasia said as she grabbed an orange juice and sat beside Sara.

Oz snickered.

Rick put an arm around her and hugged her despite her bloody, filthy clothing. "Mom and Dad must be freaking out. We need to get you guys home. Not to mention their parents." He nodded to where Hawk, Sara, and Oz sat on the rocky ground drinking orange juice.

"Transport is coming and should be here soon." Major Nelson observed them drink their juice and fidgeted with his gun.

"Where's it going?" Charlie asked and sat with a thump by Sara.

"Incirlik base in Turkey— this will take some explaining."

Charlie nodded absently as he tried to clean the dried blood from under his nails with his dagger. "The cat is out of the bag for sure," he said.

Oz snorted back a laugh. "The cat has shredded the bag and is using it for kitty litter."

Stasia rolled her eyes.

Sara sighed and leaned on Charlie.

"The website will get a billion hits," Hawk said as he lay back on the ground and put his arms behind his head. "Once word of us spreads, every fight we ever filmed will get a million hits. Wonder if we can charge for that?"

The thoughtful tone of his voice made Charlie laugh.

"This wasn't the first time you've done this?" Major Nelson asked, sounding both horrified and impressed.

"Stasia has done almost this exact thing a few times." Sara's hands hide her face, muffling her voice. "Google 'Stasis Leroy's Underhill' she pulled an entire level thirty instance, and we killed a thousand of them in twelve minutes. How long did this take?"

"Eighteen minutes."

Sara sat up straighter and drank her juice. "See, I told you we're slower now."

Oz rolled his eyes and conjured water to wash.

"Meh, that was fast enough, those bullets don't tickle," Charlie said before kissing her temple. He grabbed water from Oz and started washing. "The stealth way is better."

Oz shook his wet hands off. "Stealth is better, but I'm not going to lie, fireballing the heck out of those helicopters was rad."

One of the black-clad men snorted with laughter. "What the heck? Who says heck anymore, everyone says fu—"

"Tourney rules!" Team Valor yelled at the same time, interrupting him.

Charlie laughed at his expression.

Helicopters glided into sight. The hum of their engines heard before they were seen. Team Valor formed their attack pattern and stood waiting, almost eagerly, until Hawk said, "They're friendly."

Major Nelson spoke on the radio again. The helicopters landed, and the armored men loaded people on.

"No, we'll walk back if we have to. Rick stays with us." Charlie glared at the man trying to stop them from boarding the same helicopter as his brother.

Guthrie pulled the man aside and spoke briefly with him, and he let them board the same helicopter. All the armored men rode with them.

The sergeant leaned over to Sara and whispered, "Don't forget the advice I gave you."

She nodded and laid her head on

Charlie's shoulder. He put his arm around her and pulled her close.

When she had cell service, Sara flipped her phone open and hit a speed dial number. "Hi, Mr. Martin, it's me, Sara. We have a slight problem. If you could meet us at Incirlik base in Turkey as soon as you can…." After talking for a minute, she hung up and made another call. One of the armored men took her phone.

"This is our stop," Sara said and stood, pulling Charlie up with her.

The man gestured with his gun to her seat. "Have a seat please; we'll be there in a few minutes. After you're debriefed, you can call who you want."

Not bothering to answer, Sara cast her fear spell, and Team Valor joined hands and jumped from the helicopter.

The helicopter circled them as they floated to earth before moving away. The hillside where they landed was uninhabited. A low mountainside sparsely covered in pine trees spread out before them.

Charlie sighed. "What way Oz?"

Oz sighed too. "The hotel is that way."

With a dramatic flourish, he pointed southwest.

They joined hands and Stasia ran.

To their surprise, Charlie's mother, followed quickly by his father, spoke on the private line over their headsets thirty minutes later.

"Thank God you're back safe. Your mother and I were so worried. They just informed me you jumped from the helicopter. It's okay for you to come here to report," John said.

"You and Mom are at the base?"

Someone they didn't recognize said, "Yes, and we have your brother in custody as well."

Charlie closed his eyes, rubbed his forehead, and sighed hard. "Please, whoever this is, stop talking right now. We'll come in. We don't want to be enemies— we want to become friends, but you're making it impossible. Let me talk to my father again, please."

John answered, "Don't worry about us, your mom and I are fine. Rick is on base, but we haven't seen him. When can you be here?"

"Dad, someone better explain reputation gains to them before we come. Otherwise, they'll make it impossible for us to work with them. Right now, they're at neutral with us, but rapidly getting lower. Rep is a passive trait, so we can't control it."

"Okay, they don't understand. I'll do my best to explain it, but you have to understand how anxious everyone is here."

"Sara called her lawyer and is going to call Liz Harris and Mr. Lewis. The people we picked can help us, and we trust them. When our representatives arrive, we'll turn ourselves in. Please tell them not to do anything, um, unfortunate to any of you."

"Okay, son, we can work this out. Your mom sends her love and wants me to tell you this is project blackout."

"I love you guys, see you soon." Charlie took off his headset, and everyone followed suit.

"Okay, so Mom thinks we should maintain radio silence, that isn't necessarily a bad thing. Let's try not to let it affect their reputation with us. It's probably why she said it, she understands game rep."

"Yeah, let's not panic," Sara, agreed. "Let's make our calls and see what happens." She borrowed Charlie's phone and made another call.

Agent Lewis answered on the third ring. "Agent Lewis, this is Sara Mitchel. Can you meet us in Turkey at Incirlik Air Base? We might not have told you everything we know about that light...."

THE END OF BOOK ONE

About the Author

S. M. Savoy loves a good video game as well as a good book. Combining the two seemed like a natural progression. An avid gamer for years, she can attest to the fact that gamers, do indeed, play on their deathbeds.

R.I.P. Priestyman

A WARRIOR'S FURY

Valor: Book Two

After months of training, Team Valor is beginning to come to grips with their magic and planning for a future working with the United States Military.

When ISIS subverts a general— Charlie interferes with their plans.

Too late to stop Sara's kidnapping, he manages to warn his teammates before all can be taken. Now he'll do anything to get Sara back. A protection warrior, driven by his magic and fueled by his rage to protect those in his party, Charlie is a force the terrorists aren't prepared for.